Anna leaned back in her chair and folded her arms across her chest. "What are you afraid of?" she asked.

"I'm not afraid," Emilie said. "I have been taking care of my family for thirteen years. My father made me head of the household, and I have met that challenge head-on."

Anna leaned in closer to her. "But you are afraid to marry the man you love, my dear."

Her words reverberated through Emilie's mind. She felt herself tremble as a pain deep inside rose to the surface and commanded her heart.

"Tell me, dear," Anna said sweetly. "What is it that you fear about marrying Lorenz?"

"I don't want to marry anyone," Emilie said. "Because when you marry someone, you become a part of him. And when he's gone, you're less of a person."

Anna moved so that she sat next to Emilie and placed a gentle arm about her shoulders. "Oh, my dear," she said, "you have it all wrong. Love gives us strength. It brings us comfort. It gives us a reason to live, to face the next day."

"But he's rebellious," Emilie said, angrily. "One day he could kiss me goodbye and walk straight into a church surrounded by English soldiers and get himself exiled."

She closed her eyes tightly, willing away the image. She felt Anna's arms about her, holding her, but the relentless pain tore at her soul. . . .

Dear Readers,

Desire, dreams, and destiny—with a healthy dose of betrayal, villainy, and adventure—are the very things songs have been written about for centuries. And Ballad Romances is our love song to you: a brand-new line featuring the most gifted authors in historical romance telling the kinds of stories you love best.

This month, we launch the line with four new series. Each month after that, we'll present both new and continuing stories—and we'll let you know each month when you can find subsequent books in the series that have captured your heart.

Joy Reed takes us back to Regency England with the first book in *The Wishing Well* trilogy, **Catherine's Wish.** In this enchanting series, legend has it that, when a maiden looks into the Honeywell House wishing well, she sees the face of her future betrothed—with decidedly romantic results. Next, celebrated author Cynthia Sterling whisks us off to the American West with **Nobility Ranch,** the first in an uproariously funny—and sweetly tender—series of *Titled Texans* who have invaded America with their British nobility intact, and their hearts destined for life-changing love.

An ancient psychic gift is the key to the *Irish Blessing* series—and a maddening, tantalizing harbinger of love for the Reillys of the mid-nineteenth century. New author Elizabeth Keys weaves a passionate tale of the family's middle son in the first book, **Reilly's Law.** Finally, Cherie Claire invites us into the world of *The Acadians* in the 1750s, as **Emilie**—the first of three daughters of an Acadian exile—travels to the lush and sultry Louisiana Territory—where desire and danger go hand in hand. Enjoy!

Kate Duffy
Editorial Director

THE ACADIANS:
EMILIE

Oct. 14, 2000
Los Angeles

Cherie Claire

Manna —
To my dear
friend: Let's keep
meeting before 20 years
go by.
Love!
Cherié
aka
Cherie
Claire

Zebra Books
Kensington Publishing Corp.
http://www.zebrabooks.com

ZEBRA BOOKS are published by

Kensington Publishing Corp.
850 Third Avenue
New York, NY 10022

Zebra and the Z logo Reg. U.S. Pat. & TM Off.

First Printing: July, 2000
10 9 8 7 6 5 4 3 2 1

Printed in the United States of America

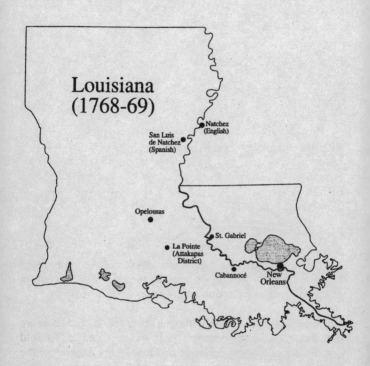

Louisiana
(1768-69)

Natchez
(English)

San Luis
de Natchez
(Spanish)

Opelousas

St. Gabriel

La Pointe
(Attakapas
District)

Cabannocé

New
Orleans

This book is dedicated to the heroes of my life:
Bruce, Joshua and Taylor.

Merci beaucoup *to my dear friends in the Maritimes—*
Susanne McDonald-Boyce, Marci Lin Marvin, Betty
Dugas, Evelyn DeCoste, Stacy Crawshaw, Cheryl
Leger, Jocelyne Marchand, Norah Wilson, Deborah
Hale, Barbara Mary Phinney and Lorraine Coyle—
and my good friend David Norwood, for help in writing
this book. A special thanks to my Louisiana ancestors
for never giving up.

Prologue

Grand Pré, Nova Scotia
1755

The harvest had been a good one, and Joseph Gallant smiled broadly as he approached his simple yet comfortable home. It was only a matter of minutes before his wife Marianne would greet him at the door.

"Beware all who trespass here," called out Gabrielle, his seven-year-old-daughter, dressed as usual in pirate garb and brandishing a willow branch in the shape of a sword.

"Dear me," Joseph replied, swinging his dark-haired child into his arms. "I didn't know we had pirates about."

"She's at it again, Father," snitched Emilie Gallant, Joseph's older daughter, who had inherited his wife's chestnut hair and hazel eyes. "She keeps going down to the Basin to look at those ships."

Joseph sent Gabrielle a stern look but secretly understood the lure of the majestic frigate anchored in Minas Basin. The English had occupied Acadia, or Nova Scotia as they called it, since the Treaty of Utrecht ceded their French country to Britain in 1713. The English allowed the Acadians to remain in Nova Scotia and practice their Catholic religion as long as they remained neutral in the French and English wars. So far, the relationship between Grand Pré residents and the English government was peaceful and cooperative. There were things to be ironed out, of course, differences to be reconciled. The right to bear arms for protection and hunting was one of those problems. All that was to be settled at the church meeting that afternoon.

"Gabrielle, you are to stay away from the water," Joseph said. "And particularly away from the soldiers. You know I have forbidden you to go there."

"But there are more ships there now," Gabrielle answered in her defense. "Several more have arrived."

For a moment, Joseph tensed. Additional soldiers had recently been called into Grand Pré, forming a large settlement around the church in town. It might be something to be concerned about, but the Grand Pré Acadians had worked repeatedly to sort out problems with the English. Only today, Joseph and his neighbors had gathered crops and fruits from their orchards to supply the occupying army with food.

"I don't care if the entire Royal Navy has come to Canada." Joseph placed Gabrielle down and sent her hurrying away with a delicate pop on her backside. "Take care of your maman and leave the ships alone."

Emilie and Joseph watched as Gabrielle bounded behind the side of the house, her long, silky black hair flying as she ran. "She won't listen to you, Father," Emilie said. "She loves the sea too much."

Joseph had to smile. His oldest, barely eleven years old, had grown so much in the past year. Emilie's tall, slim body had abandoned her one night, literally transforming her into a woman without giving her childish mind time to catch up. Emilie was caught between two worlds, on one hand trying hard to be as mature as her looks, and on the other, fighting her emerging femininity. She was more comfortable chopping wood than darning socks.

"I should have had sons," Joseph said with a laugh as Emilie picked up her neglected bucket of milk and effortlessly hauled it toward the house.

"You should have been home an hour ago," answered Marianne, looking half her age and twice as beautiful.

Joseph circled his arms about his wife's slender waist and met her lips before she could protest. "I love you," he whispered.

The light that perpetually shone in Marianne's eyes dimmed for a moment, and a look of alarm crossed her face. "What made you say that?" she asked.

Joseph pulled her toward him and squeezed. "Do I have to have a reason to love my wife?"

Joseph relieved Emilie of her load, and the two crossed the threshold into the warm cottage. Rose, the youngest daughter, barely five, sat by the enormous hearth, playing with a variety of hand-stuffed dolls and enjoying a ripe red apple. Joseph greeted his curly-headed baby, whose smile was blinding.

"Rose is so agreeable," Joseph said to his wife, who never moved from the front door. "Why couldn't all my children have been as easy?"

Emilie immediately put her hands on her hips and was ready to object when she noticed her mother's stern countenance. Joseph followed her gaze and stood.

"Marianne, what is it?"

Marianne looked as if she would faint, so Joseph quickly grabbed her elbow and guided her to a chair.

"It's nothing," she said, even though the color had not returned to her cheeks. "I thought I had a vision."

The last time his wife had a "vision," she imagined herself with child. It was a false alarm, although Ovile LeBlanc, two houses down, announced she was pregnant the next day.

"You've been working too close to the fire, *mon amour.*" Joseph brushed the auburn tendrils that framed his wife's forehead. She was a beauty the first time he set eyes on her, capturing his heart with a smile and a touch of her hand, and her loveliness had not lessened over the years.

"Don't go to town," Marianne whispered, stroking his cheek with the back of her hand. "I'm worried . . ."

Joseph laughed. "That I may visit Thomas Simoneaux's cellar on the way home?"

The light that had been part of Marianne's countenance failed to return. "Do you have to go? Can you not send one person to talk about our concerns, our needs? Why every man in the region?"

Joseph straightened and placed a loving hand on her shoulder. "The proclamation said every man and boy ten years and older must go to the meeting or risk penalty. Do you wish for us to lose our land, our livestock?"

Marianne stared at the flames. "No, but . . ."

"Colonel Winslow said the king was to communicate his wishes in this district. It's imperative that I go."

Joseph felt a shiver run through him. Marianne's dark mood was getting the better of him. He shook off the premonition.

"Papa," Emilie announced defiantly. "You tell the king we are to have our guns and ammunition whenever we please, that we will not abide by the rules the English lay out for us. If the king doesn't like it, tell him we will raise forces against him and reclaim our land."

Joseph glanced back at Marianne, who shrugged. She mouthed the name "Lorenz."

"Emilie," Joseph said as he took the large knife out of her fist. "You tell Lorenz Landry to stop putting those rebellious thoughts in your mind. We are French neutrals. We comply with the English government, give them a share of our food, and we all live comfortably with one other. We have no quarrels with the English. Do you understand?"

Emilie frowned but nodded. "I don't like them. I don't like the way they look at me."

Joseph certainly understood how young sailors would find the sight of Emilie an enticing view. For a moment he wanted to punch a few Englishmen senseless. "Stay away from them," he warned her.

Glancing at his pocketwatch, Joseph knew it was time

to go. He planted a kiss on his baby's face and was rewarded with a large hug. "Stay happy," he informed Rose, and she responded with a giggle.

He turned to his oldest. "If anything happens to me," Joseph said, mirroring his wife's fears, "you are the man of the house." He kissed the top of Emilie's head. "Take care of the family while I'm gone."

"I will, Father," Emilie said confidently, and Joseph knew she would.

He turned to his wife, who now had tears in her eyes.

"I'm afraid I'll never see you again," she whispered, then pulled him to her and held him tight. "Dear God, how will I ever live without you?"

Just then, Joseph felt it, too, a dark sense that something was amiss, a foreboding that tore at his soul. He placed a palm on the side of her head, closed his eyes and silently said a prayer.

"God watch over my family," he said aloud. "Until I return."

Chapter One

New Orleans, Louisiana Territory
February, 1768

The ship slowly made its way toward the harbor lights of
New Orleans, tacking against a bitter north wind blowing
across the wide expanse of muddy river. The Louisiana
capital, dark and mysterious lying almost below the level
of the river, appeared as if the surrounding marshland
would swallow it at any moment. Or perhaps it was the
humid air pressing on Emilie's lungs that made her feel
as if she were descending into a bog.

"I don't like it," she said to her mother and sisters
standing beside her at the ship's railing.

"That's no surprise," Marianne answered. "You said
the same thing about Maryland."

Now that the boat neared the city, Emilie caught a

variety of unpleasant odors in the wind. The stench only added to her agitated disposition.

"Why couldn't we have stayed in Maryland, let Father come to us?" Emilie insisted.

"Who's to say Father isn't hurt or ill," Gabrielle said. "We only know that he's in the Louisiana Territory at St. Gabriel. We don't know any more than that."

Emilie raised her handkerchief to her nose. Definitely the smell of rotten meat. And, if she wasn't mistaken, horse manure. Lots of it. "You just wanted the chance to be on another ship," she mumbled to Gabrielle.

Gabrielle turned to her older sister, her dark eyes expressing hurt and anger. Emilie had touched a nerve, and she instantly regretted her remark. Gabrielle would forever blame herself for their separation from Joseph, even though it was clear some other force was at work that autumn day when the English shipped them off for Maryland, forcing them to leave Joseph behind in Nova Scotia.

"I'm sorry," Emilie said, but she knew it was too late. Gabrielle retreated to the far railing, the familiar dark look haunting her eyes.

"Why did you have to do that?" Marianne said. "You know how much she blames herself."

"I'm sorry," Emilie repeated. "I didn't mean to upset her. I just don't like this place."

"It will be fine," Rose interjected. "It will be better when we join the others. Things sometimes look grim in the beginning, but turn out well in the end."

Always the optimist, Emilie thought of her sister Rose. Even when they were crowded aboard the vessel bound for Port Tobacco, Maryland, most of them sick with small-pox and half-starving, Rose never stopped smiling. She rallied through the sickness while half the ship's inhabitants failed to see their next shore.

Emilie shivered thinking back on their exile from Nova Scotia. The English capturing and holding the region's men in the church that afternoon, the fires set to their fields and homes, Lorenz crying on the shore while his mother perished in his arms, the ships coming in from New England to haul them all away.

As she had done numerous times in the past, Emilie shoved those painful memories aside. Where was Lorenz anyway? She searched the ship's deck but couldn't spot him. Lorenz was never one to miss the action.

"What have you said this time?"

Emilie swung around and nearly collided with Lorenz's broad chest, covered by his familiar long, woolen coat that hung to his knees. Lorenz Landry was one of the few men in the world tall enough to look down upon her. But not by much.

"You scared me," she protested. "Don't sneak up on me like that."

Lorenz's eyes, black as the night and complemented by equally dark hair, remained fixed on her. Emilie wondered if he would ever look at her differently again. She doubted he would ever forgive her.

"What did you do?" he demanded again.

"To whom?" Emilie asked, although she knew the answer.

Lorenz stared away toward shore, his thick, black hair, some claimed the result of a Micmac ancestor, blowing in waves across his face. They had been friends since babes, and she couldn't imagine a life without him. But if Lorenz's threats held true, their friendship had ended the night before.

"I didn't mean it," Emilie answered. "You know how sensitive Gabrielle is."

Lorenz looked back toward Emilie and sent her such a scathing look that she shivered. "And so do you, which is why you should learn to hold your tongue. Do you ever think before you speak?"

Emilie knew where this conversation hailed from, and it certainly wasn't Gabrielle. "How many times do I have to say I'm sorry to you?" she asked.

Emilie tried to keep her temper at bay, but wasn't a woman allowed to say no to a marriage proposal? Only Emilie had said no to her best friend. After she had laughed in his face.

"Lorenz, would you please let me explain . . . ," she began.

"I told you before," Lorenz said. "I don't care if you ever speak to me again. But your sister is dear to me, and I'll be damned if I sit back and watch her suffer over your callous words."

Emilie attempted a rebuttal, but Lorenz marched away and joined the men at the stern of the ship. Unmarried with no family ties, Lorenz was one of the decision makers within their community, always the one called upon to perform dangerous tasks. Emilie both adored and envied him.

Why didn't he understand? Emilie thought. He knew her so well, knew her ambitions, her desires. She hadn't meant to laugh. It was a nervous reaction to an unthinkable request. They were friends, not lovers. How could he possibly think she would say yes?

Glancing at Lorenz's back, the blue woolen coat stretched taut against his broad shoulders and his dark hair curling at the collar, Emilie felt the unwelcome emotion race through her again. He had touched her cheek so lovingly last night, kissed her without her having time to protest. Before she realized the implications, she had slipped her fingers into his silky midnight hair and let him deepen the kiss.

It had been the most incredible feeling, like summer lightning striking at her brow and shooting out her toes. And secret places had reacted shamelessly to his touch.

What had come over her, she thought, and why couldn't she get that feeling out of her head?

Heading toward the ship's main mast, Emilie knew Gabrielle would find solace at the vessel's center. She loved to watch the men sail the ship, asking about riggings and rope knots and God knew what else. Emilie knew her sister's mind captured every detail as if she were secretly planning on sailing away. But for Gabrielle, like most women, the knowledge would most likely never be used.

How alike they were, and if anyone knew her pain, it would be Gabrielle. Emilie felt doubly guilty about her insensitive remark. The last person she wanted to hurt was her beloved sister.

"Don't worry about it," she heard Gabrielle say as she rounded the corner and they made eye contact. Gabrielle was seated on the hatch, her favorite place on the ship, the center of all activity.

When Emilie didn't answer, just stared guiltily at her sister, Gabrielle took her hand and rubbed her thumb across her knuckles. "I know you didn't mean it," she said. "I don't like this place either."

Emilie joined Gabrielle on the hatch, and they embraced each other tightly. To Emilie's surprise, the tears that began to fall from hurt feelings were hers. She buried her face in the warmth of Gabrielle's woolen shawl and began to sob while Gabrielle stroked her mane of brown hair.

"I heard all about it," Gabrielle said. "Lorenz looked as if someone had cut out his heart this morning. He was more than eager to talk."

Emilie turned and rested her head on her sister's shoulder. "He asked me to marry him!" she exclaimed.

Gabrielle laughed. "Emilie Marie Gallant, you are the only person in the entire world who is surprised at this. That boy has been in love with you forever."

Emilie righted herself and wiped the tears from her cheeks. "I thought everyone imagined *I* was the one in love with him."

The sadness that routinely lingered in Gabrielle's eyes returned, and she looked at the shore, now ominously close. "That was a long time ago."

Emilie straightened her skirt. "That's just my point, Gabi. We have been living in exile for thirteen years. Thirteen years without a father, without our own homes, without rights, without knowing where our families were sent. Now we're landing in a swamp that smells like hell itself. Things like love are unimportant in these times, don't you think?''

The two women felt a jolt and knew the ship had bumped against the dock. They couldn't make out the landing for the masses of people at the railing, but they could see the chimneys of New Orleans peeking out above the crowd.

"Do you think we'll be able to sleep in a real bed tonight?'' Emilie asked. ''I know you don't mind these rolling bedrooms, but if I don't have my feet on solid ground soon, I will turn into a fish.''

Gabrielle remained silent, and Emilie wondered if she had insulted her sister again. When she turned and gazed into her face—the wisest, most remarkable face in the world, Emilie thought, despite Gabrielle's young age of twenty—Gabrielle appeared to be somewhere else.

"I have a feeling solid ground won't last long,'' Gabrielle finally said. But before she could explain her words, the sailors were shouting orders for the Acadians to disembark.

"Something's not right here,'' Alexis Braud repeated. A fear had taken hold of the man, and he would not let it go.

"We'll wait for the reply from the Spanish governor,'' Jean Depuis answered. ''He told us his wishes, and we've told him ours. Let's see what happens.''

Alexis stood and began to pace through the meager storeroom of the warehouse where the Acadians were housed, the only private place the men could find to discuss their plans. "Ulloa's not the Spanish governor," Alexis insisted, nervously dragging his fingers through his hair. "He has never officially taken over the colony, even though France ceded the territory to Spain several years ago."

"It doesn't matter, Alexis," Jean said. "He is the authority here, and his policy is to transport the incoming Acadian refugees to the frontier, to settle the areas vulnerable to English occupation."

"And keep us separated," Alexis countered. "He wants to place us upriver from the other settlements, isolated from the other Acadians. We are no better off than we were in Maryland. I say we fight this edict. We demand to go to St. Gabriel, no matter what answer this governor gives us. We must demand to be reunited with the other Maryland Acadian refugees."

"We don't have the right to do as we please," Henri Babin added. "We came to Louisiana to join our families and to recreate our homeland, but that doesn't mean we can take matters into our own hands. If the Spanish want us to defend the frontier, then we must do what they ask."

Alexis turned and stared at Henri, years of pain and anguish in his eyes. Lorenz could feel that pain deep in his gut. It was a pain he knew well.

"When have we ever been allowed to do as we please, Henri?" Alexis asked softly, followed by a silence so intense Lorenz could feel his heart beating. "We are merely asking to settle at St. Gabriel where the other Maryland exiles are. I am not a young man, and I am tired of being *sent* places. My family is at St. Gabriel. And I shall join them if my life depends on it."

Jean moved between the men, drawing slowly on his pipe. "You have sent a message to the governor of your wishes," Jean said. "Let us see what happens. We're facing exile from Louisiana if we don't do what the Spanish ask of us, Alexis. We must not act rashly."

Alexis shook his head and moved toward the door. When he threw it open, letting in a blast of frigid air, Lorenz could have sworn they were standing in his father's house in Canada, discussing the harvest and drinking wine as they did in the old days. Alexis placed his woolen cap on his head and glanced back at the anxious men, one in particular.

Honoré Braud, Alexis's brother who had originally been sent to a different county in Maryland and who echoed Alexis's thoughts about reuniting family, stood and joined his brother at the door. Lorenz knew Honoré was just as tired of having friends and family scattered to the winds. Whether their obstinance would convince the Spanish governor was another matter.

When the door shut behind them, the remaining men shivered, then began another round of discussions. It was fruitless, Lorenz assessed, but talking helped.

"Where is this Natchez district?" someone asked.

"I believe it to be about ninety leagues above New Orleans," Lorenz answered, which caused the men to stop talking and glance his way. Everyone knew Lorenz had the best sense of direction, a talent equaled by his knowledge of farming. His father used to tease him that such talents were contradictory, that the best way for Lorenz to utilize such talents was to find his way through a wheat field.

If only his father could see him now, Lorenz thought, in a humid, muddy land thousands of miles from Acadia, where a sense of direction finally came in handy.

"I have seen the maps," Lorenz added. "It's quite a distance from both New Orleans and St. Gabriel."

The other men became silent, but Lorenz could guess their thoughts. So much uncertainty. First the English, then the colonial government of Maryland, now the Spanish. Years of questions. Years of subservience to governments who promised nothing in return, where a man's word could never be trusted.

Lorenz had been old enough to accompany the men of Grand Pré to the church on that fateful day thirteen years before. He had felt honored to participate in the discussion between the Acadians and the English who occupied Nova Scotia, to feel a vital part of the decisions of his community.

"You're a man today," his father told him proudly as they walked into town. Little did his father know how true that statement would be.

The men and boys of the region entered the church at promptly three o'clock, just as the English had demanded. They greeted each other warmly, optimistic that the king would grant their requests as long as they continued to do as they were ordered.

Instead, the hundreds of English soldiers living at the church's presbytery surrounded the church, barred the doors, and promptly arrested the four hundred Acadians within as "enemies of the Crown." Then, several days later, the men were led to the beaches of Minas Basin. Reunited with their wives and children on the shore, the residents of Grand Pré were shipped away from their homeland as they watched the English soldiers burn their homes, slaughter their livestock and destroy the country they had struggled to create one hundred and fifty years before.

Lorenz shut his eyes, reliving that brutal scene. The women of Grand Pré beating at the doors of the church, his own mother begging to the soldiers for their release. The men shouting, "Cowards," at the English soldiers for trapping them as they did. His grandfather's hand on his shoulder, telling him to be brave, that even men were allowed to cry and that he shouldn't be ashamed.

Lorenz had cried that day in the crowded, suffocating church. He had cried later when he found his mother on the beach, deathly pale and trembling. Her health had always been precarious; her heart couldn't take the trauma. She had died in his arms while his father pleaded with her to hang on.

His father, a man who could work circles around his neighbors, who chopped wood effortlessly, who had a smile and a story for every occasion, had died shortly thereafter. The soldier on board the ship had said Antoine Landry had died from exposure and fever, but Lorenz knew his father had died from a broken heart.

Funny, Lorenz thought, how the heart could destroy a man when life's toils and tribulations sometimes failed to. Lorenz had survived the brutal winters of Canada, the rage of smallpox that swept through Grand Pré, and he survived *le grand dérangement,* the exile from Nova Scotia during which half of the Acadians perished from disease and neglect. He survived thirteen long years of exile in Maryland with no family to support him. But Emilie's refusal the night before was killing him.

Lorenz felt a hand on his shoulder and looked up to find Jean Depuis's concerned face. "How are you these days, Lorenz?" he asked.

Lorenz had confided only in Gabrielle, but he knew the others suspected. The men were always urging him on, encouraging him to propose. After a boisterous round of whiskey in the ship's galley the night before, Lorenz had promised the men he would finally act on his heart's desires and ask the woman he had known and loved since childhood to be his wife.

No one understood Emilie better than Lorenz, or appreciated her fiery disposition or her incredible strengths. She had kept her family going, been the backbone of the exiled Gallants through thirteen trying years. Emilie had been Lorenz's savior as well, never leaving his father's side on the ship bound for Maryland when Antoine slipped beneath death's grip, never relinquishing Lorenz's hand during his grief over losing his parents.

Asking Emilie to marry him seemed the most logical step in their relationship. After all these years, they had remained the closest of friends; it was time to move on.

But she had laughed at his declaration of love, then appeared shocked that he would suggest such a thing. The next thing Lorenz knew, Emilie was comparing marriage to a ship's anchor, with the wife being chained and dropped into an ocean of misery and despair. A "free-domless pit of drudgery once a woman says 'I do' " was how she described it.

Hell, Lorenz didn't want to change Emilie. He wanted

to love her, as she had loved him all these years. Only now, Lorenz realized with a pain more hurtful than a knife plunged through his chest, the love Emilie felt for him was simply plantonic. He doubted it would become anything else.

"She turned you down, didn't she?" Jean asked.

Lorenz closed his eyes, tilted his head back and sighed. The agony tore at his heart.

"Don't give up, Lorenz," Jean said, squeezing his shoulder. "She'll come around eventually."

Lorenz shook his head, remembering Emilie's laughter from the night before. "I can't," he said. "It's a slow death. I can't take it anymore."

Jean moved to the nearby table and poured them both a drink. "It's the first time, no? At least wait until the fifth time to give up."

Lorenz looked at Jean and wondered if he was speaking from experience. "Marie finally said yes because she was tired of me asking," Jean said with a laugh.

Lorenz accepted the glass and threw back the dark whiskey that left a tantalizing burn down his throat. "Marie loves you. It was a matter of when, not why."

Jean threw back his own glass and winced. Whiskey was not his drink of choice. "That's just my point, my boy. Give her some time. These are tough days for us. Not the best opportunity to ask a woman to marry you."

Perhaps Jean was right, Lorenz thought. Perhaps it was absurd to ask such a thing as they entered a new territory, unsure of where they would settle. And he had taken her by surprise, crossing a threshold Emilie had not anticipated.

Then there was the kiss. She had kissed him back,

hadn't she? It had all happened so fast, the details were unclear, but Lorenz was certain she had slipped those long fingers into his hair and sighed with pleasure.

Despite his logical mind telling him to find another, Lorenz wanted more of Emilie's kisses. But waiting for Emilie Gallant to change her mind would either make him insane or incite him to rage.

At that moment, Lorenz Landry wanted nothing more than to punch some sense into a certain Spanish governor.

"Do you wish to establish yourselves on the land assigned to you?" Pedro de Piernas bellowed to the group of Acadians filling the back room of the riverside warehouse. "Are you ready to give us your answer?"

When no one spoke, Jean Depuis moved to the front of the crowd. "Monsieur Piernas," he began. "Honoré and Alexis Braud have beseeched you to allow us to join our families at St. Gabriel. As they mentioned in their letter to Governor Ulloa, we came to Louisiana in the hopes of exercising freely our Catholic religion and restoring our communities. We simply want to join the others."

Piernas held up a hand to silence the elderly Acadian. "Alexis and Honoré Braud have refused passage to Natchez, left the city, and gone into hiding. They are outlaws of the Spanish crown. If anyone wishes to join them or refuses to obey this order, they will be exiled from Louisiana and deported immediately."

A collective murmur rose from the crowd, and Emilie felt a sense of panic rush through her. She grabbed Gabrielle's hand and squeezed. They had to get to St. Gabriel.

They had to find their father. But the man was talking exile.

"You will depart aboard the three vessels waiting for the journey upriver," Piernas continued. "You will settle at the fort San Luis de Natchez. There will be no more discussion on the matter."

The Acadians stood together, speechless. The Braud brothers had been their leaders since Maryland, and they had fled. There were no more choices. All diplomatic avenues had been tried and failed. There was little else they could do.

"We agree," Jean said softly.

Piernas nodded. "Then, we leave immediately."

Emilie turned toward her mother and saw the heartbreak of thirteen years reflected in her hazel eyes. Gabrielle wrapped her arms about Rose, who was trying to be brave.

They had traveled so far and were now so close. If Joseph was indeed alive, he was living and breathing only several leagues away. But it might as well be the moon if they were forced to settle at Natchez.

"We'll find him," Emilie commanded them all. "We won't give up."

Despite her brave words, panic began to consume her. She needed Lorenz. As she searched the room, Emilie found it increasingly difficult to breathe. Where was he?

Since the evening he proposed, Lorenz had refused to speak with her. Even in their close quarters, Emilie would sometimes go days without seeing him. He spent a lot of time surveying the river, talking to residents and bartering for food for the group. Emilie tried to follow him one day when he left the warehouse and headed into the

wilderness outside of town with an Acadian she did not
recognize, but she quickly lost sight of them. He was up
to something, and Emilie was dying to find out what.

Emilie finally spotted Lorenz across the room, the sil-
houette of his tall, broad frame shadowed against the back
wall. He was carrying supplies, a large satchel of some
sort, and watching the room suspiciously. It was time he
forgot this silly notion about marrying, resumed their
friendship and spoke to her, Emilie thought. They needed
each other, especially now that they were being sent
upriver to Natchez while Papa waited at St. Gabriel.

She moved toward the other side of the room, but
Gabrielle caught her sleeve. "Don't," Gabrielle warned.

Emilie wanted to demand an answer, but at the cautionary look in Gabrielle's eyes, she held her tongue. Suddenly, she knew.

"Not without me," she exclaimed to Gabrielle. The
panic rose in her throat, and Emilie thought it would
strangle her for sure. Lorenz was leaving, going into
hiding like the Braud brothers.

And leaving her behind.

"He's going to get word to Father," Gabrielle whispered. "Leave him be before the Spanish notice."

Emilie swallowed hard. "Not without me," she
repeated.

Gabrielle stared hard at her sister, then glanced back
toward Marianne and Rose, who were busy collecting
their things for the trip upriver. "You can't," Gabrielle
said. "You don't know what's out there."

"I have to go, Gabi," Emilie pleaded. "Tell Mother

I'm with Lorenz. I'll be safe with him. If anybody can find their way through this marshland, it's Lorenz.''

Emilie spotted a satchel of clothes belonging to Charles Braud, one of the younger boys in the group. Without his noticing, she grabbed the small bag and stuffed it under her shawl.

"Please, don't do this," Gabrielle said.

Suddenly Emilie felt calmer than she had in days. "I'll be fine, Gabi," she said and embraced her sister. "Tell Mother I'll see her in Natchez with Father by my side."

Gabrielle attempted to hold on to her, to keep her sister safe at her bosom, but Emilie broke free. She quickly moved through the crowd and left through the back door.

The same one that Lorenz had just exited.

Chapter Two

The men had traveled two days before they realized they were being followed. The footsteps echoed quietly behind them, so softly that they stopped several times to make sure it wasn't the wind. After the mid-morning break of the third day, Lorenz saw a shadow in the trees and knew for sure.

"You can make yourself known and enjoy our company," Lorenz yelled at the trees, "or remain hidden and force us to come pull you out of those woods."

Only the sound of the wind and the waves of the Mississippi River lapping against the shore answered Lorenz's summons.

Phillip Bellefontaine, a resident of the Acadian settlement north of New Orleans who had agreed to accompany Lorenz as far as his home, shook his head. "Why would anyone want to follow us?" he asked Lorenz. "The Spanish wouldn't bother. They would have arrested you by now. Thieves would have grabbed us in our sleep. There is no reason for a person to be hiding out in the woods following our journey upriver.''

Lorenz considered Phillip's logic. It didn't make much sense to him either. Why, indeed, would anyone bother following two poor Acadian refugees with no money, no boat and a rapidly diminishing supply of food?

Unless. . . .

''I will say it again,'' he yelled back at the trees, hoping against hope that his last thought was unfounded. ''If you don't come out and make yourself known, I will come in there and pull you out.'' Lorenz held up his rifle. ''You must have noticed by now we are armed. And I'd hate to land a musket in your head shooting at shadows.''

There was a slight rustle in the palmetto palms lining the riverbank. A body emerged from its cover, its face hidden by an enormous felt hat. The person approached them cautiously, stooped over with eyes focused on the ground.

''Who are you?'' Phillip demanded, but the intruder said nothing.

When the person emerged into the clearing where Phillip and Lorenz stood, they could tell it was a young boy. His clothes were thoroughly caked in mud and grime as if he had bathed in it. His face was completely marred with dirt and sweat.

''Stand up straight and tell us your name,'' Phillip said.

''Charles,'' the boy whispered, straightening only slightly. ''Charles LeBlanc.''

''Monsieur LeBlanc, is there a reason you are following

us?'' Phillip circled the boy, pulling off his satchel while the boy said nothing, still staring silently at his feet. When Lorenz followed his gaze toward the ground, his heart skipped a beat. The boy's britches were a good inch too short above the knee, and the shoes obviously ill-sized. The stretch of trouser tightened around the boy's hips revealing a curvaceous figure he knew only too well.

Lorenz slowly lifted his eyes to the boy's face, clouded by the brim of his equally dirty hat. But even without full sight of the face, Lorenz knew exactly who it was. Few boys, and definitely only one woman, stood that tall. Even with stooped posture, it was clear he had been followed by the one person capable of doing so.

"Mon Dieu!" Lorenz muttered under his breath. The ships had sailed for Natchez; there was no going back to New Orleans now. Which was why Emilie had followed at such a distance, he was sure. She had gotten clumsy that morning, or perhaps wanted to be found because she had run out of food.

Now what? he thought to himself. Her mother and sisters were more than likely beside themselves with worry. Did Emilie ever think of anyone else's feelings? He wanted to shake her, knock some sense into that gorgeous head of hers, make her understand reason. For as long as he had known the girl, logic was never a part of her vocabulary.

"Take your hat off," Phillip commanded.

A wicked thought came to Lorenz as he watched Emilie squirm under Phillip's dissection. If she wanted to play with the big boys, then so be it.

"Leave him alone, Phillip," Lorenz said. "He's just a boy. Probably shy."

Phillip retreated a step, but continued the interrogation. "What's your business with us?" he asked Emilie.

"I'm on my way home, monsieur," Emilie muttered in a deep voice.

"And where might that be?" Phillip asked.

"Cabannocé, monsieur."

Convenient, Lorenz thought. She picked Phillip's Acadian settlement, an area just south of St. Gabriel on the west side of the river. The exact spot they were heading. Which made Lorenz realize Emilie had more than followed them these past few days.

"So you stole our food," Lorenz bellowed, stepping close to Emilie to watch her cower. "You're the reason our supplies have been disappearing so fast."

"Now I am the one to say leave him alone," Phillip said. "Why are you accusing this boy of stealing?"

Lorenz inched closer to force eye contact, but Emilie refused to look at him. "Because up until now I thought you, Phillip, had eaten that extra bread ration."

At this news, Phillip's eyes shot up. "I thought it was you who had eaten it."

Lorenz stood so close to Emilie he could make out the rapid rise and fall of her bosom. It was outrageous, a woman of Emilie's figure trying to pass herself off as a boy. But he would play this scenario for all its worth.

"I'm sorry," Emilie whispered so only Lorenz could hear, and for a moment he imagined she was talking only to him. "I was hungry."

"And interested in where we were going," Lorenz added. "Again, what business do you have with us?"

Emilie glanced at him then, and immediately looked back at her feet. Even through the layers of mud on her face, Lorenz never could have mistaken those hazel eyes, the different shades of brown accented by specks of red that sparkled when her temper flared. For that brief moment, it had almost been his undoing. "I only wish to return home, to Cabannocé," she muttered.

"I don't know of any Charles LeBlanc," said Phillip.

Emilie said nothing, and Lorenz worried the game would end too soon. "Perhaps he's a recent refugee like myself."

Emilie glanced up quickly and nodded, then returned her gaze to the ground.

"What shall we do with him, then?" Phillip asked.

Lorenz watched as a look of fear crossed his true love's eyes. If he played his cards right, he could have a little fun and teach Emilie Gallant a lesson to remember.

"Take him with us, I suppose," Lorenz answered.

"But we have to teach him he can't be stealing bread from strangers," Phillip added.

"Absolutely," Lorenz said, looking at Emilie. "You must make it up to us."

Emilie nodded and bit her lower lip. The desire gnawing at him since she had rejected his offer of marriage resurfaced as he watched her teeth move back and forth along her lip, swollen from days in the sun. He thought of their kiss and the way her fingers had eagerly threaded into his hair, her lips opening to his. Despite her verbal objections, her body had betrayed her when they had embraced that night. Had it not been for that kiss, Lorenz might have given up all hope of ever wedding Emilie Gallant. But she had left him with a sensuous taste that was difficult to forget.

Angry at being rejected and angry at having to live with the endless wanting, Lorenz picked up her satchel and his own and threw them into her arms. "To make up for the lost bread, you carry the supplies."

Lorenz picked up the rifle and flung it over his shoulder, then kicked sand over the remaining coals of the fire. Without speaking, the two men grabbed their coats and hats and began walking the path along the river toward Cabannocé.

The sun kissed the tops of the tree line gracing the horizon before the men stopped to make camp. Since following them from New Orleans, it was the first day Emilie had seen them forgo an afternoon break. She wondered what had changed their routine; it wasn't like them to walk for hours without a rest. Wearing shoes two sizes too small made every step agonizing, but Emilie would die before she would complain.

All in all, the disguise was working well; she had managed to deceive them both. She delighted that it had taken them almost three days to discover her whereabouts. It had been her own doing, too. She had run out of food and was tired of staying awake half the night to find an opportunity to steal a meager piece of bread.

And the mud—well that was a stroke of genius. Emilie had tripped on some kind of a root sticking above the ground and muddied up her trousers and right arm. When she realized the mud gave her delicate-looking skin a rustic appearance, she rolled down a muddy ravine and covered herself with dirt. The only drawback to this clever disguise was that she was now encased in mud and the chance for a hot bath was more than likely several days away.

Lorenz and Phillip found a suitable clearing, sat down and took a long drink from their water bags. Emilie waited for them to offer her some and moved to sit on a nearby log, but before her rear end touched the wood and her bruised feet could finally rest, Lorenz shouted for her to find firewood.

"May I have a drink first?" she asked, trying to keep her voice as male sounding as possible through the fatigue.

"Firewood," Lorenz repeated.

Emilie stared at Lorenz for as long as she dared. She had never known him to be so cruel as to withhold water from a boy who had walked hours in the wilderness. Surely, he didn't mean it.

"Just one sip?" she asked.

Lorenz corked the water bag defiantly. "Firewood," he practically shouted.

"Fine," Emilie muttered as she stood and eyed the area for the driest source of driftwood. She slowly moved her throbbing feet up the bank from the river, collecting pieces of wood as she went. She wanted so desperately to sit down, to quench her thirst. What had gotten into him anyway? One slice of bread brought this out in a man?

"It's a good thing I turned him down," she muttered

to herself, grabbing another log. "You think you know a person, and then . . ."

When she entered the campsite, both men were lounging back against the side of a downed tree, sharing a slice of bread. Emilie placed the firewood in an open area and felt her stomach react to the sight of food.

"May I have some water now?" she asked, her eyes glued to the bread before her.

"Firewood," Lorenz said with a rueful smile, "is for a fire. The flint is in that satchel."

"Should we give him some bread, Lorenz?" Phillip asked.

Emilie stopped digging through the satchel and listened intently. In addition to her thirst, she was incredibly hungry.

"He already got his bread ration," Lorenz said, taking another long drink from the water bag. "He ate it last night."

Phillip nodded like a judge considering punishment to a criminal. "So he did."

"Nothing?" she asked, hoping the panic wasn't showing in her voice. "I get nothing?"

Lorenz threw the water bag at her. "You should think before you act," he said so ominously that it sent a shiver down her spine. She almost imagined he was speaking of her refusal on the ship that night.

Emilie grabbed the bag and sat down on the sand, facing away from the men. She wanted so badly to give Lorenz Landry a piece of her mind, but she had to play the part until they made it as far as the Acadian Coast. The settlements along the river above New Orleans started with the German Coast, where French and German immigrants had settled since the beginning of the colony. When Acadians began arriving in the territory in the past two years, many had developed farms just north of the German Coast, at Cabannocé and St. Gabriel.

Emilie assumed they were close to the German settlements and a few days shy of Cabannocé. She had to control her temper for at least another week. "You can do this," she instructed herself, but her impulses demanded she slap that smirk off Lorenz Landry's face.

"Did I tell you I have a niece your age?" she heard Phillip ask Lorenz. "Name's Celestine. Unmarried. You'd like her."

"What does she look like?" Lorenz inquired.

Emilie plugged the water bag and turned back toward the men. She withdrew the flint from the satchel and began creating sparks, but softly enough to hear what the two men were saying.

"Beautiful," Phillip answered. "Sweet as can be. Cooks well. Very agreeable. Would make a wonderful wife."

"Agreeable," Lorenz said with a laugh. "Now that's something I'm not used to in a woman."

Emilie hit the flint so hard both men looked her way.

"She's a little on the short side," Phillip added. "Nothing like that tall woman you're interested in."

"*Was* interested in," Lorenz said.

Emilie missed hitting the flint altogether and nearly fell over.

"What did she look like?" Phillip asked. "You said she was a beauty."

Lorenz twisted his mouth in a negative gesture that was so common with the French. Emilie knew exactly what it meant. She began hitting the flint harder because she knew nothing was farther from the truth. The desirous looks from men over the years had taught her that much.

"Nothing special," Lorenz finally said. "There are more beautiful women in the world."

With one last hit, Emilie finally threw a spark that took. She blew into the wood pile, and the spark began a fire that quickly spread. Within minutes, she had a blazing fire. She should have been proud of herself, but the conversation was eating at her heart.

"It was a childhood infatuation," Lorenz continued. "Nothing more. I finally figured that out. She was always running after me as a child, and I guess after so many years I imagined myself in love with her."

Lorenz pulled a lighted blade of palm from the fire, lit a pipe and passed it to Phillip, who took a long draw.

"Perhaps it's time to separate yourself from your childhood," Phillip said. "Meet some mature women. Start a new life."

"Perhaps you're right," Lorenz agreed. "It's time I put Emilie Gallant behind me and settled down with a real woman."

Emilie reasoned that it was the fire causing her eyes to tear, but she headed for the dark shelter of the camp's outer circle just in case. She grabbed her satchel, rolled it into a ball and lay down on the cold ground, using the satchel as a pillow. With her back toward the men and the warmth of the blaze, Emilie knew the fire wasn't to blame. With a pain so heavy pressing against her heart, she cried herself to sleep.

Lorenz tried to rest, but he kept reliving the distressed look on Emilie's face before she retreated to the far side of the campsite. He wasn't sure, but he suspected he heard weeping.

He shouldn't have been so hard on her, telling lies that he knew would cause her pain, withholding food when he knew she was hungry. He and Phillip had planned on relenting, but she had moved away before they could tell her as much.

Lorenz sighed and climbed out of his makeshift bedroll, bringing his woolen blanket with him. He left the warmth of the fire and headed for the area of Emilie's exile. She was curled up tightly, no doubt cold without benefit of a blanket, with the dirty hat still firmly planted on her head. Had she slept this way for two nights? he wondered.

God give him strength, he prayed as he gazed down on the face of the woman he so dearly loved, the woman risking her life for the chance to see her father. Despite everything, he couldn't help admire her strength and her ability to persevere. All of his anger dissipated as he placed his blanket gently over her and brushed his knuckles against her mud-kissed cheeks.

Tomorrow they would talk.

* * *

Emilie awoke to the smell of something tantalizing cooking on the fire. Sleep may have overtaken her hunger the night before, but hunger was forcing her awake.

"Hungry?" Phillip asked her when she sat up and looked his way.

"Yes, very." She nearly bounded across the distance, but managed enough sense to slip escaping tendrils back inside her hat.

Phillip handed her a skillet of pain perdue, stale French bread dipped in egg batter and fried golden brown. Alongside were two fried eggs staring at her like old friends.

"Lorenz met a farmer nearby who gave us some eggs," Phillip said, pouring her a cup of coffee. "By nightfall we should be in the German Coast. We'll get a hot meal tonight."

Emilie was eating so fast she could only nod in agreement. She had never tasted anything so good, and her body demanded that she get the food inside her as fast as possible.

Phillip stared at her hard, and Emilie wondered if her gestures were too feminine. She turned her fork around and began eating the way she saw Charles Braud devour his food when his mother wasn't looking.

"Lorenz was wrong," Phillip finally said.

Emilie wiped the food off the corner of her mouth with the back of her sleeve. "I beg your pardon, monsieur?"

Phillip smiled slightly. "You are a beauty, even covered in mud."

The bite of egg heading to Emilie's mouth stopped halfway.

"Yes, I know who you are, Emilie," he answered her unspoken question.

Emilie placed her fork down in the skillet in her lap and sighed. "How long have you known?"

Phillip took a sip of coffee and laughed. "Since the beginning. There are many women who could disguise themselves as men. You, my dear, are not one of them."

Emilie placed the skillet at her feet, no longer hungry. She rubbed her forehead and forced herself to ask the painful question. "Does Lorenz know?"

She felt a hand upon her shoulder, a sympathetic one. "Of course he knows," Phillip said. "Who do you think that lecture last night was for? I've already heard the story," he added with a groan. "Several times."

Emilie stood and threw her coffee onto the ground. "Where is he?"

"You have no right to be angry with him, mademoiselle." Phillip stood and grabbed her elbow. "You shouldn't be here."

Emilie gently but firmly pulled her arm away. "Where is he?" she asked in a calmer voice.

"He went to a coulee nearby to wash up."

"Which direction?" Emilie asked.

"Mademoiselle, I don't think . . ."

"Monsieur, I am going to find him with or without your help," Emilie said sternly. "Now, either point me in the right direction or worry that I may get lost and you'll lose time hunting me down."

She knew Phillip was eager to get back to his family and didn't want to lose time. Reluctantly, he pointed over to the right of the camp where a grouping of trees was located.

"Merci," Emilie said, straightening for the first time since they met and finding herself taller than Phillip. With those final words, she marched away.

The coulee flowed only a few hundred yards from the campsite, a better-looking stream than most in South Louisiana. Although the water was the usual muddy brown color, this stream allowed a semiclear view of the bottom.

Lorenz stood by the water's edge undressing. She could tell he was shirtless from her view above the shrubbery, but by the time Emilie had him in full sight, she realized he was removing the last leg of his trousers. Before she had time to think, he stood before her completely naked.

The sight was so alarming, and so entrancing, that Emilie froze where she stood. Lorenz Landry was the finest-looking man she had ever set eyes upon. Without clothes, he was astonishing.

A physical man as a farmer, Lorenz's broad back and shoulders were firm with well-toned muscles narrowing into a lean waist and hips. His long legs were equally sculpted and firm, rounded out by the cutest rear end that offered—Emilie almost laughed at the thought—a dimple in each cheek.

"Mon Dieu!" she whispered in awe.

Emilie took a deep breath and forced her mind to focus. She was angry, and no gorgeous male body was going to deter her from her fury. "Want some company?" she asked Lorenz.

Lorenz spun around, clutching his breeches in front of

him. *Damn,* Emilie thought when she realized she was robbed of the view.

"What are you doing here?" Lorenz practically shouted.

Emilie smiled slightly and began to unbutton her shirt. "I was going to join you in a bath," she said, keeping her voice in a deep tone. "Don't tell me you're too modest to bathe with other men?"

Lorenz's jaw tightened. "I know your game, Emilie. Now get back to camp."

"Do you, Lorenz?" Emilie pulled off her shirt, exposing a camisole that was stretched tight across her voluptuous chest. She watched as Lorenz fought hard not to stare.

Finally, his eyes met hers, and they were filled with rage. "What do you think you're doing? Phillip is only a few yards away."

Emilie removed her hat and shook the mound of auburn curls free. "I thought I'd let Phillip decide whether or not I'm beautiful since you seem to think otherwise."

"You'll do no such thing," he bellowed. "Now put your shirt back on."

Lorenz moved forward to grab her, but Emilie was faster. She scooped up his pile of clothes and moved back out of his reach, grinning slyly as she retreated.

"You're not in a position to be running about, Lorenz. Unless, of course, you want to show me those adorable dimples again." His eyes grew enormous, and Emilie felt her power returning. "When did you get so hairy, Lorenz? And so big?"

Lorenz's intense stare didn't falter. He was never one

to be outchallenged by Emilie. ''The same time you grew breasts, Em.''

Nothing Lorenz said or did shocked Emilie, but hearing such a forbidden word on his lips made her laugh. ''My mother would kill you for saying such a thing,'' she said, removing the miserable shoes. ''You know she thinks you're a bad influence on me.''

''I'm a bad influence? Your mother will kill *you* when you make it to Natchez,'' Lorenz said sternly. ''If I don't kill you first.''

Emilie threw his clothes at him, forcing him to drop his breeches. For a brief moment she got quite an eyeful. Then she removed her own clothes and quickly jumped into the water.

Chapter Three

Lorenz felt like a fool, standing naked with his small bundle of clothes clutched in front of him. The late-morning sun felt good on his face, but the brisk wind blowing down from the north chilled other parts of his body, some quite sensitive to cold. But he couldn't resist getting in the last word.

"Watch out for alligators," he said to her, then moved out of Emilie's sight and pulled on his breeches, shirt and shoes. Grabbing his satchel, which contained a bar of soap and a clean shirt, Lorenz walked toward the stream and began washing his face and neck. He hadn't washed in days, and he was not going to miss a chance because stubborn Emilie Gallant insisted on swimming half-naked nearby.

"Lorenz?"

He would have laughed had he not been so angry.

Emilie wasn't scared of many things, but alligators were another story. She had been told many tales about the dangers in the Louisiana swamps.

"Lorenz?" she called out again nervously.

How long should he make her sweat? he wondered with a devilish grin. She deserved a good scare, something to mirror her family's fear of her traveling alone in a strange wilderness full of alligators, snakes and God knew what.

"Lorenz, there aren't any alligators in here," he heard her say defiantly, then with an anxious afterthought, "are there?"

Wiping the water from his face, Lorenz grabbed his satchel and moved back to where Emilie was swimming. He strode to the water's edge, placed a boot on a nearby tree stump, and stared at the bathing beauty before him. The water was muddy enough to conceal her curvaceous features, but Emilie feared otherwise. On sight of Lorenz approaching, she drew her arms about her chest and swam backward a few feet.

"Go away," she commanded him.

Lorenz refused to move, staring intently at the exposed silky skin of her shoulders and her long, graceful neck. When he lifted his eyes to hers and the auburn curls that had sprung to life around a lovely oval face, he leaned an elbow on his knee and made himself comfortable. "I thought you were worried about alligators."

Emilie jutted her chin up. "There are no alligators in here. You're lying."

"Perhaps."

Emilie folded her arms tighter against her chest. "This

isn't funny, Lorenz. You need to go away. I have very little on. And it's wet.''

Thinking back on how she had found him naked by the stream, Lorenz felt the fire burn through his veins, but he fought to remain cool. "What's the matter, too modest to bathe with other men?" He leaned over and picked up Emilie's discarded muddy shirt. "Of course, you're not a man, just an obstinate woman stealing a boy's clothes."

"I didn't steal," Emilie insisted. "I only borrowed . . ."

"No doubt poor Charles Braud is at Natchez right now without a change of clothes," Lorenz continued, the anger rising inside him. "Did you think about what you were doing when you waltzed out of that warehouse in New Orleans? Did you think about Charles? Or your sisters? Or your poor mother sick with worry?"

"Gabrielle knows where I am. She knows I'm with you."

Lorenz placed both feet on the ground, his tall form towering over her. "You could have been killed between here and New Orleans. Any number of things could have happened to you along the way. With the distance you were keeping, you could have had your throat slit by Indians in the night and we never would have heard a peep."

Emilie turned her head and gazed at the forest behind her. "There are Indians here?"

Lorenz shook his head and sighed. She was the most insufferable woman he had ever known. "You're not listening to me."

"I am listening," Emilie shot back. "If you want to

be angry with me for refusing your hand on the ship that night, then be angry. But don't stand there and accuse me of being cruel to my family because I wish to get word to my father.''

"*I* was getting word," Lorenz said, placing a hand on his chest. "We don't need two people risking their lives."

Emilie threw her head back. "And why you? Who declared you head of this family?"

Lorenz tensed, and Emilie realized she had delivered quite a sting. She immediately regretted her insensitive remark. Since the death of his parents, Lorenz had become a welcome part of the Gallant family. If anyone was to risk his life and get word to their father, it was Lorenz. Why couldn't she ever think before she opened her mouth?

"Lorenz," she said softly. "I'm sorry. I didn't mean it that way."

Lorenz crossed his arms about his chest, but the sadness lingering in his eyes didn't leave. "You've been sorry a lot lately, Emilie. Have you noticed that?"

Emilie had had enough of their sparring. She didn't care if he could see her breasts through the cotton camisole she was wearing or notice her legs through her wet pantaloons. She had to talk to him.

Lorenz must have read her thoughts, for he pulled out the clean shirt from his satchel, held it out for her and politely turned his head. Emilie emerged from the water, turned and slipped off the wet camisole, then slid her arms into his shirt. With her back toward Lorenz, she fastened the buttons, noticing that he never moved an inch.

"I didn't mean to laugh," she said softly. "You caught me by surprise, is all."

When she turned to look into the fathomless black eyes she had adored since childhood, he stood so close she could smell the soap on his cheeks. Her mother's lilac soap. Lorenz Landry always looked, smelled and sounded like home. She knew he always would. And that was precisely the problem.

A cold breeze blew across the clearing, and Emilie shivered. Lorenz buttoned the last two buttons at the top of his shirt, then rubbed her arms to warm her. "How could you have been surprised, Em?" he asked, his anger gone. "We have been close for years."

"We have been *friends* for years," she insisted.

Lorenz stared so hard that she shivered again. "The best of friends," he whispered. "Hasn't that meant anything to you?"

Emilie broke free of his grasp and picked up her own satchel. Somewhere underneath the supplies she had managed to steal at the warehouse was a skirt, a petticoat and her own beloved shoes. It was wiser to continue wearing breeches, but she needed to feel feminine, to feel herself again. The aching that emerged like a chasm opening inside her was back, and she needed to regain her strength, her focus.

"Do you think it would be all right if I wear a skirt?" she asked him. "I'm used to my own clothes. It won't slow us down, I promise."

Lorenz looked skyward and shook his head, and Emilie imagined he felt as dark as she did. "Wear whatever you like," he mumbled angrily and moved to walk away.

Before he could back off, she grabbed the front of his cotton shirt and pulled him close. Their foreheads touched, and she could feel his hot breath on her cheek. "Don't stop being my friend," she pleaded. "It would destroy me."

Lorenz's hands were instantly on her cheeks, his thumb sliding across her wet skin, skimming the top of her lips. She could see the anguish in his eyes, feel the pain of his broken heart. But she was powerless to do anything about it.

"Marry me," he asked so heatedly Emilie closed her eyes to shut out the image. She couldn't bear watching him suffer, but she couldn't ignore the haunting darkness tearing at her own soul.

"I can't," she whispered. "Please forgive me."

When she opened her eyes, the anguish was gone in Lorenz's eyes, replaced by the now familiar anger. "A ship's anchor, eh?"

For a moment, she had no idea what he was talking about; then she remembered their conversation aboard the ship, when she had pulled arguments out of the air to satisfy his constant questions. Anything but tell him the truth. She thought to continue the lie, to remind him that she never wanted to be the property of another. It wasn't exactly a lie, after all. Why should she wish to be a powerless female married to a man who legally had all rights to property, money and decisions of the household? Since her father's disappearance on the beach that day at Grand Pré, Emilie Gallant had become head of the family, a position she both deserved and enjoyed. She liked being in charge, tending fields, working a farm. Cooking and sewing were better left to her mother and Rose.

But Lorenz wasn't the kind of man to keep her chained to a stove. He knew her ambitions, understood her tastes and desires. Of all the men in the world, Lorenz Landry would have been the perfect man to marry. If only she wanted to marry.

"I can't," she repeated in a whisper, then grabbed her satchel and walked back to camp.

Around sundown they arrived at the first settlement, a collection of small houses lined up along the riverfront with acres of farmland behind. Now that they had left the marshlands and entered into a clearing that halfway resembled a typical Maryland farm, Emilie's spirits lifted. She had tired of the endless wetlands with a thin layer of smelly green algae floating on top, the fear of snakes and alligators and the concert of bullfrogs every evening. She wanted solid ground, a place where her wooden shoes wouldn't lodge themselves in the mud every several feet.

"Those shoes don't work well here," Phillip told her when one muddy spot nearly caused her to sprain an ankle. "They are better suited to a Canadian climate."

"I figured that out," Emilie answered tersely. She hadn't meant to be rude, but everything seemed to annoy her. She was tired of the journey, tired of cold, humid wind whipping around every corner of the Mississippi, tired of finding a swamp to cross every few miles, tired of Lorenz ignoring her. Since their conversation that morning, he spoke only to Phillip, engaging in all subject matters but never including her.

Why must she be punished for not wanting to marry him? she wondered as she yanked her skirt from the clutches of a holly bush. They had led a perfect life until this point, were the best of friends. Now, because she prefered to remain unmarried, he was treating her as if she no longer mattered.

Was that all women were created for? Emilie wondered as she pulled her jacket up around her ears to ward off the incessant cold. To be married? Lorenz was never the type to suggest such a thing, but he had presented many surprises since their journey began. Maybe deep down all men were the same, despite their insistance otherwise.

"The first house is the Frederic's," Phillip announced. "They are a friendly couple, and their children are grown. I'll ask if they can spare their back rooms."

Lorenz paused while Phillip approached the house. For the first time since their conversation at the coulee, he turned his eyes toward Emilie.

"Are you going to ignore me forever?" she asked. Lorenz shrugged and looked away. "You're acting like a child," she added.

At this remark Lorenz looked back at her sharply. "You're right, Em," he said. "I am acting childish. I'm acting exactly the way a child would act when someone has trampled on his heart."

The hurt he had exhibited earlier returned, and Emilie turned away to escape those dark eyes full of pain. "I never meant to hurt you," she whispered.

"Well, you did," Lorenz said.

Phillip was greeted at the back door of the house by a stocky, middle-aged woman. They spoke for a few moments; then Phillip waved them over. Before Lorenz moved to leave, Emilie tugged on his sleeve.

"Don't do this to me," she pleaded.

Lorenz took her hand at his sleeve and rubbed it gently, despite his better judgment, she was sure. "Do what, Em? Ignore you or ask you to be my wife?"

Emilie slipped her fingers through his and held tight. "Both?" she responded sheepishly.

For a moment, Lorenz gazed into her eyes so intently, Emilie thought he might kiss her. For a moment, she hoped he would. Then he frowned and untangled his fingers from hers, whispering heatedly to her before walking toward the house, "As you said at the coulee, I can't."

"Lorenz Landry," Phillip said as they approached, "this is Madame and Monsieur Frederic."

"*C'est un plaisir*, madame, monsieur," Lorenz said, accepting the man's outstretched hand. "May I present Mademoiselle Gallant."

The husband bowed politely toward Emilie, and the woman smiled broadly. "Please," the husband said, "I am Mathias and this is my wife Anna."

"Pleased to meet you both," Anna said, still smiling. "Come in out of this horrendous cold."

Mathias held the door open for his wife, and all three men waited for Emilie to pass through. When she proceeded past Lorenz, she could still see the hurt simmering in his eyes. And like so many times in the past, his hurt reverberated into her soul.

She entered the modest house, which had obviously

been built in the early days of the colony before tools and resources were plentiful. The center of the dwelling offered a rugged floor of crudely assembled planks and a fireplace that appeared to be constructed of mud and sticks. Spoking out from the fireplace were additions constructed with more expertise, but even these more refined rooms lacked the comfort and security of a finely built home.

Despite the coarse construction and the primitive fireplace, the small house was cozy. There were braided rugs, lace curtains and a dozen carved wooden figures gracing the mantel. The homeliness of the house tugged at Emilie's heartstrings and instantly brought to mind her mother and sisters and the home they had shared in Grand Pré. More than likely her family was at the Natchez post now, living inside the Spanish fortifications.

Emilie looked back toward Lorenz, wondering if he felt the same longing for a house of his own, a place they could finally call home after so many years living under foreign governments and the charity of neighbors, but he refused to acknowledge her.

Of course Lorenz wants a home of his own, Emilie thought. *With me in it.* Emilie's heart ached for such a life. But as quickly as the thought entered her mind, she dismissed it.

"Are you hungry?" Anna asked them.

Phillip twirled the brim of his hat in his hand. "Yes, Anna," he answered with a bright smile. "We're very hungry."

Emilie couldn't imagine Anna's smile getting any bigger, but it did. She clasped her hands together, then moved into the kitchen and began placing an assortment of pots on the stove.

"She is very happy to have company," Mathias said. "Since our youngest married and began his own farm upriver, she has had no one to cook for."

"We're glad to be of service," Phillip said with a large grin of his own.

Mathias leaned in conspiratorially. "Perhaps you would care for some brandy, too?"

The men chuckled and began to talk among themselves while Mathias began searching the cupboard for a bottle. Suddenly, as was usually the case when Emilie was in the presence of men, she was excluded from all conversation. They joked, exchanged manly grasps on each other's shoulders, and turned their backs toward her. Instantly invisible, Emilie stood awkwardly on the periphery of the action, wondering if she should stay and attempt to be included or join Anna in the kitchen. She wanted to sit down and relieve her aching feet. She wanted to be warmed by a glass of brandy like the men.

Mathias raised a dusty, dark bottle above his head. "I found it," he announced proudly. He poured each man a glass, then lifted his in a toast. "To your health and happiness," he said, and the two men responded by lifting their glasses in kind.

Mathias signaled for the men to sit down at the large wooden table between the main room and the kitchen. Emilie knew it was time for her to retreat to the kitchen, but she hated leaving the warmth of the fireplace or the male conversation. Perhaps her father was right. Perhaps she would have been better off born a man.

Was this how her life would be, married to Lorenz? she wondered. Visitors would come to call, and she would be relegated to the kitchen while Lorenz enjoyed a good drink with company? She tried catching his eye, hoping he would offer her a place at the table, but he continued to refuse to look at her. Suddenly, Anna was at her side.

"Have a seat by the fireplace," Anna said to her. "I will bring you something to drink."

"But I need to help you with the meal," Emilie insisted.

Anna shook her head. "You need to get warm. Do not worry about a thing."

"I told you, she is thrilled to have the company to wait upon," Mathias said to her before turning back to the conversation at the table.

Well, at least I'm not completely invisible, Emilie thought as she sank into a comfortable chair to the right of the fireplace and inched her sore feet toward the fire.

As she promised, Anna returned with a smile and a glass. Emilie looked up to find it resembled what the men were drinking. Before she could inquire, Anna placed a finger to her lips. "Something to warm you as well," she said.

Emilie sank deeper into the chair and sipped the brandy, thankful for the kind hospitality. It felt good to be warm again, even if Lorenz's refusal to speak to her continued to chill her heart.

"So you are Acadian as well?" Mathias asked Lorenz after enjoying a long, stiff drink.

"Oui, monsieur," Lorenz answered.

The stout man laughed. "For how long?"

Lorenz appeared confused. "I don't understand, monsieur."

Mathias refilled their glasses. "First, you must call me Mathias. Second, you must realize we are a colony of many nations. I, for instance, am the son of a German, whose name was Friedrich. The French called us Frédéric and we learned their language. Just when we thought we were French, the Spanish arrived. I'm beginning to think that perhaps if I live long enough, I shall be German once more."

Lorenz smiled at his good-naturedness. He liked this man. Mathias was the first non-Acadian resident to offer good cheer and hospitality since their arrival in Louisiana.

"Be that as it may, we are still Acadians, despite our entrance into this Spanish territory," Phillip said.

"Do you consider yourself subjects of France, then?" Mathias asked.

Phillip and Lorenz looked at each other, wondering how to answer that question. They were Acadians, subject to no one but themselves. They had been Acadians a century before the English arrived, self-sufficient from their mother country.

"We are French, monsieur," Phillip began, "because we came to the New World from France. But we have lived in Acadia, our own country in Canada, since before the founding of Jamestown.

"We had a fairly good relationship with the English when they took over Acadia in my father's time," Phillip continued, "but I don't consider myself English simply because I was born in Nova Scotia when the English governed it."

"But you are in Louisiana now," Mathias said. "Which crown do you serve?"

Phillip gazed into his glass and was silent for several moments. When he looked up again, his eyes held a deep sadness. "I despise the English for robbing us of our homes and shipping us throughout the colonies, the Caribbean and Europe," he answered. "I resent the French for neglecting us in our time of need and ignoring us in our exile. And I am angry with the Spanish for welcoming us into this territory, then forcing us away from our families and friends. I have had the good fortune of settling in Cabannocé, but recent Acadian refugees have been forced to settle upriver, first at St. Gabriel, now at Natchez. It seems that every nationality is determined to scatter us every which way."

A silence hung over the room until finally Mathias spoke. "Do you not hold an allegiance to any nationality, then?"

Again, the two men gazed at each other, and Emilie wondered what answer Lorenz or Phillip would give. They were distinctly French, but stubbornly Acadian, and this was not an easy concept to understand.

"What do you think, Emilie?"

Emilie nearly dropped her glass when she realized Lorenz was speaking to her. She looked up to find three pairs of eyes waiting for her answer.

"I believe we will always be Acadians," she said. "I'm sure we'll get used to the Spanish in time, as they will get used to us. Perhaps we will call ourselves Louisianians, too. But I think we will always be Acadians."

"And why is that, mademoiselle?" Mathias asked.

Emilie turned in her seat to better face the men, glad to have their attention at last. "Our ancestors carved a nation out of the Canadian wilderness by cooperating with each other and with the natives. Over time, it caused us to establish our own culture, our own identity. We're not like other French now. And because we have been exiled from our homes, we will fight to retain our identity so our children will never forget our homeland."

Lorenz offered an appreciative smile, signaling to Emilie that he agreed. They had always been able to speak volumes to each other with merely a glance. She smiled back at him, but he frowned and looked away.

Mathias stared off into the flames, considering what Emilie had said. Then he looked up, smiled and refilled their drinks. "To the German-Acadian Coast, then," he said, lifting his glass in another toast. "And this territory of nations, whatever yours might be."

The men raised their glasses in a salute, but Lorenz turned and hoisted his glass toward Emilie. She returned the toast and felt a million times brighter seeing the semblance of a sparkle in his dark eyes. Even though Lorenz turned back toward the men and they continued talking without her, that simple gesture warmed her heart, informing her that their friendship was a long way from ending.

"You asked her again, didn't you?" Phillip quizzed Lorenz with a grin. They had eaten their fill of a hearty dinner, then retired to one of the two back rooms the

Frederics kept for travelers and visiting relatives. "You don't give up."

Lorenz wasn't particularly eager to talk about his second marriage rejection within a month's time, but it was a relief to have a confidant. "It doesn't make sense," he told Phillip. "She says no, but her eyes tell me something else."

Phillip grinned wider and placed an arm about Lorenz's shoulders. "Forget the words and the eyes, my boy. What that girl needs is a good kissing."

Lorenz had to admit it wasn't a bad idea. Nothing else was working. Under ordinary circumstances, they would have courted. He would have visited her house, taking her for walks, talking with her while her parents sat nearby serving as chaperons. But they hadn't lived under ordinary circumstances since they were children.

Besides, he couldn't picture himself courting Emilie in the traditional sense. He was practically family. Marianne had welcomed him into the Gallant family after his parents' deaths and raised him as her own. Rose and Gabrielle had been the greatest of sisters. So how was he to formally court a woman he had lived with for thirteen years? She had stroked his head and sung soothing songs while he grieved for his parents, helped him steal a basket of blueberries from the Jesuit priests in Maryland, given him his first glimpse of a woman's leg when she refused to be left behind while the men picked apples on the branches of trees. Their lives were extraordinary, and courting seemed a useless, frivolous custom.

"Perhaps you're right," Lorenz said, thinking back on what a shapely leg Emilie possessed. Not to mention the sweeping curves gracing the rest of her tall, voluptuous body. "Maybe I am going about this the wrong way."

Having pulled down the blankets of his bed, Phillip quickly threw off his clothes and jumped inside the covers. He put his hands behind his head and sent Lorenz a sly smile. "Why don't you go see how lovely Emilie is doing?"

Emilie's chamber was next to theirs, two rustic rooms extending off from the house, perpendicular to the back gallery. From the look of the rooms' contents, the Frederics used them for housing tools and food supplies when relatives were not in town.

"I really should go and see if she has everything she needs," Lorenz said, trying not to sound eager.

Phillip nodded, playing the game well. "You do that," he said before turning and pulling the covers over his head.

Lorenz tightened his coat about his chest and slipped out to the back gallery. He was immediately greeted by a blast of cold air biting down from the direction of the river. Rain appeared imminent, more than likely to be followed by more frigid weather. He thought to return to the semiwarmth of his room, but he noticed a light under Emilie's threshold. Lorenz knocked lightly.

"Who is it?"

Lorenz almost laughed. Who else would it be? "It's your footman, mademoiselle. Shall I get the carriole ready for your trip tomorrow? Or would you prefer to travel by ship?"

The door swung open, and Emilie stood before him, her reddish brown hair a cascade of curls about her broad but elegant shoulders. Her borrowed woolen night dress concealed plenty, but Lorenz could make out the shape of her ample breasts by the rapid rise and fall of her breath, which seemed accentuated by his presence. When he gazed into the hazel eyes he had adored for years, he found a light shining in them. She was glad to see him, glad to know he still cared.

He couldn't help grinning at her eager face, and she answered him with a tentative smile. Despite his logical mind warning him not to tread into dangerous emotional territory, Lorenz broke down the wall guarding his heart and entered her room. Then, while he kicked the door closed, Lorenz slipped an arm about her waist, drew her tight against him and placed his lips on hers.

Chapter Four

One minute Emilie stood in the doorway, glad to see Lorenz back on friendly terms; the next minute his lips were hot upon hers. By the time she realized what was happening, Lorenz had pulled her tight against his chest, deepening the kiss and literally taking her breath away.

She knew she should push him away. This was improper and against her wishes and better judgment. But, oh, his kisses tasted delicious, just as they had that night on the ship—hot and wild and mysterious. The sensations coursing through her body felt like riding the forty-foot tidal surge that raged through Minas Basin at Grand Pré.

Emilie decided to enjoy the ride. She leaned her head to gain better access to his demanding lips and raised her hands to thread them through his thick dark hair. When her hands reached the curls lingering at his collar, Lorenz groaned and pulled her harder against his broad chest.

"Oh, Em," he whispered as his lips began an exploratory trail across her cheeks, beneath her earlobe and down the soft reaches of her neck. "I have dreamt of this moment for years."

Emilie had always wondered what it would be like to kiss Lorenz, to experience their bodies close together. She slid a hand down the length of his back, savoring the strong, thick muscles, while her other hand stroked his magnificent hair, so wild and untamed, a mirror of himself. He felt good. Magnificently good.

When Lorenz claimed her lips again, he urged them apart and slipped his tongue inside. At first Emilie jolted at the intrusion, but when his tongue met hers, she could have sworn she heard herself moan. A spasm passed through her, melting her insides, all the while creating a heightened sense of something undeniably new and thrilling. She wanted more of this lovemaking, even though they were treading on dangerous territory.

Lorenz drew away slightly and rested his forehead against hers. When she looked into his haunting black eyes, they were glazed with desire. Emilie wondered if hers revealed the same longing.

"Where did you learn to kiss like that?" she asked him.

Lorenz answered with his trademark lazy smile while the deep recesses of his eyes twinkled. "From you," he said. "In the barn behind Paul LeBlanc's house."

They were so close Emilie could see every detail of his ruggedly handsome face: the sharp lines of his chin, his long, regal nose, the fullness of his lips which had brought her so much pleasure. Without thinking, she placed a hand on his cheek and brushed her thumb across those hot, insistent lips. Lorenz instantly placed a hand over hers and captured her thumb with his mouth, pulling it inside where his tongue gently circled the tip. The sensation that simple gesture caused made her knees weaken.

"I was only eight when you kissed me in the barn," she said feebly, hoping to focus on anything but what his tongue and lips were doing to her fingers. "I'd say you've learned a lot since then."

Lorenz pulled her hand away and placed it at his waist. Then he placed his hands at her waist and drew her closer. This time, she wasn't being held only against his chest. Now other parts of her body were rubbing his. "Why don't we learn it together?" he whispered so fervently that Emilie shivered.

She knew she should demand he leave her room, but she wanted to see what else Lorenz had learned since their childish kiss in the barn.

Lorenz didn't disappoint. His lips met hers again as he pressed the small of her back so that their bodies merged at the hip. In that instant Emilie knew Lorenz's desire and her own. She parted her lips further, and Lorenz took the bait. His kisses were wild, his tongue probing deeper, his teeth nipping on her bottom lip.

Just when Emilie thought she would abandon her defenses, Lorenz drew back, gazed one more time into her eyes, and tucked a wild strand of hair behind her ear. "Good night, Em," he whispered and quickly left the room.

Emilie stared at the door as if a gale force wind had

suddenly blown through her room, then died altogether. She placed a hand on her chest to try to stabilize her breathing. Then she remembered her weakened knees and sat down.

What had just happened?

She almost became angry, imagining herself a victim of a man vindictive after being spurned, teasing her with lovemaking only to reject her as she had rejected him. But those kisses had been anything but retaliatory. He had been as excited as she was. Was he scared of what might transpire or just hoping to set a spark that would linger and burn into a flame? If the latter was true, he had succeeded. Emilie wanted more. Much more.

Suddenly cold and shivering, Emilie climbed into bed and pulled the blankets tight against her chin. She extinguished the candle and lay back against her pillow, staring up into the intense darkness. Outside the rain pelted the house, and the wind howled through every hole in the wall. She could hear Lorenz entering his room next door and climbing into his own bed. What was he thinking at this moment? she wondered. Was his heart beating as fast as hers?

Emilie could still feel the heat on her neckline and face where his kisses had touched her skin. Her lips tingled from Lorenz's kisses.

"What do I do now?" she asked no one, wishing her mother and sisters were nearby to give her advice. Mother would know what to do, she thought, and Gabrielle would understand Lorenz's mind. Rose would be optimistic that there was a solution to every problem, even though Emilie doubted there was an answer to this one.

The thought of her family traveling upriver in an open boat or sleeping inside a frigid Spanish fort only made Emilie sadder. Suddenly, she felt incredibly alone.

She turned on her side and hugged her pillow. When times were dreary, Rose would sing them all a soft, romantic song, sometimes stroking Emilie's hair until she fell asleep. If only her family were with her now, they would tell her what to do, explain how to react to Lorenz and his insistent demands to be married.

As myriad emotions fought within her, Emilie gently touched her lips and thought how nice it would be if Lorenz were lying next to her, touching them himself.

"This is not acceptable," Joseph Braud announced. "This country is not habitable."

Rose watched as Pedro de Piernas cringed and rubbed his forehead with his thumb and forefinger. They had been in the fort at Natchez for less than a week, housed in the upper story of the barracks and given liberal use of the fort's kitchen. No one at the fort had better quarters than the Acadians. Yet, daily the exiles voiced their disapproval to the Spanish commandant.

"The land is perfectly fit for settlement," Piernas returned. "Not only have I and Governor Ulloa deemed it good land for farming, but one of your own has inspected the land and said so."

"There are better lands," Joseph countered. "Ones closer to New Orleans."

Rose had joined the men when they inspected the land surrounding the fort and found it quite habitable, but she knew the majority of the settlers wanted to be closer to the other Acadian refugees. Nothing Piernas would say would make them feel otherwise, and they would find every excuse to convince him to send them downriver to St. Gabriel.

"Send three of us to New Orleans, let us talk to the governor," Joseph demanded. "Give us some boats and men and let us have a chance to present our case."

Piernas stared at his feet, an aggravated look upon his face. Rose wondered if he would agree to let the three men travel to New Orleans just to be rid of the hotheads. Joseph Braud and two other men had taken it upon themselves to keep defensive feelings high. Every time the Acadians began to settle in to their surroundings, Joseph and the other men incited them to rebel. Rose was as tired of the complaining as Piernas, even though she wanted nothing more than to be reunited with her father at St. Gabriel.

Suddenly, Piernas looked her way as if he remembered something, staring hard first at her and Gabrielle, then their mother.

"I will grant you this request," he said, turning back toward the men. "You will take three of my smallest boats, and I will give you men and provisions. You have forty-five days to travel to New Orleans and back. I will draw up the papers now."

Piernas moved to leave the room, but stopped where Rose and her mother stood. "Madame Gallant, I wish to speak with you and your daughters, *s'il vous plaît.*"

Marianne nodded, and Piernas left the room for his

private quarters. When she turned toward Gabrielle and Rose, she reached out her hands for their comfort.

"It can't be about Emilie and Lorenz," Gabrielle insisted as they followed the commandant through the garrison. "They would have said something by now."

"I don't like this," Marianne whispered back. "Something's not right."

Piernas entered his quarters and motioned for the women to sit down. "I prefer to stand, if you don't mind," Marianne said.

Piernas sighed heavily and rubbed the top of his nose. Rose had witnessed the same gesture many times; obviously the man suffered from some form of headaches, most likely given to him by the consistently bewailing Acadians.

"Willow bark tea would help those," Rose offered.

The piercing stare Piernas gave her made her swallow hard. "I beg your pardon, mademoiselle," he said.

"I've used it many times for headaches," Rose said. "I will be happy to bring you some."

Piernas laughed, which startled the women. "I'm sorry," he said, when he noticed them flinch. "But I believe you are the first Acadian to worry about my discomfort or to offer me any kind of assistance. I would rather command an army than six of your families."

Rose felt her mother's hand tense in hers, and Gabrielle folded her arms defiantly across her chest.

"Please, sir," Rose began, hoping to ward off any angry words her mother and sister might throw his way. "You must understand that some of our families are at

St. Gabriel. Our father, whom we haven't seen in thirteen years, is suspected of being there.''

Piernas looked at each of them, clearly surprised at the news. ''This is the first I've heard of it,'' he said.

''Alexis Braud told the governor of our situation,'' Marianne explained coldly. ''How is it that you have no knowledge?''

Piernas rubbed the back of his neck, obviously another sore spot. ''The governor wishes to settle the Louisiana frontier with families so that we can stop English aggression. Those were my orders, nothing more. Surely, you can understand his position and mine.''

''We are one family,'' Gabrielle pleaded. ''Would one family make a difference?''

''You are one family, and Joseph Braud and his wife are another,'' the commandant insisted. ''Henri Babin is another. The LeBlancs. The Depuis. Where do we draw the line, mademoiselle?''

''Señor,'' Marianne said, stepping forward. ''Why do you wish to see us?''

The dark Spaniard placed a hand at his hip and stared at the mass of papers before him. ''You have another daughter, have you not?''

Rose felt her throat constrict and her heart race. She immediately prayed that Emilie and Lorenz hadn't been caught and deported from Louisiana.

''Yes, I do,'' Marianne said proudly, her chin held high. Rose felt her mother's hand shaking, but knew her mother would never let him see her weak. ''Why do you ask?''

Piernas remained silent for a moment, then met her stare. "Please sit down, madame," he said softly.

Suddenly, Marianne's shaking was clearly visible. "Has something happened?"

"No, madame," Piernas assured her, grabbing her elbow and leading her to a chair. "And we hope nothing will."

Gabrielle placed a hand on Marianne's shoulder and squeezed. "What do you know of Emilie?" Gabrielle asked.

Piernas leaned back on the corner of his desk. "I received a list of passengers aboard the *Guinea* from Maryland. Your daughter and Lorenz Landry were two who did not arrive here in Natchez, besides the Braud brothers." He moved to the front of his desk and picked up an official paper. "The number of passengers bound for Natchez was reported in New Orleans. I am not the only one who knows that there are members of this party unaccounted for. The governor wants my report."

"They have gone to St. Gabriel," Marianne said anxiously. "They only want to get word to my husband. They will join us as soon as they find him. You have our word on it."

Piernas rubbed the bridge of his nose again, this time more furiously. Rose felt the man's anguish. He was only performing a duty to his governor, making the best for a group of settlers who should be happy to have land and the freedom to practice their Catholic religion. Instead, he was housed with dozens of complainers and complications. Without forethought, she reached over and took his free hand.

The Spaniard's eyes shot up, and Rose instantly regretted her instinctual move. She was forever acting on impulse, never thinking things through. She had only wanted to express some gesture of gratitude and understanding, but as she had done so many times before, she had crossed a cultural and diplomatic boundary.

Piernas pulled his hand away at the same time Rose removed hers. But to her amazement, he seemed neither embarrassed nor alarmed.

"I will send word that your daughter and Monsieur Landry became ill en route and will be joining us at the fort as soon as they are able," he said. "If they are not at Natchez within two months' time, I will have to report them missing. If they are found, they will be tried and possibly deported."

Marianne stood and covered her mouth to keep her emotions at bay. "Thank you, sir," she finally whispered.

"They'll be here," Gabrielle assured him.

Piernas nodded and dismissed them with a wave of his hand. "Let's hope so, for your sake and theirs."

Marianne and Gabrielle bowed and left the commandant's quarters, but Rose paused and glanced up at the Spaniard one last time. "I'll have the tea brought to you as soon as possible," she said. "You should try a hot compress on the back of your neck as well."

Feeling rather embarrassed, as if she had stepped over the line yet again, Rose bowed awkwardly and moved to leave. Before she reached the threshold, she heard a faint reply. *"Gracias,* mademoiselle," the commandant said.

* * *

"Two months," Gabrielle repeated, pacing the floor of the barracks. "How long did it take us to get here?"

"Sit down, Gabrielle," Marianne ordered. "You're making me nervous."

"Oh, why didn't I stop her?" Gabrielle paused and placed a hand on her forehead. "I should have shouted out. I should have called someone after her."

"You would have risked both their lives," Rose said. "Stop blaming yourself."

Marianne stared hard into the fire as if in a trance. Rose was used to her moments of "sight," but she had become ominously silent since their meeting with Piernas. "They'll make it," Marianne whispered, closing her eyes. "I see them with us. But your father . . ." Marianne's eyes shot open, and she gasped.

"What about Father?" Rose asked, bending down to look at her mother's face.

Marianne's face constricted in pain. "I see him going away from us," she said anxiously, grabbing her daughter's hand. "He's leaving us."

Gabrielle kneeled down on the other side of Marianne and took her other hand. "That's not possible, Maman. We got word that he was at St. Gabriel. We'll find him."

Marianne shook her head, tears pouring down her face. "Perhaps," she said, wiping them away. "But not this year."

Gabrielle and Rose gazed at each other over their mother's lap, and Rose felt a chill travel up her spine. Holding on to their mother's hands, both daughters felt the energy leave her body. After every vision, Marianne collapsed, sleeping for hours afterward. Rose wondered if it was the power of such a gift that stole her energy or the memory of that fateful day in Grand Pré.

Gabrielle and Rose helped their mother to bed, the tears still fresh on her face, then retired to the fireside. Neither one could hope for sleep after such an image.

"It's been a long time since I've felt this low or seen mother in such a state," Gabrielle finally said. "I wish Emilie and Lorenz were here."

Rose stood next to her sister and placed Gabrielle's head at her bosom. While she stroked her sister's long, dark hair, supposedly a replica of their father's, Rose began singing the first stanzas of "Sept Ans Sur Mer," a soft French ballad about a shipwrecked family.

Emilie was awakened by the sound of the men leaving to tend to the animals, the lilt of Lorenz's laughter rising above the rest. Wanting to see him and make sense of what had happened the night before, Emilie threw her legs from the covers and jumped out of bed. As soon as her feet touched the ground, however, she knew she could not make it as far as the door. Swollen, bruised and cut from days of wearing Charles's shoes, her feet had finally declared mutiny.

She sat back down on the bed, massaging her throbbing feet. In the distance she heard the men walking in the direction of the barn and fields. *Probably just as well,* she thought, as her stomach voiced its own disapproval of being neglected. In all likelihood, Anna was creating a massive breakfast for them all, and she should help out in the kitchen.

Emilie struggled through dressing, gently slipping her woolen stockings over her damaged feet. When she stood, she was amazed to find she could hardly walk. She limped through the process, holding on to whatever she could find. By the time she entered the main house, she was ready for assistance. Anna immediately caught sight of her, snaked an arm about her waist and led her to a chair by the kitchen table.

"What on earth has happened to you, child?" Anna exclaimed as she placed Emilie into a chair and removed her stockings. Peering down toward her war-torn feet, even Emilie was surprised at their condition.

"I wore shoes two sizes too small for days," Emilie explained. "Then I switched to my own shoes, which probably added to the injury."

Anna examined each foot, particularly the joint areas around the big toes where blisters had formed and oozed blood and pus. She glanced up at Emilie with a bewildered look. "And you never noticed this happening?"

Emilie wondered how to explain her predicament. Gazing down into accepting, maternal eyes, she decided to tell the truth. "I wasn't supposed to travel with the men," she began. "I followed them for days dressed as a boy in case they saw me, which they eventually did."

To Emilie's surprise, Anna nodded knowingly. "You stay put and I'll get you a plate of breakfast," she said, rising. "Then I'll get a bucket of hot water to soak those feet in."

Emilie watched as the older woman went about her business, obviously not too concerned that Emilie had disguised herself as a male and run away from her family.

"It was important to me that I go to St. Gabriel with them," Emilie continued, feeling a need to explain her defiance to her mother, her sisters and the Spanish governor of Louisiana.

"I understand," Anna said, placing a heaping plate of food before her. "Coffee?"

Emilie nodded and watched in bewilderment while Anna poured her a cup of steaming coffee. "You do?"

Anna sat down across from Emilie at the table and folded her hands in front of her, the same gesture her mother used when she wished to discuss matters of importance. "I've seen how you two look at one another," Anna began. "Of course I understand."

In between bites of eggs and a thick and juicy blood sausage, Emilie gazed up at the kind woman who had shown her unending hospitality. She dreaded asking the next question. "Understand what?"

"My dear," Anna began, placing a maternal hand on her wrist. "I am old enough to be your mother. I can see when two people are in love."

Emilie nearly choked on her breakfast. She was sure a piece of sausage had lodged in her throat. When she tried to argue, her voice emerged in a whisper. "It's not what you think."

Anna rose and poured herself a cup of coffee, then grabbed a sugar bowl and small pitcher of cream before sitting back down. "Of course not, dear."

"No," Emilie said, her voice finally free of the obstruction. "We're just friends."

"Friends." Anna spooned sugar into her coffee and motioned to do the same for Emilie's cup.

"Oui, merci," Emilie said. "Madame Frederic . . ."

"Anna. Cream?"

"Oui, merci, Anna." Emilie swallowed hard to clear her throat and her senses. She had to be distinct on this point. "You must understand. Lorenz and I have been good friends since childhood. It's nothing more than that."

"So were Mathias and I." Anna rose and picked up a cast-iron skillet from the stove. "More sausages?"

"Oui, merci," Emilie said, wondering if Anna was hearing her. Anna placed an enormous sausage on Emilie's plate, knowing well that Emilie was hungry enough to eat it, then sat down and folded her hands together as if waiting for the truth to be told. As with Marianne and possibly all mothers, Emilie knew there was no lying to this woman. "He asked me to marry him," she said.

Anna instantly brightened. "How wonderful," she said, grasping Emilie's hands and squeezing. "You must be very happy."

"I turned him down." Emilie watched as Anna absorbed this information. "Twice."

Anna didn't flinch. She appeared more disappointed than astonished. "Why?" she asked with such emotion, Emilie felt a strong tug on her heart. Tears lurked precariously close to the surface.

Emilie stared down at her plate, the appetizing sausages quickly becoming a blur. "Because we're friends," she stated firmly, hoping her words would restore her emotional equilibrium. The statement gave her strength, and she looked up, releasing her hands from Anna's grip. "We've always been friends."

Anna leaned back in her chair and folded her arms across her chest. Emilie didn't like the way she was being scrutinized by the kind woman; she felt guilty meeting the older woman's eyes. *Definitely a maternal trait,* Emilie thought, thinking back on how her mother could send such scathing messages with only a look. If Anna was anything like Marianne, she feared what arguments would come next.

"What are you scared of?" Anna finally asked.

"Scared of?" This was not what Emilie had expected. She was scared of nothing.

"Yes, I asked what you are scared of."

Emilie laughed, folding her own arms about her chest. "I'm not scared of anything. I have been taking care of my family for thirteen years. My father made me head of the household, and I have met that challenge head-on."

Anna unlocked her arms and leaned in close. "But you are scared of getting married to the man you love, my dear."

Her words reverberated through Emilie's mind, bouncing off and bringing to life denied fears she refused to think about, let alone believe in. She trembled as a pain deep inside her rose to the surface and commanded her heart.

Anna placed her hands on Emilie's arms and pried them apart. Then she held her hands tightly.

"Tell me, dear," she said sweetly. "What is it that you fear about marrying Lorenz?"

"I don't want to marry him," Emilie reiterated, hoping to convince herself as much as Anna. "I don't want to marry anyone."

"But why?"

Emilie felt the tears roll down her cheeks and the words lodge in her throat more painfully than her breakfast. "Because when you marry someone, you become a part of them," she whispered. "And when they're gone, you're less of a person."

Anna moved so that she sat next to Emilie and placed a gentle arm about her shoulders. "Oh, my dear," Anna said. "You have it all wrong."

Emilie shook her head. "I've seen it in my mother. She and my father were so much in love, and it's destroying her being apart from him so long."

Anna lovingly placed Emilie's head on her shoulder and began stroking her hair. "Your mother and father did become a part of each other when they fell in love. But that doesn't mean they lose a part of their souls when they are apart. Your mother became *more* of a person by knowing your father. His love gives her strength, not the other way around."

Emilie wanted to sit up straight and make her point, but it felt good to have someone to confide in, someone to comfort her in her mother's absence. Still, she wasn't completely convinced. "Mother cries herself to sleep," Emilie said. "I've heard her. Sometimes she is so sad she doesn't speak for days. She claims she can feel Father's pain, almost hear his thoughts."

Anna leaned her head and brushed a cheek against the top of Emilie's head. "You get that way when you love a person for a very long time. Sometimes I know what Mathias is going to say before he says it."

Now that Emilie considered it, she often knew what Lorenz was thinking before he put his thoughts to words.

"But you must understand," Anna continued. "Love gives us strength. It brings us comfort. It gives us a reason to live, to face the next day. Don't fear it for what may or may not happen. You and Lorenz may live to be one hundred years old, and what comfort will you have then if you don't allow yourself the pleasure of loving him now?"

This time Emilie did sit up. "He's rebellious," she said angrily. "He's always doing things he shouldn't be doing, being in places he's forbidden. And naive—God how he is naive. Anyone could talk him into doing something foolish, something wrong. One day he could kiss me goodbye and walk straight into a church surrounded by English soldiers and get himself exiled."

Emilie closed her eyes tightly, willing away the image. She hadn't meant to bring that horrid memory to the surface. She felt Anna's arms about her, holding her, kissing her forehead, but the relentless pain tore at her soul.

"It's behind you now, dear," Anna whispered while Emilie fought back the sobs. "Don't fear the future and risk your happiness because of what happened years ago."

"But the Spanish government threatened us with exile," Emilie insisted, wiping away the tears.

"I doubt the Spanish government will deport a young,

beautiful Acadian who wishes only to find her father,'' Anna interrupted. ''Nor will they find much fault in a young man who wants to protect his fiancée and reunite his future family.''

Emilie thought of how Lorenz had always managed to get into trouble, and amazingly escape it, in the past. Would he escape this time? ''I hope you're right,'' she whispered.

Anna pulled up her apron and wiped Emilie's eyes. ''He's a nice boy and you're a nice girl. You should be together.'' Then she moved Emilie's neglected plate closer. ''The next time he asks you to marry him, don't tell him no. If you can't say yes, tell him you need more time. He'll understand.''

Emilie wanted to say that two rejections usually didn't bring about another proposal, but Lorenz's kisses the night before proved he was anything but defeated.

''Perhaps after we get to St. Gabriel,'' she offered, amazed that relenting could feel so good.

Chapter Five

Emilie had just finished her third helping of breakfast when the men arrived, a joking Lorenz pulling up the rear. His smile disappeared when he caught sight of her feet dangling in a bucket of steaming water.

"What happened?" he asked, rushing to examine her.

"It's nothing," Emilie said. "Just blisters from the walk."

Lorenz bent down to get a better look, his face turning serious when he investigated the shape of her feet. "Blisters? You won't be able to walk with those sores."

Emilie bolted to a standing position, nearly knocking the bucket over. "Of course I'll be able to walk," she demanded. "Lorenz Landry, don't you dare think you are going to leave me behind."

Lorenz stood, crossed his arms and steadfastly met her gaze, but surprisingly he didn't mean to argue. "We're not going anywhere, Emilie, so sit down and give your feet a rest.'' When Emilie refused to move, Lorenz placed a gentle hand on her shoulder and pushed her back into her seat. His large hand caressing her evoked images of the night before, and a thrilling sensation ran through her before she could consciously send it away.

"What do you mean we're not going anywhere?" she asked.

Lorenz returned to his stooped position, focusing back on her damaged feet. "Emilie, you are one stubborn female," he said, shaking his head. "If you had stayed with your family, this wouldn't have happened."

Emilie ignored the remark. She was tired of being female and consistently left behind. "What did you mean we're not going anywhere?" she repeated.

Lorenz raised one of her feet and contemplated the broken skin surrounding her toes. He slid his fingers over the blistered area and down the delicate curve of her arch, massaging her damaged tendons. Emilie felt the tension leave her body as his fingers caressed her foot. It was a simple gesture, one that could easily be interpreted as medicinal, but Lorenz's massage reminded her all too much that his touch could send sensual feelings coursing through her. She began to react as she had the night before, her pulse increasing and her breath catching. She feared a heavy sigh would soon escape her lips and reveal her passionate thoughts, so she swallowed and focused back on their conversation. "Lorenz, why did you say . . . ?" Emilie asked, trying to keep her mind on track.

Lorenz looked up, his wild hair falling about his forehead, apparently a victim of the wind howling around the house. "The rain is flooding the area, and it doesn't look like it will let up anytime soon," he said. "We have to wait it out until the weather improves. With the shape your feet are in, I'd say the rain is a blessing."

He removed her other foot from the bucket and began to massage it as well, and Emilie felt her insides melt. With his head bowed over, Emilie wanted so badly to run her fingers through his soft raven hair. There were other things she wanted to do, too, which scared her even more.

When had this enormous change occurred? she wondered. When had Lorenz, her best friend since childhood, suddenly become a suitor, one capable of bringing forth such wild, aberrant feelings? They were buddies, confidants, not courting lovers. She wasn't interested in him that way. She wanted friendship, not marriage, just as she had explained to Anna. But despite all her logic, her emotions betrayed her, her heart reeling at his every touch. And the words Anna had imparted kept echoing in her mind. She would wait until St. Gabriel. She would not refuse him. For now.

"I think she's had enough soaking," Anna said, waking her from her ardent thoughts and Lorenz from his sensual handling of her feet. She handed Lorenz a towel, and Emilie pulled up her feet while Anna removed the bucket. Lorenz gently placed her feet on the towel and began patting them dry.

While he gently ministered to her, a lock of his hair fell about his forehead. Emilie couldn't resist anymore. She brushed the dark curl aside, letting her hand pause in the process, reveling in the feel of the thick, satiny hair through her fingers.

In an instant, Lorenz captured her wrist and kissed the inside of her palm, sending a tidal wave of sensations through her. Before she had time to see if Anna was watching, Lorenz returned to his duty at her feet, but a mischievous grin played on his lips.

"Where are the men?" Anna asked. Emilie held her breath, thinking that Phillip and Mathias might have seen that kiss as well.

"Most likely changing their clothes," Lorenz answered, glancing about the cabin and finding them absent. "It's been raining hard since daybreak."

It was then Emilie noticed Lorenz's soaked shirt, vest and breeches. "Don't bother with my feet," she admonished him. "Go warm yourself."

Lorenz looked up with a sly smile. "I am warming myself," he said in a heated whisper.

Anna placed a cup of coffee on the table beside them and cleared her throat. "This will help," she said to Lorenz. "I'll go see about Mathias."

"Merci," Lorenz said, and Emilie wondered if he knew Anna was allowing them their privacy.

When Anna entered her bedroom and pulled the curtain across the threshold behind her, Lorenz met Emilie's gaze. In his eyes a familiar light sparkled from the depths of the blackness, like sunlight shining on obsidian. He leaned forward so that his hands were on the arms of her chair, pinning her in her seat, the devilish glow still glistening in his stare. "Did you sleep well, Em?" he said so seductively, a wave of goose bumps traveled up her arms.

Emilie wanted to punch him hard, the way she used to when they played as children and he claimed she wasn't as strong as the boys. "Of course I didn't sleep well, thanks to you." The response only fueled the fiendish look he was sending. "Did you?" she returned.

With that remark, Lorenz pulled back slightly. "Hardly," he said, and for a moment she believed he had suffered as much as she had.

"Why did you leave so suddenly?" she asked.

The glint disappeared, replaced by the desirous stare he had delivered the night before. "Because if I hadn't, I might never have."

Emilie swallowed hard, recalling her careless actions in his arms. Even though the thought of sharing a bed with Lorenz sent a bolt of desire racing up her spine, she knew things would never have gone that far. It was absurd to think of such a thing; two friends experimenting with kissing was one thing, but serious lovemaking? Despite her promise to Anna, Lorenz was still her best friend. And only her best friend. Until they reached the others, she was not going to think otherwise.

"You assume a lot, don't you?" she finally said, raising her chin in defiance.

Lorenz wasted no time placing a thumb on her chin and bringing her face level with his. Before Emilie could object, he kissed her. It wasn't insistent, wild and passionate as before, but gentle and delectable like warm cream on ripe, sweet strawberries. He lingered at her mouth, too, brushing his lips softly against hers, teasing her with tiny nips on her lower lip. Emilie could have sworn hours had passed before Lorenz finally backed away and their eyes met. If her expression mirrored the desire reflected in his eyes, they were in deep trouble.

"Emilie," Lorenz whispered, and Emilie leaned forward, hoping for another kiss.

Instead, Lorenz slid his hand against her cheek and gazed deeply into her eyes. "Darling," he said so seductively that Emilie quivered. "What can I do to convince you to marry me?"

There it was again. That word. Emilie cringed and shut her eyes to remove the vision of Lorenz asking for more than she was able to give. She heard him sigh and opened her eyes to see the familiar pain shining in his gaze.

"Please, Lorenz," she begged him. "Please stop asking me."

"Why?" he asked, the anger emerging in his voice. "Can you at least tell me why?"

It was Emilie's turn to place her hands on his face, to caress the rough skin marred by cold, windy weather and a poor razor. Funny, she thought. She loved that face, dreamed of holding it just that way since her first confirmation, when Lorenz had teased her about her new clothes and pulled her hair in church and called her names in front of his friends. She had vowed she would marry him that day, to follow him for the rest of his life. Now the tide had changed, and Emilie couldn't fathom how to explain it.

"Will you wait until St. Gabriel?" she asked him. "Will you promise not to ask me until then?"

"Why . . . ?" he began earnestly.

"Please," she implored him. "Give me some time. At least until St. Gabriel and our search for Papa is over."

Lorenz covered her hands with his and kissed them both. "As long as you promise not to say no until then."

Emilie smiled and rested her forehead against his, reveling in the comfort that only Lorenz could offer. He smelled of leather, manly perspiration and wet wool. He felt like home.

A deep shiver began in Emilie's gut and traveled outward through her. Home, or the lack of it, was not a welcome thought. Anna was right. She was scared of marrying Lorenz, and it would take a lot of convincing to change her mind.

"I'm getting you wet," Lorenz said, moving away and standing. He held out his hand to raise her from her seat, which Emilie gratefully accepted. She stumbled slightly and grabbed Lorenz's wet sleeve for support.

"You're going to catch cold in those clothes," she told him. "You must go change into dry things."

Lorenz didn't move, still staring at her with those fathomless eyes. Emilie feared another serious conversation about marriage and home was imminent. Then the customary twinkle appeared.

"Proposals are one thing," he said. "But does this mean kisses are forbidden, too?"

Emilie couldn't help but smile. There was no doubt she enjoyed his lovemaking. "I suppose a kiss now and then—"

Before she could finish her sentence, his lips covered hers, this time more urgent and pressing. She meant to push him away, to remind him that although he tasted like heaven itself, there were other people in the cabin, ones who would not think much of two unmarried people

embracing in their living room. But Lorenz retreated as
fast as he had kissed her, raised one of her hands to his
lips, bowed, then departed for the back room.

Watching his tall, robust figure walk through the back
door, Emilie knew it was going to be a long road to St.
Gabriel.

Piernas held the bottle of prized rum in his hands and
felt his spirits lift. Civilized luxuries were hard to find on
the frontier, and alcohol a rarity. Thank God for neighbors.
Even English ones.

"Got it from that damned pirate Bouclaire," Coleman
Thorpe said. "Charged me a pretty piastre for them."

Piernas smiled and threw Coleman a box of his finest
cigars. "He would be kinder if you weren't English."

Coleman raised the box of cigars to his nose and smiled.
Despite what cost he incurred for the rum, the Spanish
cigars made it an equal exchange.

"I hope you will grant me another wish," Piernas said.
"The English governor of West Florida is at your fort
on the other side of the river. He wrote to me, asking to
visit our garrison."

"All in good friendship, I'm sure," Coleman said.

"Yes, I do believe he is sincere in that regard." Piernas
placed the bottle in a secret compartment of his desk,
then closed and locked its door. "What I was hoping is
that you would accompany me three nights hence and
help translate at the dinner I'm giving in his honor."

An apprehensive look crossed the Englishman's face
as he considered this request. "Pedro, I don't mind doing

business with you, but you must have realized by now that my father is a devout English patriot.''

''An English spy, you mean?''

When the young man's eyes grew bright with worry, Piernas wondered how involved Coleman was in his father's espionage. Richard Thorpe was a notorious English patriot, plantation owner and first-class bastard. He couldn't imagine a man as honest and kind as Coleman following in such footsteps. If Coleman was helping to spy for the English, he wouldn't have admitted as much about his father; he would have gladly accepted the invitation to dinner and hoped to gain as much knowledge from the Spanish as possible.

''There is no love lost between my father and myself,'' Coleman said, as if reading Piernas's thoughts. ''I do not share his politics either.''

''Good. Then, I'll see you here for dinner?''

Coleman rose and extended his hand, which Piernas accepted. The Englishman's eyes were direct, his handshake firm. Piernas couldn't help gaining satisfaction that despite the troublemakers, loyalist spies, government bureaucrats and complaining settlers he dealt with each day, there was always a person or two who stood out above the rest and offered comfort in the thick of chaos. The empty cup of birch tea sitting on his desk was another prime example.

''There is something else you can do for me,'' Piernas said, thinking back on the angel who visited twice a day to bring him his tea. ''There is a family here who has been separated from their patriarch. Perhaps you can help them.''

The young man frowned at the suggestion. "You want me to help one of the French families?"

"One of their daughters," Piernas began, thinking of the way Rose had offered her hand on his in comfort that afternoon, "is remarkable. She brings me tea for my headaches."

Coleman glanced at the cup before him, his smile broadening. "Are you sure it's not laced with poison?"

Piernas laughed. "I assure you, this woman has a heart of gold. She reminds me of you, señor, which is why I'm asking."

The smile lingering on Coleman's lips faded fast. "I assure you, sir, I have no heart of gold."

The light shining in the young man's eyes disappeared, and the cold tone in his voice sent a shiver through Piernas. Perhaps he was wrong about the Englishman. He hoped not.

"They have fewer luxuries than I," Piernas continued, hoping to dispel the dark mood that had descended upon the conversation. "The angel and her mother sew shirts for extra money." Piernas withdrew a wooden cross from beneath his shirt. "The oldest daughter creates these beautiful crosses. Since you're a man of means, perhaps you can help."

Coleman stared down at the cross held in Piernas's fingertips. "I'm a Protestant, señor. What would I want with a papal cross?"

Piernas laughed again. Englishmen and Protestants were such an intense lot. "You don't have to convert to Catholicism," he said. "Just buy one and help the poor family. Or barter as you do with me. I'm sure you can part with some items from that vast plantation of yours.''

"That vast plantation belongs to my father," Coleman said, the bitterness again emerging in his voice. "I have no authority there."

Only minutes ago the young man's eyes were full of life, his demeanor friendly and kind. Now a sadness and anger distorted his countenance. Piernas was determined to one day learn the Englishman's story.

"Rose will be helping with the dinner," Piernas said, placing a fatherly hand on Coleman's shoulder and walking him to the door. "I will introduce you, and you can decide for yourself. Agreed?"

The shadow that had crossed the Englishman's face departed, and the Coleman Piernas knew returned. "Just make sure this Rose doesn't serve the tea to the Englishmen," he said with a slight smile. "Or it may be a quick dinner."

As Piernas watched Coleman make his way toward the waterfront, a fear crossed his heart as he considered Coleman's final words. Perhaps having Rose help with the meal wasn't such a good idea. Spaniards and Acadians arguing over settlements was one thing. But the differences between the English and the French were quite another.

The early morning sun bathed Rose's cheeks as it peeked through the house's hastily constructed walls. It wasn't yet April, and the weather had turned warm and sunny. With the change in temperature, Rose was certain

Lorenz and Emilie would easily meet up with their father and be on their way north to Natchez.

Rose needed their stabilizing influence, Emilie's take-charge attitude and Lorenz's masculine comfort to bring their mother out of her melancholy. Since Marianne's vision before the fireplace more than a week before, she had refused to talk and ate very little. Even the prospect of their own home brought little comfort. If it hadn't been for Pélagie Leblanc's crazy superstition regarding dreams of grooms, Marianne might never have improved.

"Did you dream of him?" Gabrielle whispered.

Rose turned and found her sister equally basking in sunlight, only from a different hole in the wall. "We must do something about those walls," Rose answered. "The next time it rains we'll have water everywhere."

"Mud and moss works as an insulator," Gabrielle replied. "I heard the men discuss it. I'll have one of them help us as soon as they're able. Now, did you dream about him or not?"

Rose turned her head and stared at the ceiling, equally spotted with holes. Dreaming of an intended on the first night in a new house was a silly superstition. "Doesn't matter," Rose finally said. "I didn't see his features."

Gabrielle leaned on her elbow and gazed down into Rose's face. "You counted the bed's joists, just like Pélagie said to do?"

Rose rolled her eyes. She couldn't believe Gabrielle accepted such nonsense. Still, it was amazing she had had such a vivid dream. "Yes, I counted them. And I dreamed of a fair man, one who liked to remain apart from the crowds. I never saw his face."

"Blonde," Gabrielle said. "Why was he away from the others?"

Rose had a good idea, but she didn't want to give voice to it. "I don't know. He was standing apart, as if he didn't belong. Then the next thing I know he's wearing ragged clothes, working a field and singing. And quite happy to do so."

Gabrielle sat up and propped herself against the wall. "What was he wearing before?"

"I don't know, Gabrielle," she said, rising from the bed and sliding on her cotton stockings. "It's a ridiculous superstition. The man in my dreams was most definitely not the man I am going to marry."

At this Gabrielle smiled. "Why are you so sure? Is he someone you know?"

It was no one she knew. It was no one she was going to know. "He spoke English," Rose finally admitted, watching her sister's countenance change from jovial to astonishment, then disgust. "And if you tell mother I'll never forgive you."

"Tell me what?" Marianne asked as she entered the house, her arms full of clean clothes.

"That she didn't dream of the man she is to marry," Gabrielle answered, sending Rose a conspiratorial glance.

Marianne placed the clothes on the bed and stared hard at first Gabrielle, then Rose. "Why is that such a secret? Why are you afraid to tell me that?"

Rose didn't want to think of the Englishman, let alone speak of him. She decided to change the direction of the conversation. "Because we know how much it means to you for us to have visions like you do."

Marianne brushed the tousled hair from Rose's face and at the same time reached out and took Gabrielle's hand. "I want you girls to find love," she said. "I was hoping that being in a new place would bring you happiness much like your father . . ."

Marianne grew silent and swallowed hard, fighting back tears. When Pélagie had explained the maiden superstition the night before, after the priest had blessed their meager home, for the first time in days Marianne had come alive. She had helped them dress for bed, sung a couple of old French songs passed down from her grandmother and tucked them into bed. Now Rose feared the sadness had returned.

"We haven't heard from Gabrielle yet," Rose said, hoping to bring her mother back to a happier subject. When she turned toward her sister and watched Gabrielle's face turn pale, Rose realized her blunder. If Gabrielle's dream had differed from the usual nightmares she experienced, she would have told Rose first thing.

Marianne turned toward her middle child. "Anything new besides the ship dream," she asked gently. "A man's face this time perhaps?"

Gabrielle shook her head. She had been plagued by dreams of sailing ships since their deportation, of a dark, faceless man at her back as they drifted off to distant lands. Marianne placed an arm about her shoulders and squeezed. The sadness that lingered between them was more than Rose could bear. She couldn't stand to watch her mother and sister suffer through the memories, to carry such pain. She wanted to make them happy, to see them both smile once more.

Emilie called her the eternal optimist. Perhaps it was because she didn't remember the atrocities at Grand Pré. She barely remembered Papa, save for the sound of his hearty laughter and the smell of apples about him. Maybe she couldn't feel the pain in the same way her sisters and mother did because she hadn't suffered as they had. But despite all their history, Rose believed life was what you made it, no matter what horrors befell you. She wasn't about to linger in sadness or watch those she loved endure grief without her intervention.

"Shall I bring you pastries from the dinner tonight?" Rose asked the women. "The cook said there will be a five-course meal and plenty of food left over. Perhaps there will be chicken and we can make a *rapure* with our potatoes, just like in Acadia."

Marianne brightened at the thought of their traditional dish, and Rose was glad the memories were now good ones. "That would be nice," Marianne said. "Perhaps some of those red peppers as well. Your Spanish friend the cook was right about them livening up the food."

"I'll be sure and tell her," Rose said, digging through the pile of clothes Marianne had brought in from the line.

Marianne slapped her hand aside. "You will wrinkle everything, and then you won't look your best for the commandant and his guests." She pulled Rose's bright striped skirt, white shirt and blue vest from the pile and handed them to her. "Who is coming to this dinner anyway?"

Rose blanched at the question. She knew Piernas was entertaining Montfort Browne, the English governor of West Florida, who commanded the English territory from the other side of the Mississippi to the Atlantic Ocean, but she hadn't felt comfortable disclosing that information. Rose remembered little of the "lobsterbacks" who had patrolled her homeland, and she didn't fear them as the others did. She only wanted to help with the dinner, to assist Piernas and her new friend in the kitchen.

Rose also knew the other Acadians would insist on Rose acting the spy. She spoke a little English, learned from the Jesuit priests at Port Tobacco. It was only enough to conduct business in town; she was barely able to carry on a conversation past the price of butter. Better to keep quiet about the English, help serve the meal and inform the villagers later, Rose surmised.

"Military men," Rose answered her mother. "I'll tell you all about it tonight when I return home."

Marianne accepted the explanation and began to brush Rose's hair. Gabrielle, however, was not so easily placated.

"Watch out for blondes," she whispered to Rose before grabbing the water pitcher and heading for the outside well.

The spring sun slipped behind the ridge of cypress trees, casting an eerie glow through the moss blowing in the dusk breeze. Coleman felt his spirits dissolve as the sunlight slowly left the earth. How had Piernas managed to talk him into entertaining the stuffy English governor and his collection of career soldiers?

He had spent the afternoon watching the Spanish troops assemble for their guests, the artillery saluting the gover-

nor and his men, and Piernas treating them all as royalty.
Such pomp and protocol, such meticulous detail to honor.
The two countries could destroy each other tomorrow,
but by God today they would be civil and follow every
formality and convention called for in such circumstances.

The games colonial nations played disgusted Coleman.
Innocent people were always the victims; rich aristocrats
and royals would forever rule the earth and divide the
wealth of its people. He had learned that lesson firsthand.

As he watched the governor and his entourage parade
through the garrison's courtyard, heading for the dining
room, Coleman imagined how easily one could shoot the
governor from his concealed place at the window. If the
Spanish, or anybody for that matter, could adopt the fighting mannerisms of the Indians, they could defeat any
enemy. The English fought in America as they always
had in Europe: bright, colorful uniforms in wide-open
spaces, marching to the enemy in regulated lines like
lambs to a slaughter. If the Indians could hide in trees
and bushes, shooting the marching Red Coats like fish in
a barrel, surely the Americans could do the same.

Coleman rubbed the back of his neck. What was he
thinking? Such traitorous thoughts. Despite his wishes to
free North America of the tyrannical colonial governments, he was still a subject of the English crown.

"So this is where you are hiding," Piernas said,
approaching him from the rear. Behind him Coleman
saw the governor and his men helping themselves to
Coleman's rum in the fort's rustic dining room.

"Getting some air," Coleman answered.

"You could have gotten air in the courtyard with us," he replied.

"That's doubtful," Coleman said. "Too much hot air in one small area."

Piernas laughed, then frowned at his loss of control. Coleman knew the Spaniard shared his view of the English. "Why is it you feel more comfortable with me than your own kind?" Piernas whispered.

Coleman watched the stout English governor throw back a glass of overpriced rum, then immediately refill his glass. "Because they are not my kind," Coleman said.

Piernas stared hard, and Coleman wished he had thought first before speaking. Piernas may be a friend, but he was still the commandant of the Spanish garrison, not exactly a man to confide in. "Someday I hope to learn your story," he finally said.

"That would be a first," Coleman said softly. Then with more authority, he added, "Unlike your guests, I don't speak of myself."

Piernas appeared as if he wanted to further the conversation; but something caught his eye, and he smiled. Coleman knew his exile at the window was over and it was time to translate small talk over dinner. Instead, a young woman approached with a bottle of wine and glasses.

"Rose," Piernas said when the petite woman reached them.

When Rose looked up and met Coleman's gaze, her face went pale, and her brown eyes enlarged with fright. He knew his stocky build and blond hair exposed him as English, but he hated her thinking he was the enemy simply because of his nationality. Rose recovered her initial shock and curtsied before the two men, but she continued to stare at Coleman in fear.

Piernas made an introduction of sorts to Rose in French. When Coleman heard his name mentioned, he bowed slightly toward the bright-eyed Acadian. "It is my pleasure, madame," Coleman said.

To his surprise, Rose smiled, and a blush spread across her cheeks. She was rather charming, this angel of Piernas's. Of medium height, ordinary brown hair and eyes and a curveless figure, Rose would hardly turn heads, yet she seemed to glow with an inner light that warmed him, made him comfortable to be in her presence. The freckles surrounding her nose and the dimples gracing her cheeks were additional endearing traits. Coleman found himself entranced.

"The word is mademoiselle," Piernas corrected him in English.

The Spaniard had said something, but it took Coleman several seconds before he comprehended it. "I beg your pardon," Coleman said when the words sank in. "It is my pleasure, *mademoiselle,*" he said with a more formal bow.

Rose's dimples grew deeper, and Coleman began to hope her distrust of him had ended. Her chestnut eyes glistened in the candlelight. "Do you speak English?" Coleman asked.

Rose frowned and stared down at her feet. "A little," she uttered, clearly uncomfortable with the subject.

"Do you speak French?" Piernas asked him.

Rose gazed up at him expectantly, and for the first time

in his life Coleman wanted nothing more than to be fluent in the language. Unfortunately, he had refused to learn French at the same time he refused to help his father spy for England. "No," he answered. "I do not."

"Well, this will be a short conversation," Piernas said.

Rose handed Piernas and Coleman the glasses, then poured them each a glass of wine. Piernas moved to the governor and his men, announcing that he would like to propose a toast. Before Rose could move away, Coleman grabbed her free hand.

He didn't know why he did it; the French were as far removed from his life as Mother England, and certainly Rose wouldn't take kindly to an Englishman's touch. But he had to make her trust him, let her know he was not to be feared.

"I am an American," he said.

Surprisingly, Rose understood. As she gazed into his eyes, he felt a connection between them, an understanding.

"I am an Acadian," she answered him. In that moment before Rose left his side and retreated to the kitchen, Coleman felt a hopeful spark ignite in his heart, so long dead to emotions and joy since the death of his mother, the only brightness in his life.

Coleman joined the toasts at the opposite side of the room, lifting his glass to the queen and His Excellency, Spanish Governor Antonio de Ulloa. But he swore that before the night was over, he would learn more about Piernas's angel and how he could help reunite her family.

Chapter Six

The early morning sunshine reflected on the endless puddles and streams of water filling the fields, making the scene so bright Emilie had to turn her head. Only hours before, the cold wind had howled around the house as rain fell like bullets on the roof. Now a warmth filled the air, reminding Emilie of early summer in Grand Pré.

"Strange weather," she muttered.

"What did you say?" Lorenz asked from his place behind the horse stall.

Emilie carried her egg basket laden with breakfast into the barn. Since their arrival several days before, she and Lorenz had made themselves useful. "I said it's strange weather," Emilie repeated. "I don't like this place."

Lorenz pitched the soiled hay from the horse stall, then placed his pitchfork on the ground and leaned into the handle, wiping his forehead with his sleeve. "So tell me something new."

"There's water everywhere," Emilie exclaimed. "The ground is drowning."

Lorenz laughed and grabbed his hat, placing it tightly on his head. "There was water everywhere in Grand Pré, or don't you remember?"

Emilie grasped the basket's handle with two hands and leaned back against the cow's stall. "Of course I remember. But it wasn't like this. It didn't rain for days and turn everything into a swamp. We had diked our land. The water was manageable."

Lorenz leaned the pitchfork on the side of the barn. "We had forty-foot tides and endless winters," he said as he marched past her on his way to milk the cow. "Give me warm weather any day."

Emilie placed the basket on the barn floor and accepted the extra milking stool Lorenz handed her. "You can't be serious," she said as she sat beside one cow and Lorenz began milking another. "You don't really like Louisiana?"

"I saw a herd of deer this morning, Em," he said as he effortlessly brought forth milk. There was little Lorenz could not do. And most everything he did, he did well.

"You were always a good hunter," Emilie replied, struggling to get the milk flowing. "Besides, the rain probably brought them out."

Lorenz laughed. "I saw wildlife everywhere. Wild turkeys, rabbits, even Canadian geese."

Emilie stopped milking and turned. "You didn't kill any, did you?"

Lorenz peered around the side of the cow. "Emilie, it's been thirteen years."

"What does that have to do with anything?"

Lorenz stared hard, and Emilie knew what he was thinking. He had always thought her ideas on relocating to Canada ludicrous. She lifted her chin defiantly, then turned back toward her cow. "I don't think it's improbable to return to Nova Scotia. We've heard of others doing it."

Lorenz sighed and returned to his work. "They went to New Brunswick, Montreal, Quebec, where the French are, not Nova Scotia," he said. "The English forced us out of our homeland, *cher.* I doubt they will ask us back."

"You know what I mean," she stubbornly continued.

"No, I don't."

Emilie squirted the milk into the pail a little too hard, and the cow bellowed. "I want to go home," she practically shouted.

The barn became quiet, and Emilie looked over to find a pair of leather shoes at her side, topped by woolen stockings and a pair of breeches tied at the knee, clothes her mother had lovingly made for Lorenz last spring. The thought of home, of her parents so long separated, of her sisters toiling at Natchez without her, brought tears to her eyes, and Emilie looked up to Lorenz for support. He instantly took her hand, raised her and covered her in a tight embrace.

"Oh, *'ti monde,*" he whispered as she fought back the tears. "This is our home now."

Emilie enjoyed the feel of his strong arms about her, then pulled away and walked to the barn door. She gazed out at the secluded farmhouse and the arpents of cleared land made fertile by the ritual overflowing of the river. The conclusion of rain had brought about a cacophony of music from songbirds, and the land was littered with robins, birds Emilie had never seen before May. Despite the appearance of greenery and wildlife so early in the year and the sunlight warming her face, the flat, wet landscape failed to appeal to her.

She felt Lorenz's arms about her again, and she captured his arms tightly. He felt good holding her close, like a lifesaver to cling to in a storm.

"Look at it, Em," he said to her, his breath warm at her ear. "It's beautiful."

Emilie tried to see the charm of the land, what Lorenz kept describing as paradise, but it consistently reminded her that she would never return to Grand Pré.

"What is that gray stuff hanging from the trees?" she asked him.

"Anna calls it *barbe espagnole* because it reminds her of the beards of the Spanish," Lorenz explained. "They seem to be fond of facial hair."

Emilie laughed at the reference, feeling slightly better.

"I think it's some kind of moss."

"And those trees." Emilie pointed toward a grouping where the Spanish moss was especially thick. "I keep stumbling on their roots sticking out of the ground."

"Cypress," Lorenz said. "Those roots are the tree's 'knees.' And if you would wear the moccasins Anna made for you instead of your wooden sabots, you wouldn't be stumbling."

Emilie wiggled out of his embrace and turned. "They're the only thing I have left of Grand Pré," she insisted. "I suppose the next thing you'll want me to do is change my name." At this remark, Lorenz brightened, and a sly sparkle glistened in his eyes. "You know what I mean," Emilie quickly added.

Lorenz captured a loose strand of her hair and placed it behind an ear, caressing her check with his thumb in the process. "We'll never lose Grand Pré," he said softly. "It lives within us. No matter where we go, Emilie, we'll always have Grand Pré. Like you said to Mathias, we'll always be Acadians."

It sounded so simple. Head for Louisiana and start over. But it was all so different, this swampland filled with trees with knees covered in Spanish beards. And they had yet to be reunited with Papa.

"I wish it was that easy," Emilie said, feeling the anxiety regarding her future wash over her again. She feared giving words to the thoughts that they might never find her father, that voicing such apprehension might make it come true.

"I know what you're worried about," Lorenz said, pulling her against his chest and kissing her forehead. "I've worried about not finding him, too." He slid his large hands up her back, and Emilie responded by wrapping her arms about his neck and savoring the comfort of his embrace. Leave it to Lorenz to read her thoughts.

"What will we do if Father's not there?" she whispered, hoping the words wouldn't cause an outbreak of emotion.

Lorenz hugged her so tightly she could barely breathe, but Emilie didn't care. "We'll find him," he said confidently. Emilie shut her eyes and rested her head against the broad shoulder that had been her solace since the deportation.

They stood there for what seemed like an eternity until Lorenz pulled back slightly. "What are you washing with?" he asked seductively. "You smell incredible."

Emilie looked up into his raven eyes and found pleasure knowing she could produce such a reaction in him. "Anna makes soap with herbs," she said with an equally seductive grin.

As he had done so many times during the past week, Lorenz scanned the horizon for witnesses, then leaned down and delivered a deep kiss. Each time Emilie felt it in every inch of her body.

This was becoming too familiar, she thought. They could never keep their hands off each other. Ever since that kiss in her room three nights before, they had found every chance to sneak a little privacy and engage in lovemaking. And usually, when the kisses started, so did other things. Emilie worried their self-control would fail them one day and they would cross a dangerous line.

Lorenz moved a hand to Emilie's bottom and pressed her tightly against him. She knew instantly how deep Lorenz's desires were and was surprised to find herself equally aroused. So this was what all the fuss was about, Emilie thought. Perhaps marriage wasn't such a bad idea.

Suddenly, the cow bellowed, unhappy to have its milking interrupted. Emilie pulled back and gazed at the cows. "We shouldn't have started something we couldn't finish."

Lorenz smiled slyly. "I'd be happy to finish it," he whispered.

"I was talking about the milking." Emilie pushed him away and gave him a playful punch on the arm, just as she had a hundred times before as a child. This time, Lorenz caught her arm and pulled her close, delivering one last, satisfying kiss before he let her go. They moved away from each other then, the heat still lingering between them.

"This wouldn't have to end if we were married," Lorenz reminded her.

"You promised," Emilie replied. "You said you wouldn't speak of it."

A silence followed, but Emilie knew it wouldn't last long.

"Damn it, Em," Lorenz said. "Will you at least tell me why?"

Emilie slid her stool into place and resumed milking. "No," she stated firmly.

"You are the most stubborn female I have ever met."

"I'm stubborn?" Emilie asked. "I'm not the one who proposed marriage three times."

She shouldn't have said it. It was insensitive and mean-spirited, but the words took a life of their own, flying out of her mouth before she had time to think of the consequences. She started to apologize, but knew it was too late.

"You're right," Lorenz answered, the hurt apparent in his voice. "I must be crazy to keep asking you."

Emilie continued milking while an aching settled in her heart. She was so confused. She didn't wish to speak of marriage, yet she didn't want Lorenz to stop asking. She wasn't ready to agree to matrimony, but she didn't want to stop being close. The only thing Emilie knew for sure was that she wasn't ready to agree to anything except continuing on to St. Gabriel and finding her father. Why couldn't Lorenz leave well enough alone for now?

"Lorenz, I didn't mean to . . ."

Emilie heard Lorenz rise, pulling a full bucket of milk with him. "Forget I asked," he said as he picked up the basket of eggs and left the barn.

A few more pulls and she would have it, Emilie thought as she glanced down at her near-filled bucket. She had to catch up with him, so she quickened the speed. As the last drops of milk emerged, Emilie grabbed the bucket and ran after Lorenz, catching up with him only a few steps from the house.

"Wait," she cried, breathless from the run. "Please don't leave it this way."

Lorenz turned, but his eyes stared at the horizon behind her.

"All I'm asking for is a little time," she implored him.

Lorenz looked at her then, his anger still brewing inside him. "And all I'm asking for is a simple explanation."

"I don't have a simple explanation," Emilie insisted.

Lorenz placed the bucket and basket at their feet and grabbed her shoulders. "It's very clear. You either love me or you don't. How hard is that to explain?"

Emilie pulled away. "You promised."

Lorenz shook his head and sighed. "Yes, I promised," he uttered through gritted teeth. "Until St. Gabriel."

Emilie hated to see his anguish, but she wasn't going to give in. She needed time, and that was that. Lorenz was a big boy, capable of delivering one small promise.

Still, she hated to see him suffer. "I'm sorry," she whispered.

To her surprise, Lorenz smiled, but it wasn't the reaction Emilie had hoped for. A darkness lingered in the depths of his eyes, and his smile was obviously forced. "I'm sorry, too," he said coldly, sending a shiver through her. Then he picked up the buckets and headed into the house.

The road to the Mayer store rolled on forever. Just when Lorenz thought the next bend would reveal the building, he was greeted with more fields along the road that followed the curving Mississippi River.

When yet another farmhouse came in view, Lorenz began to hum "J'ai Passé Devant Ta Porte," a song he learned in childhood. It was an appropriate tune for his dark mood, of a lover who laments that his sweetheart does not care, refusing to answer when he passes her door and wishes her good night.

"Typical," Lorenz muttered, his anger fueled by the fact that men had had difficulties dealing with women for centuries.

One simple answer. All he asked for was one simple answer.

Lorenz kicked a pinecone lying across his path and sent the item flying. He was tired of Emilie's game, tired of waiting, tired of the mystery of it all. He knew she cared for him—her kisses told him so! Why, then, wouldn't she consent to marriage, to consummate a relationship they had shared since they were old enough to speak? Nothing made sense.

The sun was beginning to set, and Lorenz picked up his step. He had to make it to the store to exchange Anna's bread for supplies and return before dark. The store couldn't be much farther. Anna had said it was only a few leagues. But the sun was quickly setting, and there was to be no moon that night.

He knew Emilie would worry if he was late. She always worried. There wasn't a time when Lorenz failed to make a meal or was detained that Emilie didn't come rushing out the door to greet him and assure herself he was not harmed. How could a woman who cared that much and kissed that passionately not love him in return and wish to spend the rest of her life married to him?

Lorenz pulled back his foot and sent another pinecone sailing through the air. He felt powerless and frustrated and wanted nothing more than to punch something and punch it hard.

He thought of Colonel Winslow in the church that afternoon in Grand Pré. There was a prime target. Winslow, in his frivolous red uniform, had offered up a half-baked apology that what he was about to do was distasteful to his "make and temper," as if that could alleviate the suffering he later inflicted on the Acadian town.

Lorenz remembered every detail of that fateful afternoon when the English soldiers had marched in and taken positions at the door and windows while Winslow announced the royal order that all Acadian families were to be removed from the country. The men had argued, then begun to plead when the realization that they were trapped set in. For the first time in his life, Lorenz had wanted to beat an English soldier senseless. Thirteen years later, he still did.

The store finally appeared in the latest turn of the river, but Lorenz had not managed to walk off his anger. He was tired of being helpless, tired of living in exile, tired of obeying the commands of foreign governments. And he was tired of being rejected.

When he entered the store and placed the warm loaves of bread on the counter, Lorenz failed to see the Spanish soldiers to his rear. When they startled him with questions, getting his attention by poking him in the side with a bayonet, Lorenz was all too happy to comply.

"What do you mean he's being detained?" Emilie asked. "Where is he?"

Phillip pulled on his coat and grabbed his hat, heading for the door. "I'll let you know as soon as I find out. All the man said was Lorenz is being held at the store."

"Who said this? Where are you going?" Emilie felt the panic rise in her chest, threatening to cut off her air. Lorenz was in trouble. She knew it.

"Our neighbor, Pierre Bourgeois, said the Spanish soldiers had detained Lorenz at the store," Mathias explained, pulling on his boots. "We'll investigate and let you know."

"I'm going with you," Emilie said, grabbing her own coat. There was no way she was going to be left behind.

Mathias placed a fatherly hand on her shoulder. "Don't worry, *mon amie*. We'll bring him back."

"Not without me," she insisted. There was absolutely no way they were leaving without her.

"Don't be ridiculous child," Anna said. "Let the men deal with the soldiers. You and I will wait together."

"I'm tired of waiting," she practically shouted. She hadn't meant to be rude to her new friend, but she had spent thirteen years waiting. She couldn't be left behind. "You have to take me with you."

Phillip opened the door and paused on the threshold. "Nonsense, Emilie. You'll only slow us down. Be a good girl and wait here. I'm sure everything is fine. We'll be back with Lorenz before you know it."

Be a good girl? Emilie was livid. "I'll follow you," she warned him. "I'm going to the store whether you like it or not."

Mathias looked over to Phillip, who was clearly shocked at Emilie's behavior, but the kindly German seemed to be relenting. Phillip's return glance reproached Mathias for giving in to her crazy demands.

"I *will* follow you," she repeated. "You can't keep me here."

Phillip threw up his hands and headed out the door.

"Come on," Mathias said to Emilie.

Emilie didn't wait to be asked twice. She bolted through the door, pulling on her coat in the process. "Be careful," she heard Anna cry out as the three entered the dark, moonless night.

"Stay close," Phillip barked out to her, clearly upset that she was accompanying them. "You won't do Lorenz any good by getting lost and having us hunt you down."

"Why is he being detained?" she asked them, rushing to keep up with their long strides. "What did he do?"

"Pierre didn't elaborate," Mathias said quietly.

The men said nothing more, causing Emilie's imagination to run wild. The panic returned. What would she do if something happened to Lorenz? What if he was to be exiled, like the Spaniard at New Orleans had warned them? The Spanish more than likely knew that she and Lorenz had jumped ship; they knew of the Braud brothers' flight. They could be preparing to send Lorenz into exile.

The panic intensified. She should have expected as much from Lorenz. He was always walking the fence between safety and trouble. He was nearly arrested in Port Tobacco for theft from the English merchants, routinely reprimanded by the Jesuits who tried to teach him. He balked at most authority figures. Her mother had spent many a day convincing others of Lorenz's worth when he was caught at crimes or talking back to adults. Things had gotten better as he matured, but Emilie knew there was a fire brewing inside him, an unrelinquished anger waiting to emerge.

She had refused him once again, delaying his questions on marriage. It was just the spark he needed.

And that was precisely the problem. Why would she want to marry a man who would lose his temper so easily and likely lose his life in the process? Why would she wish to end up like her mother, alone in the world, waiting?

Damn him, she thought. *How could he be so senseless?*

"Emilie?" Mathias called out, making sure she was keeping up.

"I'm right here," Emilie answered. The panic had subsided, replaced by anger. If Lorenz wanted answers, she would give him some. As soon as they got him safely back home.

Emilie nearly collided into the back of Mathias when the men halted. "Someone's approaching," Phillip said.

For a moment, Emilie feared for her own safety. Spanish soldiers could easily arrest her as well. Her lack of forethought, much like Lorenz's, might get her exiled.

She felt Mathias's hands on her arms, making sure she was behind him. "Say nothing," he whispered.

"That sounds like Phillip Bellefontaine," she heard Lorenz call out in the darkness.

"Lorenz," Phillip answered. "Are you alone?"

"Yes," Lorenz said, his voice now in their company.

"Merde." Emilie heard Phillip follow with a few more choice words as he slung his rifle onto his shoulder. "Damn it, Lorenz, you gave us a scare."

Emilie might have been shocked at such vulgarity used in her presence, but her thoughts resembled Phillip's. She was ready to give Lorenz her own dose of reproach when the men started back toward the house.

"What happened?" Mathias asked, his voice taking on a stern tone Emilie had not witnessed before. "You had us all worried."

"It was nothing," Lorenz said. "The Spaniards asked me some questions, wanted to know where I was from and where I was going. I didn't like being interrogated, and so I refused to answer. They weren't too happy with me, naturally, but after our tempers cooled, we came to an understanding."

"Tempers?" Phillip asked. "How heated did this conversation get?"

Lorenz laughed solemnly, and Emilie's heart quickened. She recognized that laugh; it was the one he delivered after being caught at a misdeed. "Let's just say they look worse than I do."

Emilie nearly met with Mathias's back for a second time. "Are you crazy?" Mathias shouted at Lorenz when he stopped short. "You are traveling illegally through this colony, one administered by these men, and you have the nerve to put your life and that of your fiancée in jeopardy?"

"You don't understand," Lorenz began, the mirth in his tone long gone. "They were harassing me."

"I don't care what they were doing to you," Mathias continued. "They have the power to put you and Emilie in jail or expel you from the colony. They could jail me and Anna for harboring you."

A silence lingered in the Louisiana darkness. Emilie wanted to view Lorenz's face, to hope that he at last could understand the folly in his hasty actions, but all she could make out in the night were dark shapes hovering before her.

"I'm sorry, Mathias," Lorenz finally said. "I never meant to harm you or your wonderful wife. I will be forever grateful for your hospitality.

"But," he continued solemnly, "I am weary of colonial governments telling me what to do. I know you will never understand this, but I will never allow a soldier to force me to do anything ever again. I will die first."

A silence befell the group until Emilie heard Mathias

sigh. "These soldiers are not your enemy," Mathias explained. "They are not the English, my friend. They have allowed you to settle on their land and given you food and tools to do so. Do not be hasty in your anger and cause harm to the wrong men."

Emilie felt Mathias leave her side and heard the men following. She could barely make out the road at her feet, but followed it, listening for the men's voices to guide her.

"Do the soldiers know who you are?" Phillip asked.

"I used my father's name," Lorenz answered. "They are looking for Honoré and Alexis Braud, the brothers who went into hiding. They mentioned others, but didn't give names."

"Then, you must leave immediately," Mathias said softly.

Emilie knew Mathias hated sending them away; they had all become good friends in the three days spent at the Frederics' homestead. But if the soldiers were searching for them, it was best for all that they head north that night.

"I'm sorry," Lorenz repeated. "I never meant to cause harm to anyone."

"See that you don't anymore," Mathias said.

The foursome neared the house, and Emilie could make out the silhouettes of the men before her. When they reached the door and the light shone forth, Lorenz turned toward Mathias.

"Please don't tell Emilie about this," he said. "She worries so much about me."

Mathias placed a fatherly arm on Lorenz's shoulder

and squeezed, then opened the door to his home. "I won't have to," he said and entered the house.

Phillip followed, sending Lorenz a scathing look as he passed. Lorenz paused at the threshold, afraid to turn around, knowing somehow that she lingered at his back. When he finally sighed and gazed back toward Emilie, she gasped in horror. His right eye was badly bruised, turning a deep shade of purple and swollen shut. Blood had hardened about his nose, the result of a fist blow, she was sure. And there were cuts about his chin.

"It's not that bad," he began, but Emilie didn't let him finish.

"I'll never marry you, Lorenz Joseph Landry," she said, the tears pouring in torrents down her face. "Not if you were the last Acadian man in Louisiana."

Chapter Seven

"It won't be much farther now," Phillip said for the third time that morning. "I distinctly remember this bend in the river."

Lorenz felt the fire burn in his temple. Phillip had said the same thing about the last two curves in the Mississippi. He didn't mind that the older Acadian's memory was amiss; what he minded was Phillip's insistence on small talk.

"The sunny weather's holding up nicely," Phillip continued. "If we're lucky, we should have a warm evening."

Lorenz didn't want to be rude, especially after being the cause of the three of them fleeing in the middle of the night, following the river road north without the help of a moon. But he was dreadfully tired, his head throbbing from the injuries inflicted on him by the soldiers. If Phillip

Bellefontaine uttered another word, he would lose his mind for sure.

"This has to be the last bend," Phillip said. "I recognize the grove of oak trees."

Lorenz gritted his teeth, stopped and turned back toward his companion. Since Emilie had refused to talk to him, she kept a good distance to the rear. The way he was feeling, he didn't care what she did. Now if only Phillip would do the same.

Phillip pulled the rifle from his shoulder and placed the butt on the ground, leaning into the barrel for support. From the look on his face, Lorenz knew Phillip got the message. "Just attempting to make conversation," Phillip explained. "God knows I'm the only one trying."

Emilie caught up with the men and exchanged a quick glance with Lorenz. Her eyes still burned with the wrath of the night before, still angry over his loss of self-control with the soldiers. Lorenz thought of Emilie's ultimatum, of her refusal to understand that his motive with the soldiers was as strong as her refusal to offer an explanation for her constant rejections of marriage.

This morning, he was too tired to care whether Emilie approved of anything. He was tired of her games. If she wanted to be angry, let her stew in her own discomfort. Let her walk ten paces to the rear in silence.

"You're not listening, are you?" Phillip asked, when he noticed Lorenz's mind wander back to Emilie.

Lorenz looked at his friend with his good eye, trying to keep the impatience out of his voice. "As you said, Phillip, we have to put some leagues between the Frederic's homestead and Cabannocé."

Lorenz picked up Phillip's rifle, flung it over his shoulder and continued down the road, praying that the beating inside his head would cease along with Phillip's endless prattle. But Phillip had other plans.

"We should stop for a while," Phillip said. "We've been walking since midnight, and I'm famished."

Emilie caught up with the men, and Lorenz could hear her wooden shoes beating a patter against the mud behind him. "Stubborn female," he muttered.

"Did you say something?" It was the first time Emilie had spoken to him since the previous night. Normally, Lorenz would have been thankful for the break in the ice, but he was in no mood to spar with her.

"Can't lunch wait until we reach another settlement?" Lorenz asked Phillip. In his mood, it was best to keep walking.

"No, it can't." Emilie threw her satchel on the ground and sat down on a nearby stump. She withdrew her feet from the sabots and began to rub them, while Phillip unloaded his satchel and joined her. It was clear they were going nowhere, so Lorenz admitted defeat, dropping his own supplies and sitting on the damp ground.

"You really should wear those moccasins Anna made for you," Phillip said to Emilie. "Leather is better for traveling. It's less harsh on your feet."

"Don't bother," Lorenz said. "Logic doesn't work with her."

Emilie shot him a fierce look. "You have a lot of nerve," she retorted. "You threatened all of our lives last night because of an incident that happened thirteen years ago and you're saying I'm illogical?"

Lorenz wasn't in the mood for an argument. He had explained his actions, made his apologies. He felt remorse for his mistake, ashamed that he had put their lives in jeopardy while thinking only of personal revenge. He should have been more careful, but his anger had snapped inside him like a dry twig under his foot.

But of all the people in the world who should have understood his actions, it was Emilie. Yet she joined the rest in their condemnation. For that reason, Lorenz couldn't bear to speak to her. He felt betrayed, abandoned. How much pain could one woman inflict upon a man? In Emilie's case, the amount seemed endless.

"I wanted conversation," Phillip piped in, "but friendly conversation please."

"It's not possible," Lorenz said, standing. "I'm going to search the area for food."

"Anna gave us plenty," Phillip said. "We have only to enjoy it and be on our way. Now sit."

Lorenz paused, gazing out on the Mississippi River sparkling in the midday sunshine. *Such an enormous river,* he thought. *Such a wild, untamed land.* It wasn't home, but a man could get used to such limitless possibilities. Especially if he had a woman by his side.

When Lorenz sent his gaze back toward Emilie, her chestnut hair curling loosely about her shoulders, her dress hugging every curve of her voluptuous figure, Lorenz felt his heart constrict. She was a beauty to other men, something lovely to look upon and dream about. To him, Emilie was more than a pretty face; she encompassed his heart and soul. Lorenz sighed, thinking of the torture she inflicted on him, the waiting, the accusations. The woman was pure poison.

Emilie must have heard his painful exhalation, for her hazel eyes looked his way. Lorenz's fury returned when he realized her anger lingered.

"Sit," Phillip commanded.

Lorenz sat back down, but he refused to look at Emilie. "So what was the name of your niece?" he asked Phillip.

"Pardon?" Phillip cut a slice of apple and handed it to him.

"Your niece," Lorenz continued. "You said you have an agreeable niece who is of marrying age." Through the corner of his eye, Lorenz saw the apple wedge pause before Emilie's open mouth. "The beauty," Lorenz added, enjoying his own form of torture. "The one who's a master in the kitchen and sweet as honeysuckle."

Phillip said nothing and continued slicing the apples. It was fun jesting when Emilie was caked in mud and pretending to be a man, but now that Phillip had witnessed Emilie in all her feminine glory, he would be a difficult accomplice.

"Celestine. Wasn't that her name?"

Phillip sighed. "Yes, Lorenz. Her name is Celestine."

Lorenz wanted to make Emilie jealous, to prove that he wasn't going to wait while she observed his every fault as a reason not to marry him. In his anger, the thought of meeting a beautiful Acadian girl, an agreeable one at that, became enticing. He almost convinced himself it was time to move on, to consider marrying another.

"Celestine," Emilie remarked between bites of apple. "A name suggesting heaven or divinity. She would be perfect for you, Lorenz. She would have to be a saint if she would be your wife.''

Lorenz almost smiled at the comment. Maybe an argument was just what he needed. "Well, a saint would be a nice change," he told her. Emilie didn't react, keeping her wits about her, a trait Lorenz had always admired. Today, however, he wanted to see her suffer. "Of course," he continued, "it would be a drastic change considering what I've been used to."

Emilie rose and dusted the dirt from her skirt. "You have my blessings, then." She picked up her satchel and headed for the river, turning one last time to get in the final word. "And dear Celestine has my condolences."

The men watched her tall, elegant form, rounded out by generous curves at her bottom, disappear toward the river. Lorenz saw the appreciation in Phillip's eyes, and for a moment he wanted to knock the desire from his friend's gaze. Instead, he aggressively combed his fingers through his hair, nearly yelling when the action caused a cut at his forehead to rip open. Lorenz stood and kicked the satchel before him. When he realized it contained the pots and pans, Lorenz did yell.

"For God's sake, son, haven't you had enough agony for one twenty-four-hour period?" Phillip asked.

Lorenz couldn't comprehend which hurt more, his head or his big toe. He could only point toward the river. "She is going to be the death of me," he muttered.

Phillip rose and offered Lorenz his tree stump. When Lorenz stubbornly refused to sit, hopping around on one foot, hoping the pain would relieve some of his frustration,

Phillip firmly but gently pushed him onto the stump. "*You* are going to be the death of you," Phillip insisted.

Realizing his fury was getting him nowhere and exhausting him in the process, Lorenz let his shoulders slump, dropping his head into his hands.

"You're tired," he heard Phillip say. "You need some rest."

Rest was exactly what Lorenz needed, rest from the constant pain Emilie inflicted on his heart.

"He needs more than rest. He needs a good dose of common sense." Lorenz felt Emilie's skirts brush his legs as she sat next to him, but he wasn't about to give her the pleasure of responding to her remarks.

"Move your hands, Lorenz, so I can clean you up."

Lorenz glanced sideways and found Emilie posed with a strip of wet petticoat in her hand.

"Move your hands," she commanded him.

Lorenz grudgingly sat up straight and placed his hands on his lap, and Emilie began to wipe the dried blood from his face. The cool water relieved some of the pain at his eye, or was it her long fingers caressing his temple that seemed to alleviate the pounding headache? Lorenz didn't care; he closed his eyes and gave in to her ministrations.

"Stubborn man." She uttered it in anger, but Lorenz detected a note of sorrow in her voice.

He should retort, he should try and explain, but he was too tired to speak. And too focused on the delicate hands stroking his face. What he really wanted to do was guide those exploring, nurturing fingers to other parts of his body.

"What is my father going to say when he sees you?" Emilie asked, breaking Lorenz from his illicit thoughts.

"He would be proud of me," Lorenz slurred as Emilie wiped the cut above his lip.

"My father never raised his hand against another man in his life."

Lorenz opened his eyes and stared at her hard. "Maybe that was the problem."

Emilie threw her cloth into his lap and stood, hands fisted at her waist as she towered above him. "Just because I wasn't at the church that day, Lorenz Landry, doesn't mean that I don't know what happened. I do know that nothing you or my father could have done would have changed what happened to us."

Lorenz joined her, as always finding it ironic that they practically stood eye to eye. "We let them take our land away. We practically handed it to them on a platter."

"That's not true." Emilie crossed her arms defiantly, but Lorenz noticed tears forming in her eyes. "Papa told me himself there was little else we could do but comply with the English. No one knew they were going to trick us like that."

Lorenz felt the fire rising up inside him. Thirteen years and he would never forget the feeling of hopelessness he had encountered that fall, trapped inside a church for days while the English looted their village and the women cried at the church door. Or the beseeching look in his father's eyes as he watched his wife slip away on the cold, wet beach.

"We had the best land, Emilie," he said, trying to keep his fury at bay. "We were multiplying like rabbits and refusing their religion and their language. Do you honestly think the English would have let us stay in Nova Scotia while their own suffered on less fertile land? And what did we do while they plotted to ship us off to all points of the world? We fed them. We obeyed their laws.'' Lorenz leaned in closer to emphasize his last thought, the most ironic aspect of their history. ''We gave them our arms.''

Now Emilie was crying—despite her better judgment, he was certain. ''We had to,'' she said. ''They made us.''

Lorenz shook his head. It couldn't have been that easy. ''We never should have let it come to that.''

The headache returned tenfold, and Lorenz winced at the pain. He felt Phillip's hand on his shoulder. ''It wasn't that easy, son. You were too young to realize what was happening. Emilie's right. We had no choice.''

Lorenz knew in his heart that what Phillip said was true; but he was angry, and time had failed to relieve his heartache. Now Emilie was adding to it. God, Lorenz thought, why hadn't his blow to the Spaniard's face made him feel better?

''It's time to go,'' he said gruffly, picking up his rifle and satchel and heading down the path.

Lorenz didn't look to see if the others trailed him, but he knew they weren't hurrying to follow. Probably meant to give him space. Just before he turned a curve to place him out of their view, he heard Emilie remark, ''I pray my sisters have better luck with men than I do.''

Funny, Lorenz thought, he was thinking the same thing. Only he wondered why he never had the sense to fall in love with Rose or Gabrielle.

* * *

Captain Jean Bouclaire surveyed the stretch of Mississippi, taking in the sight of his flat-bottomed *radeau* moored just off the shore of Fort San Luis de Natchez. Provisions were getting slim, so his boat rode high in the water, a welcome sight. As a result his breeches pockets produced a nice jingle from the sound of English and Spanish coins. All in all, the trip upriver had produced a hefty profit. A few more plantations to service, a few more Spaniards looking for alcohol, and Jean could retreat back to New Orleans and reclaim his prize schooner.

"Damn insufferable governments," Jean cursed at the wind. A Spanish frigate had fired on his ship several months ago, and Jean had acted in self-defense, never knowing that Louisiana had become a Spanish colony and that the Gulf waters near the mouth of the Mississippi were under rigid Spanish rule. Winning the skirmish, Jean had every right to pick the Spanish ship clean, according to the law of the High Seas. But the Spanish hadn't seen it that way. They were all too happy to confiscate *La Belle Amie* when it arrived in New Orleans.

While he waited to raise the funds to retrieve his ship, Jean sailed his pitiful boat up and down the Mississippi, selling hard-to-come-by supplies to the colonists at four times the cost. In time, he would have enough to bribe the right officials and regain his beloved ship, but for now he was doomed to relieve Louisiana residents of their money at primitive outposts like Natchez.

The young Englishman was a prime source, he thought as Coleman approached him. He was all too eager to part with his currency for a case of rum. The blond, blue-eyed man had that desperate look about him that morning. Too bad Jean had sold his last bottle the night before.

"You're too late," Jean told him. "I'm out of rum."

Coleman appeared confused. "I need your help," he said.

"I told you, I'm out of rum."

When Coleman came closer, he repeated his statement slowly and louder as if Jean hadn't understood. "I need your help," the Englishman said.

God, but Jean hated the English. They were such an annoying bunch. Aggressive, demanding, always expecting everyone to understand their language even though America had been colonized by the French years before their lot had landed in Virginia. This upstart was a good example, living on the border of a previous French colony, one comprised of French citizens, yet he didn't speak a word of the language.

"I heard you the first time," Jean said slowly and loudly in English. "I have no more rum."

"I don't wish for rum," Coleman answered. "I need your help."

Now, this was a new one, Jean thought. What possible help could a Frenchman give an Englishman, the son of a notorious spy, no less? As if he read his mind, Coleman answered the question. "There is a person I wish to speak to and I need a translator."

Jean eyed him curiously. "Why not ask your father? I understand he speaks French."

Coleman thrust his hands into his breeches and stared

out at the river. "I am not on speaking terms with my father."

Chalk one up for the French, Jean thought. Still, he wasn't keen on helping the man. "I'm not a cheap translator," he said, hoping that would deter the Englishman and send him on his way.

"I can pay."

"You were hard pressed to buy the rum," Jean answered.

Coleman withdrew two cigars from his breast pocket, grimacing at the thought of parting with his beloved tobacco. "You may have the last of my cigars."

Now, this was something new. Jean couldn't remember the last time he enjoyed a good smoke. He grabbed his waistcoat and pulled it on. "Where to, then?"

"There's a family of women who have been separated from their patriarch," Coleman explained. "I hired them to repair and launder my shirts."

"You wish to communicate instructions or prices?" This sounded fishy. Money was a universal language.

"Among other things."

As if uncomfortable divulging more information, Coleman set off down the path toward the Acadian settlement. The Spanish had awarded land grants to the Acadians, and slowly the men were constructing houses along the nearby bayous to accommodate the families. Jean's better judgment urged him to ignore the crazy Englishman; but the taste of a fine cigar lingered in his mouth, and he was interested in seeing what the Canadian French had done with their land. They had an interesting way of doing everything, including speaking French, which made him constantly wonder why one hundred plus years in Canada had made them so unique.

Jean followed Coleman up the muddy slope leading from the river. When he caught sight of an Acadian woman, her rosy cheeks glowing from beneath her *garde de soleil,* or sunbonnet, Jean knew exactly what the Englishman was up to.

"It's a woman," he said to Coleman's back.

Coleman paused and waited for Jean to reach his side. "Rose and her mother mend my shirts, nothing more."

Jean snorted, and they both continued walking. "So why hire me to translate?"

Coleman remained silent, and Jean wondered what the Englishman was scheming with this poor Acadian family without protection of a man. "I want to know if there is anything she needs," he finally answered. "I want to know if there is something I can do for her."

Jean grabbed his arm and swung Coleman around. "You're out of your mind if you think I'll be party to this," he said.

Just as furiously, Coleman yanked his arm from Jean's grasp. "Party to what?"

"I know what you're up to," Jean said, leaning in close. "You can't marry the woman, so that leaves only one recourse. You want the helpless woman as your mistress."

Coleman's eyes lit with a fiery fury, and it was he who now leaned menacingly close. "Damn you, sir," he said between gritted teeth. "How dare you speak of the lady in such a fashion."

Dear God, Jean thought, the man was in love. He recognized that rabid look in Coleman's eyes. But there were oceans of differences between them, not to mention the fact that Coleman was English, the same nationality that expelled this Rose from her home.

"I don't expect anything," Coleman said, as if he knew what Jean was thinking. "I just want to be of service to Rose and her family."

Service? To a French Catholic? There was trouble brewing here, Jean knew it. "The best thing you could do for her is leave her alone." He meant it as a threat to this brash Englishman, but it emerged as friendly advice. His congenial tone surprised him as much as Coleman.

"I shall," he answered solemnly. "But I would first like to do what I can to help her."

They walked the remainder of the path in silence, welcomed by a middle-aged Acadian woman, a beauty in her own right, at the door.

"*Bonjour,* Monsieur Thorpe," the woman said.

"*Bonjour,* Madame Gallant," Coleman answered awkwardly, glancing at Jean for support. Obviously this was the extent of his French.

"*Bonjour,* madame," Jean said, bowing. "I am Captain Jean Bouclaire. Monsieur Thorpe has asked me to accompany him today so that he may be able to speak with you."

Madame Gallant sent Coleman a look much like the one Jean had delivered at the riverbank. Jean wondered if she knew her poor daughter had attracted the attention of a love sick Englishman.

"Please come in," she said.

The rugged cabin, with its walls thick with tiny beams

of light shining through, offered a homey feeling despite
its absence of refinement. The women had clearly made
the place cheery, but Coleman was right. There was a lot
a man could do to help.

Before Jean could offer his services, Madame Gallant
picked up a pile of pressed garments and handed them
to Coleman. Jean nearly laughed when the young man's
face dropped. Two cigars and this Rose wasn't even home.

Just then two young women entered the house. A petite
woman with a long braid of brown hair trailing down her
back while curly tendrils framed her face crossed the
threshold first, and her face beamed when she caught
sight of Coleman. Clearly this fairylike child was Rose,
and Jean could easily see how the young man had become
enraptured in her warm and engaging smile.

He heard Rose's mother offering introductions and
waited for the fairy to meet his eyes. Instead, the second
woman entered the house, a raven-haired goddess, and
her eyes lifted suddenly to his as his name was mentioned.

"Captain?" she asked.

"Captain Jean Bouclaire," he answered, bowing.

Her dark eyes, as enchanting as the dark waters of the
Gulf at midnight, glistened as she examined him. He had
captured the dark beauty's attention, but he wasn't sure
why. "I'm sorry, mademoiselle, I didn't catch your
name."

The second daughter placed the clothes basket on the
table, straightened the front of her skirt and extended her
hand. "Gabrielle Gallant," she said, still gazing at him
intently.

For a moment, Jean wondered if they had met before.

She seemed so familiar, this regal enchantress with an angelic name. Without thinking, Jean leaned forward and kissed the top of her hand. The mother bristled, unhappy with the intimate gesture, but Gabrielle never blushed, her black eyes staring at him as if she approved and wanted more. A bolt of energy ran through Jean, filling his senses with this woman, and he wondered if she felt it, too.

Jean let go of Gabrielle's hand, a little too late for proper company, and admonished himself for his actions. He wasn't interested in women. They were bad luck. He wanted only to recapture *La Belle Amie* and return to sea. But now he had cigars to earn.

"Madame," he continued, turning toward the mother. "As I was saying, Monsieur Thorpe has asked me to translate for him."

"What does he want?"

Jean read concern in the mother's face, a look to be expected. He felt pity for this woman. An Englishman wished to court one of her daughters, and he, himself, wanted nothing more than to carry off the dark-haired angel. If Madame Gallant had any sense, she would rid her household of both of them immediately.

"What did she say?" Coleman asked him.

"What do *you* want to say?" Jean asked Coleman impatiently. He found himself seeking out Gabrielle's eyes, and the attraction for her scared him. Especially since she was doing the same. "Coleman?" Jean asked again, waking the Englishman from his own thoughts of attraction. "What do you wish to ask these gentle women?"

Coleman gazed at Jean silently, then turned toward the brown-eyed fairy in the center of the room.

"Tell her," he began softly, "that I wake every morning with thoughts of her."

Jean stared at him as if had lost his mind, certain that the young man would retract his intimate and improper thoughts, but the Englishman only continued.

"Tell her that her resplendent face is in my mind every waking moment," he went on. "That I sleep with her image in my dreams."

Coleman paused and swallowed, and Jean swore he could hear the beating of the young girl's heart. "Tell her I love her more than life itself," Coleman continued passionately, never taking his eyes from his beloved's face. "That she is the only light in my dark existence."

The silence that followed was deafening. Jean stood at a loss over what to do. He knew the man had feelings for the petite woman, but he never expected such an outburst of affection. Still, Coleman had asked for him to play translator. He began slowly, "Monsieur Coleman said—"

"No," Coleman shouted, staring down at the hat held tightly between his fingers. "Please ask them if there is anything they need," he added tersely.

Jean turned again toward the women, their eyes as wide as pecans, and translated the request.

"*Non, merci,*" the mother stated firmly, and Jean caught every bit of its message.

Jean nodded that he understood her meaning and grabbed Coleman's arm to leave. Until the fairy blocked their path.

"A violin," Rose said in French. "We could use a violin."

Coleman brightened instantly and rested his gaze on Rose's face. "A violin," he repeated in English. "She wants a violin?"

"We have no music," Rose explained to Jean. "We left Acadia with practically nothing, including our instruments. And we so love our music. Our men have spoken of nothing else since we arrived."

Jean continued looking at Rose, such a small frame of a woman filled with such vitality, but he spoke to Coleman. "Yes, your lady wishes for a violin."

Rose looked over to Coleman, and the affection that passed between them was blinding. Coleman smiled and bowed. "Please tell her she shall have her wish."

Jean conveyed the message. Rose smiled, blushing profusely as she offered a curtsy. Jean then wished Madame Gallant good day and bowed to Gabrielle, who blushed as well. Her flirtatious smile caused a tightness in Jean's trousers, so he grabbed a starry-eyed Coleman and pushed him out the door. As the men left the meager house, and the eyes of the beautiful Acadian women, Jean sent up a silent prayer. "God help us," he muttered.

What had just happened? Gabrielle thought. She glanced at her mother and read fear in her eyes, which confirmed her own. If she wasn't mistaken, that Englishman had just professed his love to Rose.

Rose stood there grinning, as if an Englishman courting her was as common as the sunrise. Maybe she was mistaken. Maybe she was reading more into this than had actually happened. There was only one way to find out.

Gabrielle bolted through the door and ran after the men, thankful that Coleman had taken the lead. She caught up with the captain and touched his sleeve to halt his step. But when his enormous eyes met hers, she felt her knees weaken, just as she had inside the house when he had first gazed on her, and suddenly Gabrielle was at a loss for words.

"Mademoiselle," he said, capturing her hand and raising her fingers to his lips once more. This time he didn't just kiss them, but slowly brushed his lips against her fingertips. The prickly sensation caused by his mustache forced her breath from her lungs, and Gabrielle wondered how she would ever speak.

"How may I help you?" he asked deeply, and Gabrielle shuddered, thinking of ways in which he could.

She swallowed. "Did Monsieur Thorpe say what I thought he said?"

Jean let go of her hand, and Gabrielle instantly missed the warmth of his touch. "I'm afraid our Englishman is smitten with your sister."

Gabrielle placed a hand at her heart and sighed, as much to release the tension the captain was causing as for concern over Rose's welfare. "What are we to do?" she asked him.

"Perhaps it will pass," he said, gazing intently into her eyes.

"Do you approve of this man?"

At this, Jean laughed, and Gabrielle delighted in the sound of it. She wondered what he was like at the helm of his ship. "He's English," he said with an infectious grin. "Although he seems better than most. I'll keep an eye on him, if you wish."

The thought of seeing Jean again made Gabrielle's heart race. She nodded in agreement, afraid that her voice might betray her inner feelings.

"Bon," Jean said, placing his hat on his head and tipping it. "Good day to you, mademoiselle."

He moved to leave, and Gabrielle realized he had answered only one of her questions. "Are you a ship's captain?" she called out.

The captain turned and gazed back curiously. "I own a schooner," he said. "Why?"

Gabrielle thought of her dream, of sailing off to uncharted lands with the sea wind in her hair and the strong chest of the man at her back. The man whose face was never clear. "I was wondering, is all."

Jean walked back toward her. "Do you like to sail?"

Gabrielle wanted to gush enthusiasm, that she adored the sea, but that wasn't something a woman was supposed to enjoy. Besides, it was the lure of the sea that had caused the family's separation at Grand Pré, when Gabrielle's fascination for the ships at Minas Basin had forced Marianne to come looking for her, at the same time losing track of Papa on the crowded beach. She would not let it happen again. "Yes, I like to sail," she answered quietly. "Although I doubt I will do it again."

"I know the feeling," Jean answered. "But perhaps . . ."

Gabrielle's heart skipped a beat, waiting for the next word, but Jean only smiled, tipped his hat and rejoined Coleman on the path. She watched as Coleman handed the captain two cigars from his breast pocket and the captain returned one of them while slapping the Englishman on the back. Perhaps Coleman Thorpe could be trusted. She hoped the captain was trustworthy as well.

"He's a pirate. Piernas told me so." Rose joined her and slid an arm about her waist. Gabrielle wrapped her arm about Rose's shoulder, and the sisters watched the two men disappear down the road, both sporting smoking cigars.

Gabrielle wanted to laugh, but the prospects were anything but funny. "We're being courted by an Englishman and a pirate."

Rose leaned against her shoulder and sighed. "What would Emilie say to that?"

Emilie would have their hides.

"If only falling in love was as easy as Emilie and Lorenz," Gabrielle said. "I'll bet they are halfway to the altar by now."

Chapter Eight

Phillip Bellefontaine was right, Emilie thought gazing at the delicate woman before her. Celestine Bourgeois was quite a beauty. She owned all the grace and gentleness that Emilie had never mastered, and Lorenz delighted in it all. He stared adoringly at the petite girl, laughing at her innocent remarks.

"What have you done to yourself?" Celestine asked, rising onto her toes to wipe the dirt from the cuts at his face. "And why have you let this black eye go unattended for so long?"

Lorenz leaned in close to the doe-eyed girl. "I've been neglected," he whispered, grinning slyly while sending Emilie a look filled with arrows.

Emilie grimaced and looked heavenward, praying that God would grant her patience along with the other feminine traits she lacked. Looking down at her filthy skirt and muddy shoes, Emilie realized she was no match for the likes of Celestine.

Why would she even think such a thing, she chided herself. She didn't care what Lorenz did or who the obstinate man flirted with. She shouldn't find fault with the girl, who was more than likely finding men appealing for the first time in her brief life. *God help the woman who marries Lorenz Joseph Landry and his stubborn bull-headedness,* Emilie thought. He could marry the Queen of England for all she cared.

Still, it annoyed her that the one woman to catch Lorenz's eye would wear such neat clothes, arrange her silky hair without so much as a pin out of place, and possess feet so intolerably small. It just wasn't fair.

"You poor thing," Celestine said to Lorenz as he bowed to allow her access to his facial scars. "You must let me clean you up when we reach the house. You said you were traveling two days with such wounds?"

Emilie gritted her teeth, fighting back a reply. If only little miss perfect knew.

"Celestine, where are the men of the village?" Thankfully Phillip interrupted the scene the two were making. "We need to have a word with them."

Celestine straightened, but never took her eyes off Lorenz, frowning as if fearful he might disappear while she fetched her father. In all truthfulness, Emilie didn't blame the girl for her attention. Lorenz was by far the finest-looking man Emilie had ever met. Very few women passed Lorenz by without noticing his sturdy build and strikingly dark features. And Lorenz answered in kind by delivering an equally appreciative glance their way. His flirting skills were as remarkable as his appearance.

"We need to find out some information about St. Gabriel," Lorenz said to Celestine, as if assuring her he would not vanish while she located her father.

"I will see you later at the dance, then?" she asked with a pout.

Lorenz bowed, then kissed her hand. While Celestine released a long sigh, Emilie rolled her eyes. "Your father," she reminded the girl.

Celestine stared at Emilie as if she was caught doing something wrong and had no idea what it was. She retrieved her hand from Lorenz's grip and led the group toward the village.

"That was uncalled for," Lorenz whispered to Emilie as they followed Celestine into the clearing.

"Was it?" Emilie asked. "I thought we were here to find my father."

Celestine glanced back toward the trio, but it was clear she had eyes only for Lorenz. "Still here," he said with a grin.

The girl giggled and continued on, offering small talk as they labored across the field. Emilie didn't know how the girl did it. The cypress knees, her faithful enemy, were no longer the problem, but there were holes everywhere, capped off by protruding mounds of mud. Celestine dodged them without looking; but even with careful scrutiny of the earth, Emilie's wooden shoe lodged into one, and she hit the ground, face first. She raised her arm just before impact, but her body slid through the mud, still saturated from the rain.

"Oh, my," she heard Celestine exclaim above her. "Are you hurt?"

Emilie felt Lorenz's hands grab her and effortlessly right her. When she realized he howled with laughter, she yanked her body from his grip.

"She's fine," Lorenz said between chuckles. "Stubbornness does that to a female."

Turning to face him, Emilie meant to deliver a solid piece of her mind and maybe turn the other eye blue, but when she realized the extent of her accident, mud staining the entire length of her vest and skirt, the fire drained from her words. Staring at Lorenz the whole time, she plucked off her sabots and continued toward the town barefoot.

"Are you all right?" Celestine asked. The poor child was practically running to keep up with Emilie's long strides. For a moment, Emilie almost liked the girl.

"I'm fine, thank you," she answered. "All I need is a good bath." With a look behind her, she added, "And some pleasant company."

"My mother will take care of you," Celestine said, breathless. Emilie decided to slow down, give the poor girl a chance. "She'll find you some clean clothes."

Emilie stared at the top of Celestine's head. It was doubtful the mother was taller. "Thank you, but there are few women who can share their clothes with me."

At this Celestine giggled. "I beg your pardon, but I've never seen a woman as tall as you."

Whatever kind feelings Emilie had acquired for Celestine began to dissipate. "I suppose you don't have shoes my size either.'' When Celestine resumed giggling, Emilie vowed she would never like the girl.

''Wear the damn moccasins,'' Lorenz yelled from behind.

Emilie gritted her teeth. She was tired, sore and now dirty, and in no mood to listen to a man who had argued relentlessly for three days. ''What are those mud holes anyway?'' she asked Celestine, hoping to change the conversation away from her faults that everyone, save dear Phillip, seemed to find humorous.

''Crawfish,'' Celestine said, her skirt sashaying as she walked.

''Crawfish?'' Emilie asked, wondering what unique animal lived inside a mud hole.

''Miniature lobsters,'' Phillip said with a laugh, holding up his fingers to indicate two inches. ''We boil them.''

Trees with knees, alligators, Spanish moss and boiled miniature lobsters. What would Louisiana offer next? Somewhere behind the small villages they had visited and upriver were Indians, according to Anna, including a tribe of cannibals west of the Great Swamp. Emilie prayed they would reach St. Gabriel soon. She had to find Papa and convince him to take them home to Grand Pré. She didn't care what possibilities this new frontier offered. Emilie wanted to go home.

She was exhausted. The tears lingered precariously close. Fighting them off was causing her a headache. If she could take a bath, alone, and have a good cry, perhaps she might feel better.

Then there was still the problem of Lorenz. Despite her vow to never marry her best friend, the thought of him furious with her and flirting with another woman fell heavy on her heart. Celestine was pretty and agreeable, but Emilie was the only woman who was right for Lorenz.

Emilie felt a comforting hand about her shoulder. "You go with Celestine," Phillip said. "I'll go talk to the leaders of Cabannocé and see what I can find out."

"Find out about Papa," Emilie insisted. "And a boat to get us to St. Gabriel."

Phillip squeezed her shoulder. "Don't worry," he said. "I will find out everything I can and come back to you later. Right after I check on my family."

Emilie had forgotten this was Phillip's homecoming, and that he had been delayed because of the rain. She felt guilty at not considering this sooner. "Your wife must be sick with worry," she said.

Phillip smiled warmly, and Emilie realized she was going to miss her friend, especially the calming influence he offered when she and Lorenz launched into argument. "Do get some rest," Phillip said. "It's Saturday, and there is always a dance after the sun goes down. You wouldn't want to be too exhausted to have a turn with me later."

Music, Emilie thought. When was the last time she had danced? She couldn't remember. Tears formed in her eyes, and this time she didn't bother wiping them away. Phillip pulled her close and kissed the top of her head. "Everything will be fine," he assured her, then headed for the north side of the village.

"Where's he going?" Lorenz asked, coming to her side. "And why are you crying?"

Emilie wiped her nose with her sleeve, smearing mud

INTRODUCING *BALLAD*,
A BRAND NEW LINE OF HISTORICAL ROMANCES

As a lover of historical romance, you'll adore Ballad Romances. Written by today's most popular romance authors, every book in the **Ballad** line is not only an individual story, but part of a two to six book series as well. You can look forward to four new titles a month – each taking place at a different time and place in history.

But don't take our word for how wonderful these stories are! Accept our introductory shipment of 4 Ballad Romance novels – a $22.00 value – ABSOLUTELY FREE – and see for yourself!

Once you've experienced your first four Ballad Romances, we're sure you'll want to continue receiving these wonderful historical romance novels each month – without ever having to leave your home – using our convenient and inexpensive home subscription service. Here's what you get for joining:

- 4 BRAND NEW Ballad Romances delivered to your door each month

- 25% off the cover price (a total of $5.50) with your home subscription

- a FREE monthly newsletter filled with author interviews, book previews, special offers, and more!

- No risks or obligations...you're free to cancel whenever you wish... no questions asked.

To start your membership, simply complete and return the card provided. You'll receive your Introductory Shipment of 4 FREE Ballad Romances. Then, each month, as long as your account is in good standing, you will receive the 4 newest Ballad Romances. Each shipment will be yours to examine for 10 days. If you decide to keep the books, you'll pay the preferred home subscriber's price of $16.50 – a savings of 25% off the cover price! (Plus $1.50 shipping and handling.) If you want us to stop sending books, just say the word... it's that simple.

If the certificate is missing below, write to:
Ballad Romances, c/o Zebra Home Subscription Service, Inc.,
P.O. Box 5214, Clifton, New Jersey 07015-5214
OR call TOLL FREE 1-888-345-BOOK (2665)
Visit our website at www.kensingtonbooks.com

FREE BOOK CERTIFICATE

Yes! Please send me 4 Ballad Romances ABSOLUTELY FREE! After my introductory shipment, I will receive 4 new Ballad Romances each month to preview FREE for 10 days (as long as my account is in good standing). If I decide to keep the books, I will pay the money-saving preferred publisher's price of $16.50 plus $1.50 shipping and handling. That's 25% off the cover price. I may return the shipment within 10 days and owe nothing, and I may cancel my subscription at any time. The 4 FREE books will be mine to keep in any case.

DN070A

Name _____

Address _____

City _____ State _____ Zip _____

Telephone ( ) _____

Signature _____

(If under 18, parent or guardian must sign.)

Orders subject to acceptance by Zebra Home Subscription Service. Terms and Prices subject to change. Offer valid only in the U.S.

Get 4 Ballad
Historical Romance Novel:
FREE!

BALLAD ROMANCES
Zebra Home Subscription Service, Inc.
P.O. Box 5214
Clifton NJ 07015-5214

IIl..l..lll..l.ll.l.l..ll.l.l.l.l.l.l.ll.l.l.l.ll.l.l.l..ll.l..l across her face. *"Merde,"* she shouted, stomping her foot.

Celestine's eyes grew enormous at her use of vulgarity. Lorenz shot her a look of consternation. "What?" she asked him angrily.

When Lorenz glanced over her shoulder, Emilie's heart sank. She turned to find Celestine's entire family staring at her, including several children and an elderly woman cupping the ears of the youngest child. Emilie wished a crawfish hole would open up and swallow her whole.

"I am Lorenz Landry, and this is Emilie Gallant of Grand Pré, most recently of Port Tobacco." Lorenz extended his hand, which thankfully turned their attention away from the large, cussing woman with a filthy face and bare feet. The father shook Lorenz's hand and welcomed them, but it was clear he was not pleased with Emilie's unladylike behavior. The mother, an older mirror image of Celestine, cautiously welcomed Emilie into their house.

"She needs a bath, Maman." Celestine unhesitantly slid her arm into the crook of Emilie's elbow, helping her into their home. Emilie protested that Celestine's help would only smear mud onto her own shirt, but Celestine insisted with a smile. Emilie sighed, giving in to the forces at work that day. She was competing with a saint after all.

The sun began to disappear between the live oak trees, and still her clothes remained damp. *A fitting end to a horrendous day,* Emilie thought. After Celestine and her mother had removed her clothes and insisted upon helping her with her bath, the two women had asked the nearby families for clothes, only to return home empty-handed. Emilie wouldn't have minded wearing her *jupon,* or petticoat, until her clothes dried, but even her undergarments had been caked in dirt. She had ended up wearing one of Celestine's father's shirts, which draped over her torso like a priest's cloak, and Charles Braud's tight breeches, which threatened to suffocate her. And as if to mock her and all her inadequacies, her large feet protruded from the inches-short trousers like those dreadful cypress knees. She would have cried, but she was past tears.

"The dance is going to start soon," Lorenz said as he approached. "Will your clothes be dry by then?"

When Emilie glanced up at Lorenz's towering figure, dressed in a clean, pressed shirt and breeches and a dark blue vest, and looking every bit as handsome, the tears returned. Despite his height, Lorenz never had trouble finding clothes to borrow. And there would be dozens of women eager to catch his hand in a dance that evening, looking as breathtaking as he did. But Emilie wouldn't be one of them.

"My clothes are still wet," she said, not caring of the emotions emerging in her voice.

Lorenz sat down next to her on the back stairs leading up to the house. Emilie pulled her exposed shins up underneath the enormous shirt, and Lorenz sent her a sly smile. It was a fruitless gesture; he had witnessed her legs many times before.

"It's not proper, you seeing me like this," Emilie said anyway.

"True," Lorenz replied, twirling his hat in his fingers.

"Since we don't intend to marry, it's best we stop enjoying the liberties we've shared before."

Emilie felt the tears rise in her eyes, thinking that not only would Lorenz forget their passionate secret kisses and marry another, but their lifelong friendship would be over. It was all well and good. He was better off with the likes of angelic Celestine. But she couldn't bear the thought of it.

"Have you heard news of Papa?" she said, fighting back the anguish.

"There are men here who remember him," he said softly.

Emilie's hazel eyes shot up to his, and Lorenz felt the power of her gaze deep in his soul. God, how the woman could move him, even after three days of endless arguments or refusals to talk sense. Her power over him was a constant mystery. Every logical thought in his brain urged him to move on, to marry another, to find a sensible girl who would be happy to marry a healthy, hard-working man. But Emilie owned a piece of his heart, and no matter how hard he vowed the contrary, she would always do so.

She appeared so lost in her oversized shirt and boy's breeches, so fragile, so emotionally raw. This was not the typical Emilie he knew and loved, not the woman who had helped him bring in the crops last autumn or the rallying force on the ship from Maryland when storms set in and the children grew afraid. Emilie the undefeatable he called her, only now she appeared as if misery had taken the upper hand.

He wanted to believe she pined for him, that his attention to Celestine was the cause of her sadness, but he knew she was only concerned for her father's welfare. He didn't blame her for that. He knew she had fears for their future, that they might have traveled to Louisiana in vain. But he so much wanted dearly to hold her close, to offer her comfort and be a safe haven no matter what the future brought.

"A man of your father's description was in the village several months ago," Lorenz began. "He said he had arrived in Louisiana with Joseph Broussard, with the first boatload from Halifax."

"Halifax?" Emilie asked, eager to hear more. "Why would he have been in Halifax?"

"According to what the men told me today, Joseph Broussard, who some call BeauSoleil, led a group of men into hiding in the Canadian wilderness when the English exiled us. Some went to New Brunswick, others to Isle Saint Jean. Your father, if this man was your father, went with Broussard."

Emilie's eyes brightened, and she sat up straight, her long, slim legs emerging from beneath the shirt. Lorenz smiled. Even at her worst, dressed as half man, half boy, the woman's sensuous beauty was awe-inspiring.

"They led ambushes against the English, but they eventually surrendered when they ran out of food and proper clothing," Lorenz continued. "They were imprisoned at Halifax."

"Then, how did they get here?" Emilie inquired.

Lorenz grinned broadly. Acadians weren't the richest or the most educated people in the world, but damned if they weren't smart. "It seems the English brought in their own people to live on our land, but they didn't know how to operate our dike system. So they paid your father and BeauSoleil to teach them how. Of course, your father and BeauSoleil and the rest of the imprisoned men charged them a pretty penny for the lesson, enough to pay for a passage to Louisiana and freedom from the yoke of the Crown.''

Emilie smiled then, proud that her father had outsmarted the English. "So, is he near here? Is he at St. Gabriel waiting for us?"

Lorenz glanced back down at his hat. He honestly didn't know what to expect. "A man of Joseph's description came through here, Emilie . . ."

"Is he here, Lorenz?" she asked anxiously.

"He came through here, but no one knows for sure where he is now." He stared at her troubled eyes, her smile gone. "He said he had a land grant out west of the Great Swamp, that he was traveling across the territory to find his family. But the last they saw of him he was heading toward New Orleans."

"New Orleans?" Emilie's eyes grew enormous, and she shook her head. "We got word that he was in St. Gabriel. That's only a few leagues more up the river, no?"

Lorenz grasped both her hands and rubbed his thumbs across her fingers. "I told you before, my love, we'll find him."

The tears finally broke through Emilie's resistance and flowed down her cheeks. Lorenz moved a hand to gently wipe them away, relishing in the feel of her soft countenance.

"What if we missed him, if he was in New Orleans all the time . . . ?"

"I sent out inquiries when we were there and received nothing," Lorenz assured her. "He would have met the boat, Em. He would have known we had arrived."

"But, then, where . . . ?"

Precisely the question Lorenz wanted answered. "I don't know. We'll continue on to St. Gabriel and keep our hopes up." He brushed her cheek with the back of his hand. "Emilie," he whispered. "If it takes the last breath in me, I'll find him."

Emilie reached inside his breast pocket and retrieved a handkerchief, then blew her nose soundly. "That's what I'm afraid of," she said, wiping the rest of the moisture from her face.

"What?"

Emilie pulled away from his embrace and looked away. "Doesn't matter. You'll never change."

He wanted to demand an explanation, but Lorenz heard voices approaching the rear gallery. Emilie threw him the handkerchief and scurried behind the clothesline, well hidden behind the billowing sheets and dresses.

"*Bonjour,*" Celestine said happily as she exited the house. "I didn't expect to find you here."

"I've come to talk to you," Lorenz answered. The young girl's cinnamon eyes nearly doubled, and her face exploded in a smile. "It's about Emilie," he added.

To her credit, Celestine didn't so much as blink. Perhaps she envisioned Emilie as merely a friend of the family. He wished he could think the same. Marrying a sweet, attentive woman like Celestine would be a nice alternative to the relentless pain of Emilie's refusals. If that was what he wanted.

Celestine's mother joined them on the rear gallery. "Lorenz," she said as happily as her daughter. "So good to see you again."

He was in trouble, Lorenz thought, as he absorbed the two women's overeager smiles. Better to state his case and be gone. "Madame Bourgeois," he answered, bowing. "I have a request to make of you. It concerns Emilie."

"Anything," Victorine Bourgeois answered less enthusiastically. Lorenz almost laughed, thinking back on Emilie's use of vulgarity in front of the Bourgeois family. He was sure they would offer no obstacle to his demand.

"Louis Hébert has left on a hunting trip and is not expected back for several days," Lorenz began. "I have been given the use of his cabin in his absence. I can sleep anywhere and would be happy to use the barn, so I was hoping I could offer the cabin to Emilie instead." Lorenz swore he heard a gasp from behind the sheets, and he fought the urge to smile. "She needs it more than I."

"But we can't let poor Emilie sleep in a man's cabin by herself," Celestine retorted. "She would be lonely."

Now Lorenz did smile. "I beg your pardon, mademoiselle, but Emilie is in need of solitude these days. I doubt she will be lonely. You may have noticed her disagreeable nature this morning. Searching for her father has not been easy for her."

"All the more reason for her to be near other people," the mother said. "We shouldn't let her out of our sight."

For a moment Lorenz feared his good intentions had backfired and that the two women would be more attentive to Emilie than before. "Emilie has long taken care of herself, her mother and two sisters," he insisted. "And I will make sure she wants for nothing."

"You are very sweet, Lorenz." Celestine sent him an adoring look. "But women need to take care of their own kind."

He had to arrange this, Lorenz thought. If he was the cause of Emilie being made over by two insistent females, she would never speak to him again. For a moment, the revenge was tempting, but he knew Emilie was in no emotional state for such a game.

"Madame, mademoiselle," he began earnestly. "Surely you have noticed that Emilie is not your typical female." When the women remained silent, he almost laughed. "Then, let me impress upon you, since I have known her since childhood, that the best thing Emilie needs now is solitude and peace. We shall be moving on to St. Gabriel, and only God knows what we will find there."

Lorenz hated speaking the words. They pierced his heart, and he knew Emilie felt their power from behind her thin shield of laundry.

"We will bring her meals," the mother began. "Every day. And make sure she has clean clothes."

Celestine moved toward the clothesline. "I'll get her clean sheets," she said.

"Let me." Lorenz grabbed the end of the sheet from Celestine's hands, and their contact brought a bright blush to the young girl's cheek. While she fought to regain her composure, Lorenz slid the sheet off the line with his back to Emilie, watching Emilie move out of sight through the corner of his eye. He slowly folded the sheet, then turned in Emilie's direction and sent her a wink. "All taken care of," he said before heading toward his cabin.

"What a thoughtful man," Emilie heard Victorine remark as Lorenz strolled down the lane leading to the other houses. "I wonder if Emilie realizes what a friend she has in Lorenz."

They didn't know the half of it, Emilie thought. No one, save her mother and sisters, would ever know her as well as Lorenz did. And there were times when only Lorenz understood the inner workings of her soul.

She watched his tall form disappear around the bend of the path and felt his absence intensely. She had sent him away, most likely for the last time, but she felt helpless to change the course of fate. Despite what Anna insisted about love giving one strength, Emilie felt defeated and empty. Lorenz and his brush with the soldiers had nearly destroyed her. Knowing that he could have been sent away for his insubordination had robbed her of all rational thought that night. Her chest had constricted, her breathing labored. A knife in her gut would have been a preferred choice of pain than watching Lorenz being exiled.

And now, in a sense, he was going away. He would be happier with the likes of Celestine, she assured herself. That was what he wanted: a home, a family, a woman to love him.

Emilie shut her eyes tightly to ward off the image of Lorenz in another woman's arms. Despite her best intentions, she couldn't let him go.

*   *   *

The fiddler concluded his mournful ballad about a lover waiting for her soldier to return from war and launched into a joyful tune. Most of the village women lit up with excitement, and the men responded gaily by grabbing them for a turn around the fire. Several of the men, as was usual, eyed Emilie throughout the dance, waiting for a signal. Brave souls even crossed the void to where Emilie sat with the older women of the village and asked for a dance. But Emilie refused every time.

"Why don't you dance, *cher?*" Widow Melancon asked. "The men are dying to make your acquaintance."

Emilie knew well what the men were dying to do, and she wasn't interested in playing those games. She wasn't up to small talk and requests for further courting from men who appreciated her figure and most likely little else. If she was in the market for a husband, which she wasn't, the man was already bought and paid for. Of course, she had practically given her merchandise away, gift wrapped.

"I much rather enjoy hearing *la 'tite causette,*" Emilie answered the elderly woman, remarking on their constant stream of gossip. "It's gratifying to hear news of people I haven't seen since childhood. Not to mention that I met three people here tonight that I knew in Grand Pré."

"And I'm sure you will meet more when you get to St. Gabriel," Widow Melancon added. "But now you need to dance."

Emilie glanced across the stretch of field laid flat by the beating of the dancers' feet, highlighted by a blazing fire in its center. Lorenz never missed a chance to turn a girl around the camp fire, asking Celestine for at least three dances. Amazing how he could delight in other women's company when she had no desire to so much as talk to another man.

The familiar pain returned, like a blow to the chest. He wanted a wife; no doubt he was working his way to the altar. But was that all she meant to him, a love to be cast off so soon?

Stupid girl, she berated herself. *What did you expect him to do, wither up and die at your feet?*

"Yes," she practically said aloud. Their separation was nearly killing her, and he was the one who first proposed marriage. Why wasn't he suffering as she did?

"You love that boy, don't you?" Phillip asked as he approached her for a drink.

"Who?" Emilie moved her gaze back to her work filling mugs of water and cutting slices of *gateaux de syrup,* a cake laced with a Louisiana syrup, one that came from cane growing from the ground instead of the kind that dripped from maple trees.

"Don't be coy with me, silly girl," Phillip said with a fatherly grin. "Remember how we met? You were covered in mud and pretending to be a boy, just so you could follow that man upriver? Or follow that man anywhere perhaps."

Emilie filled his mug and met his gaze as she handed it to him. "I had to get to St. Gabriel to reunite my family. And as you can plainly see, Lorenz doesn't seem to be missing me, nor I him."

Phillip took a long drink, then returned the mug to Emilie. "You're both fools," he said. "Life is too short for such nonsense. You two should have learned that in the past thirteen years. Be glad you're alive and that you have each other. So many of us were not as lucky.''

Emilie's gossip session with the older women had revealed that many of her neighbors and friends in Grand Pré had perished in *le grand dérangement*. Phillip had a point, one they would take to heart if Lorenz and Emilie were rational people.

"I'll keep that in mind," she told him.

Phillip smiled and took his wife's hand for a slow dance. Out of habit, Emilie searched for Lorenz through the crowd. When she spotted him returning a young woman to her mother's side, she noticed his smile disappear and a cloud pass over his eyes. It was then Emilie recognized the song.

"A La Claire Fontaine" was a soft ballad Lorenz's mother used to sing to them at bedtime. Emilie had heard it many times when their mothers had visited and the children were put down for naps around the Landry's enormous hearth. Her voice had been exquisite, much like Rose's in its clarity and range. The children had actually delighted in naps just to hear Lisette Landry's magnificent voice.

They were so young then, seventeen, eighteen years ago, their daily concerns were merely which willow tree to climb or tracking the tides so they could collect crystals when the waters receded. She and Lorenz had been inseparable, even when they grew older and their peers had encouraged them to dislike the other gender. And their parents, always present, had been a steady light in the darkness to guide them home.

An intense despondency overtook Emilie, and she again searched the crowd for Lorenz. She had to find him, to hold him close, to relish the comfort that only his embrace could offer.

She looked at the spot where Lorenz had stood, but he had disappeared. She glanced around the fire, but he was nowhere to be found. A panic commenced in Emilie's stomach and grew outward, threatening to rob her of her breath. Her chest constricted. He couldn't leave her. She couldn't live without him.

Dear God, she thought, she did love Lorenz. Not a young girl's adoration or a friend's esteem, but a passionate, soul-encompassing love. As though they were soul mates—two people destined to be together.

Emilie hurried through the crowd, searching for his face, but found nothing but strangers. Where was he?

Off to the side of the fire, Emilie noticed several laughing men moving toward a grouping of trees. Upon closer scrutiny, she realized they were enjoying *un petite coup,* a taste of some sort of alcohol. Lorenz had more than likely accompanied them into the woods, sampling whatever it was that they distilled in the swamplands of Louisiana.

She couldn't follow him there, and her heart was too heavy to return to the dance. Thankful for the solitude of her cabin, Emilie wrapped her shawl about her shoulders and headed for bed, the image of happier times in Grand Pré still vivid in her mind.

Tomorrow she would talk to Lorenz, she vowed. Talk sense into his impulsive, hard head. Maybe it wasn't too late. Lorenz Landry, for all his passionate confessions of love, couldn't be that eager to replace her with another woman. Not after a lifetime of companionship.

The prospects of the coming day failed to lighten her melancholy. As she entered the meager cabin, her eyes downcast from the weight of her dark mood, she didn't comprehend at first the lighted candle on the floor or the man's boots by its side. By the time the items registered and she raised her eyes to his, Lorenz had captured her hand and pulled her solidly into his embrace.

Chapter Nine

She should have questioned why he was there alone in her cabin or at least inquired about the haunting sadness lingering in his eyes just before he pulled her into his arms, but Emilie didn't want to speak. She only wanted Lorenz.

He was sitting on the edge of her bed, his hair tangled as if he had disturbed it with his nervous hands. His thick hair always got the brunt of his agitated moods. As his arms encircled her waist, Emilie ran her fingers through his tousled hair and pressed her cheek against the top of his head, reveling in the masculine scent that was all Lorenz.

"Oh, Em," Lorenz moaned as his face leaned into the warmth of her body.

Emilie pressed his head against her bosom while Lorenz made a larger space for her between his legs. He then

wrapped his arms so tightly around her, she could barely
breathe, and it was difficult to determine where one person
began and the other ended. But she didn't care. It felt so
good to be held, to be back in the safe confines of Lorenz's
embrace, to be near the man she so dearly loved.

Lorenz relinquished his tight hold on her, sighed and
caressed the length of her back. When he looked up, she
knew his mother's song was the reason he had disappeared
from the group as she had. The pain reflected in his eyes
caused a shiver to run down her spine. He looked as he
had that day on the beach when his mother had slipped
through consciousness or the night on the ship when his
father had been buried at sea, his covered form disappearing beneath the dark ocean surface within a heartbeat.

Emilie ran her knuckles against Lorenz's cheek and
kissed his forehead. She wanted so very much to erase
his suffering. And she wanted to ease the pain plaguing
her own soul.

Staring down into Lorenz's face, she noticed his gaze
shifting, the midnight irises now emitting a hungry, determined stare. Lorenz moved his legs farther apart and
pulled Emilie forward until their bodies were completely
united. Emilie could feel Lorenz's desire pressed against
her. They were nearing dangerous territory.

Tonight, Emilie vowed, she wouldn't say good night.

Lorenz must have read her thoughts, for he slipped his
fingers into her braid hanging across her shoulder and set
her hair free, the flowers Celestine had woven between
her strands floating to the floor like petals on the wind.
Then Lorenz leaned back while cupping her face and
brought it forward until they kissed.

There was nothing chaste or exploratory about Lorenz's kiss. It spoke of insistent passion. Emilie wound her fingers through his hair until she had a good grip and matched his wild kisses with equal fervor. Someone moaned— she wasn't sure who—and Lorenz deepened the kiss, his tongue relishing the soft reaches of her mouth. When Lorenz drew away and alternated between kissing and nipping her lips, stopping to place her lower lip between his teeth and savoring the length of it with his tongue, Emilie knew the next moan was hers. She began her own line of kisses along his jaw line, taking a playful bite on his earlobe.

Lorenz leaned his head forward and buried his face within her chest while he slid a hand underneath her skirt and savored the curve of her calf. When his hand reached the back of her knee, then her thigh and the top of her woolen stockings, Lorenz slipped his fingers under cloth until he met bare skin. Emilie gasped as his immense hands slid even farther beneath her undergarments and captured the roundness of her bottom.

She had to have more, she thought as his fingers traced the curves of her bottom. She wanted his hands everywhere.

Emilie leaned back, her breathing labored as she gazed into eyes that mirrored her desire. There was something else looking back. Worry perhaps? She almost smiled thinking that dear Lorenz would be concerned about her virginity, even though their union would assure their marriage. He had the power to force her hand, to bring her to the altar with kisses and sultry caresses, yet she knew he would never want her consent that way. And with the fire raging inside her, he didn't have to.

Emilie lowered her hands from Lorenz's hair, stroking his newly shaved face and delivering a kiss before moving to the buttons of her vest. She slowly released each button, then removed the garment and let it fall onto the floor.

Lorenz comprehended her meaning instantly, his hands quickly freeing her legs of her stockings. As he reached her ankles, however, his face exploded in a smile.

"Well, I'll be damned," he said as his fingers grasped the leather moccasins and slid them off her feet. Emilie punched him in the arm, knowing well he got the better of her, but she returned the smile.

"Stubborn woman," he muttered.

"Stubborn man," she answered before he claimed her lips once more.

This time, while their kisses brought them back together, Lorenz flattened his hands against the soft material of her blouse and cupped the sides of her breasts, his thumbs circling the now taut nipples. Free of the tight-fitting vest, her abundant bosom rose with each arduous breath as if aching to fill his palms. Lorenz's hands eagerly responded by squeezing the nubs between his forefingers and thumbs, then massaging each breast first softly and delicately, then roughly as if he would burst from the contact.

Emilie had to breathe, to emit the sigh building inside her. She straightened, exhaled the pent-up steam and leaned her head back to allow Lorenz more room. Much to her surprise and delight, Lorenz lifted her shirt and raised it over her head. Before Emilie could address what had taken place, his lips were on a breast, his tongue teasing a nipple, biting, sucking.

Emilie felt her knees weakening from the waves of exultation breaking over her. One hand on her bare back, his mouth on her breast, another hand caressing her thigh beneath her skirt—Emilie thought she would burst from the sensations. When Lorenz cupped both breasts and began to alternately devour each one with his tongue, she knew for sure her legs would not support her.

"Lorenz."

His name emerged more as a moan than a whisper, and Lorenz instantly caught its meaning. He undid the ties at her waist, but glanced up to make sure she was prepared for what was to come. When she slid her hands through his hair and caressed his cheek, leaning into his embrace to feel the warmth of his chest against her bare skin, she felt her skirt loosen and fall to the floor. With a deft movement, her undergarments followed suit.

She stood naked before him, but felt neither embarrassment nor shame. Instead, the pose seemed natural, as if being united with Lorenz was as planned as their births. How could she have doubted this union, believed that their lives, so intertwined, would not lead to this moment?

Lorenz moved his hands along her body delicately, as if savoring the feel of her skin, the soft curves of her hips, thighs and breasts. When his eyes met hers, they were filled with wonderment and gratitude.

Emilie would have giggled from the serious look on his face had not the stimulation of his fingers caused myriad reactions throughout her body, beginning with the hot, fiery sensation burning at her core. When his fingers moved lower toward the fire's center, stroking a hidden nub lying in its midst, Emilie felt a shiver of pleasure overtake her and her knees weaken once again.

"Lorenz," she said more commanding this time. "The bed."

He smiled so seductively she wondered if she would melt in his embrace. When he rose from the bed and carried her up into his arms, she gasped. How he managed to kiss her while turning to place them both on the bed, she would never understand. But his kiss sucked the air from her lungs and made her giddy with anticipation. As he placed her on the freshly cleaned sheets and pulled the cotton blanket over her, he rubbed his lips against hers.

"Now tell me you don't love me," he dared her, his black eyes glowing in the darkness of the moonless night.

The candle remained on the floor, but Emilie could still read the heightened passion in the depth of those eyes. "You know I do," she whispered.

Lorenz straightened and unbuttoned his vest, then removed both it and his shirt. Emilie wasted no time reveling in the dark hair covering his broad, strong chest. "Tell me," Lorenz said as he began to unbutton the *clapet* of his breeches. "I want to hear you say it."

Emilie didn't doubt her feelings, but her mind concentrated on his fingers circling the buttons of his breeches. She wondered if it was true what the married women said about tall men with large hands. She wondered if there would be pain.

She felt a gentle hand on her chin, lifting her face upward. When her eyes met his, she blushed at being exposed. But Lorenz wasn't thinking of her curiosity. "Tell me," he insisted.

Not caring that the blanket fell away, Emilie slid into his lap and hugged her body to his. Amazed at how wonderful his thick chest hair felt against her breasts, she wiggled into his embrace and began to nuzzle his neck.

"Tell you what?" she answered teasingly, while he moaned and grabbed her bottom, pulling her tighter against him. "That you're the most incorrigible man I have ever met in my life?"

Lorenz pulled back and met her lips with a heated kiss, his tongue dancing inside her mouth before he released her and led a wild path of bites along her cheek and neck. His massive hands fondled her breasts, capturing them in his palms as if their size was created specifically for his embrace. Emilie slid her legs around his waist, her fiery center tingling with the close contact of his desire.

"Tell you that your head is as hard as the rocks of Cape Blomidon back home?" she continued, taking a piece of skin at his nape between her teeth.

Emilie wiggled some more, and the *clapet* loosened. She could feel his manhood set free, bulging at the entrance to her own desire. She could sense his hands raising her bottom at the same time his tongue encircled a nipple. She knew their union was upon them, and she closed her eyes, bracing herself for the impact.

Lorenz looked up and took her face in his hands, then kissed her gently.

"Are you ready, my love?" he asked her, wild desire burning in his dark eyes. She knew his restraint was taking every ounce of his strength, but Lorenz would never take more than she was willing to give.

Emilie nodded and lowered herself onto him. The intrusion was painful at first, but Lorenz entered slowly, one hand at her waist guiding her down, the other at her face, always caressing. He passed his lips once more against hers. "Tell me," he pleaded.

Emilie exhaled and tightened her legs around his waist, pulling him deeper inside her. A roar like the sound of the tide returning to Minas Basin pounded in her head as they moved to a synchronized rhythm. The fire that had begun at the center of her body now reached outward, and she could feel the licks of the flames singeing her skin, stealing her breath.

Lorenz slid his hands against the small of her back and thrust her down upon him. As the fire threatened to consume her, Emilie wiggled once more, rubbing her breasts against his rock-solid chest. The fire burst forth, sending sparks throughout her body. Emilie leaned her head back and savored the savage emotions surging through her.

This was it, she thought. Everything she had ever dreamed of with Lorenz. And it was better than anything she could have imagined. For that one blissful moment, when the world exploded in light, Emilie let her defenses down. There were no painful memories here. Only Lorenz and the promise of a bright future.

"I do so love you," she said as Lorenz joined her on her way to heaven.

* * *

They lay in silence, tight within each other's arms, until Lorenz noticed the candle's light flickering. He kissed Emilie's forehead, then left the warmth of their bed.

"Shall I find another candle or do you wish to sleep?" he asked, hoping she was as eager to remain awake as he.

Emilie propped herself on an elbow, her eyes glistening in the weak light. "Are you tired?" she asked, and Lorenz thought he heard a thread of disappointment in the words.

Lorenz searched the sparse cabin for a candle, determined to make the night last forever. He found one on the night table, which he lit and placed in its holder. "No, I'm not tired," Lorenz said, watching the candle's glow reflect off the red highlights in Emilie's hair and her shoulders bask in the golden light. He grew hard at the sight of her. "I'm not tired at all," he reiterated firmly.

"Marie Bergeron says all men go to sleep afterward," Emilie said. "That Pierre falls asleep on top of her."

Lorenz slipped back under the sheets, hoping Emilie wouldn't notice just how awake he was. He bolstered his face on an elbow so that they were eye to eye. "I'm not most men," he said with a sly smile. "And I doubt you and I are the kind to waste time sleeping."

Emilie smiled broadly and raised a hand to his cheek. Her long, elegant fingers caressing his skin nearly undid him. He wanted her to touch him everywhere, and he wanted to resume what they had started. But right now, he wanted answers.

"Emilie," he began, and her smile faded at the tone of his voice. "Emilie, I need to know . . ."

She pulled her hand away and lay on her back, her eyes staring heavenward. Damn, but the woman was infuriating, even after all they had just experienced.

"Why won't you tell me why you won't marry me?" Lorenz pleaded.

Emilie refused to answer, so Lorenz sighed and moved onto his back, his eyes staring at the same spot in the ceiling as she. Strange, he thought, how two people could stare ahead in the same direction, yet maintain a wall of silence and ignorance between them.

"You're too impetuous," she finally said.

"Impetuous?" he repeated.

"Yes, impetuous and impulsive."

Now, this was something new, Lorenz thought. "I thought that was what you liked in me."

Emilie sat up, holding the sheet to her breasts, but she still refused to look at him. "Perhaps when we were children," she stated harshly. "It's hardly an admirable trait in an adult."

His anger returning, Lorenz sat up and folded his arms across his chest, their tense shoulders touching. "I apologized for my action with the soldiers. I was wrong and I admitted it. But that was days ago. You had refused me before then, and if I remember correctly, your reasons had nothing to do with my impetuousness."

Emilie looked at him then, her eyes filled with emotion. "You stole apples from our English neighbors in Port Tobacco and nearly got thrown into jail. The Jesuits were always furious with you over skipping church. You were so insistent over deck privileges on the boat from Maryland that the captain considered confining you to quarters. You lost your rations three times.''

"What did you expect me to do?" Lorenz answered, his own heated emotions getting the better of him. "We were starving in Maryland. We were too congested on that blasted ship. And who gives a damn about going to church when God has forsaken us.''

The fire burned in his temple, and Lorenz could feel the familiar thumping in his chest. He threw his legs over the side of the bed and leaned his forehead in his hands.

"I'm raked with fury," he said, his voice quivering, amazed to be admitting his secret aloud. "You can't imagine what it's like to witness your parents slip away in your hands and be powerless to do anything about it.''

Lorenz felt two long arms wind themselves about his waist and a cheek rest upon his shoulder. "Of course I do, my love. I was there, remember?''

"Em, you have family," he said. "God forbid, if we never find your father, you will always have family. My cousins, my aunt, her husband, my mother's father, they were all sent away in different ships. I have no one left.''

Emilie straightened and moved to his side so she could look him in the eye. "Lorenz Joseph Landry," she stated. "We are your family.''

The anger subsiding, Lorenz circled an arm about her shoulder and pulled her into his chest, kissing the top of her chestnut hair. "All the more reason to marry me, Emilie. We can make it official.'' The silence that lingered sliced through his heart harder than any knife. "Is it really because you think being married to me would be a freedomless pit of drudgery?''

Emilie drew back, raising the sheet to cover her. She refused to look at him, and Lorenz barely made out her answer. ''I don't want to become like my mother,'' she said softly.

Lorenz started to answer that he didn't understand, but realization quickly hit. Why hadn't he thought of that before? Emilie had spent thirteen years waiting for news of her father, watching her mother's anguish in silence. She would dread marriage for fear of the same fate befalling her. But surely, she didn't imagine him experiencing the same end as her father. ''You're afraid the same thing will happen to me as happened to Joseph?'' he asked.

Emilie glanced at him for a moment, then lay down facing the far wall. ''I don't want to wither away waiting for you to return, wondering where you are, if you're alive, if you're well. Crying myself to sleep because I'm so alone.''

''It won't happen,'' he argued.

''It might,'' she said, her voice cracking. ''You practically made it so three nights ago. Why didn't you just ask the soldiers to place you on the next boat out of Louisiana?''

Lorenz lay down next to her, lightly caressing her arm with his fingertips. ''I promise you I won't act foolishly again.''

A long silence ensued. Lorenz brushed her hair from her face, savoring the feel of her shoulders and the deep curve of her elegant neck. He kissed the top of her shoulder, sliding a hand down the length of her arm. ''I love you," he whispered. "I will promise you the moon if that's what it takes."

"Prove it to me," she answered.

Lorenz pushed her shoulder back so he could see her face. "I'll be glad to," he said with a smile. "Before this night is over, I will kiss and love every inch of you."

Her eyes flickered passion at the suggestion, but the hurt remained. Lorenz sighed, knowing he still had a long distance to travel before she would relent. "I promise," he said. "I will prove to you that I can change my impulsive nature."

Emilie raised a hand to his cheek. "Do you mean it?"

Lorenz stared into the eyes he had adored since adolescence. "Yes," he said. He couldn't mean anything more.

Emilie smiled slightly, placing his hand on her breast. "Then, you may start kissing here."

Feeling an enormous weight lift from his shoulders, Lorenz did exactly that.

Chapter Ten

The sunlight beamed into the tiny cabin, pouring warmth on Lorenz's face. Under normal circumstances, he would have welcomed the unusually temperate spring sunshine and returned to the blissful state of sleep, but the realization of dawn jolted him.

''They're coming with breakfast,'' he said, remembering his conversation with Victorine Bourgeois the afternoon before.

How long had it been since the sun rose? he thought anxiously, jumping out of bed and grabbing his discarded clothes off the floor. The second candle was nearly extinguished, and daylight seeped in through the cracks in the walls. After Lorenz pulled on his breeches, he opened the shutters and cautiously peered outside the cypress walls. Thankfully, there was no one about.

''Where's the fire?'' Emilie said to his rear.

"It's dawn," he said, leaning out slightly to peer around the corner of the house. He breathed a sigh of relief upon seeing no one in the common area between the houses, until a chicken skittered across the path. If the chickens were awake, it was certain some of their owners were as well, despite the late-night dance.

"*Merde,*" Lorenz said. "I've got to get out of here before Celestine and her mother arrive."

Emilie giggled as she watched him throw on his shirt and button his vest in the wrong holes. "Watch your mouth, Lorenz. A woman could pick up bad habits from the likes of you."

His deep eyes sparkled as he cast a quick glance and a smile her way, but his attention remained on getting dressed. "Emilie, I wish to spend my life sharing bad habits with you. Unfortunately, I don't have time to do it right now."

Emilie sat up, tucked the sheet under her arms and began to correct his hasty dressing. While she worked at the buttons of his vest, he tucked in his shirt and reached down to affix the ties at his knees. When his head was next to hers, he sneaked a kiss, memorizing the softness of her mouth for the long passage of time when he wouldn't be able to hold her. Her hands on his chest, Emilie returned the favor, then beamed when she raised her eyes to his.

"God, I love you," he said, feeling the words reverberate throughout his soul. He grazed her cheek with the back of his hand. "I never thought it was possible for you to be lovelier, but today I believe you are."

Before Emilie could react, he kissed her once again, then seized his shoes and bolted out the door.

The bed that had been ablaze with their lovemaking now felt cold and empty. Emilie slid back between the sheets, but even the woolen blankets did little to replace the warmth of Lorenz's body next to hers. She leaned into the pillow they had shared and breathed in his scent. She knew now that it was impossible to live without him.

He had promised her he would change. He had sworn he would not act foolishly and put his life in danger. Their future together was not an impossibility, just as Anna had said.

Emilie snuggled into the pillow and smiled. What a glorious night. What an amazing morning. If only Gabrielle and Rose were here to share it with her. If only her mother were present to confide in. Marianne would be furious with them, and for good reason; she and Lorenz had enjoyed what should have been saved for the wedding night. But Emilie knew her mother would understand. Emilie had overheard Pélagie Leblanc joke to her mother about Emilie's birthdate and Emilie had always assumed her presence in the world was the result of a liberty her parents had taken before their marriage. They never could keep their hands off each other. It was a wonder she had only two sisters.

Emilie hugged the pillow to her chest, remembering how her father used to arrive home, lifting Marianne into the air and kissing her warmly before greeting the children. The way her mother rested her head on his lap while he recited stories by the fireside. The light that perpetually shone in their eyes when they looked at one another. She could have the same life with Lorenz, couldn't she?

The sound of two women talking outside the cabin caught Emilie's attention, and she remembered Celestine and her mother promising to visit at first light. For the first time since she had arrived in Cabannocé, Emilie longed for their company. She wanted to be around women this morning. If not her dear mother and sisters, then another caring mother and daughter. The way they had fussed over her the night before, pressing her clothes and braiding her hair with wildflowers! Emilie looked forward to the breakfast.

Suddenly she remembered her state of dress, and a panic filled her. What would they think if they found her naked, her clothes strewn about the cabin? Emilie sat up and searched for her nightdress but found it nowhere within reach. As the voices got closer, she feared she could never dress that fast, but she had no choice. She inhaled deeply, then threw back the sheets and began pulling on pieces of clothing. As she rushed through the buttons of her own vest, she wished she hadn't laughed at Lorenz.

"Emilie," she heard Celestine call out. "May we come in?"

"Just a moment," Emilie answered, hoping the panic in her chest wasn't evident in her voice. "Let me straighten up a bit in here first."

Footsteps could be heard on the wooden steps leading up to the cabin. "No need for you to do that," Victorine said. "We're all friends here."

The vest finally buttoned and the ties at her waist fastened, Emilie quickly glanced around the cabin while Celestine opened the door. Just before the young girl looked up from carrying Emilie's breakfast on a tray, Emilie spied Lorenz's hat lying on the floor. With a deft motion, she kicked it under the bed a second before the women made eye contact.

"How are you this morning?" Celestine asked, placing the tray on the nightstand.

"Did we wake you?" Victorine asked as she followed behind her daughter into the cabin.

Emilie brushed her hair with the palm of her hand. "Just dressing," she said. "Forgive me for not being presentable. It's been a long time since I have slept late."

"Don't be silly, child," Victorine said. "We were hoping you would have a nice, long sleep. I trust you slept well."

The thought of Lorenz leaving a long trail of kisses down her body flitted through her mind, and Emilie could feel the blush spreading across her face. "I slept very well, thank you," she assured the older woman, who smiled broadly at the news.

"Bon," Victorine said. "Lorenz assured us a quiet night alone would do wonders for you, and I'm happy to see he was right."

Emilie couldn't help but match her smile. "It did wonders for me all right."

"We have brought you breakfast," Celestine inserted. "Are you hungry?"

Famished was a better word, but she couldn't forget her manners. "Please, sit down," she said, motioning for the women to sit on the cabin's only chairs. Emilie sat on the bed, glancing down to make sure Lorenz's hat was well concealed.

Celestine removed the towel covering the tray, and a large array of bread, fruit, select meats and a slice of the *gateaux de syrup* emerged before her. "It's more than you could possibly eat," the petite girl explained. "We brought along more than enough, plus some leftovers from last night in case Lorenz happened along."

Emilie gazed at the platter of food and stifled a laugh. She knew she could eat each and every morsel. *"Merci beaucoup,"* she said before tearing off a piece of the bread and biting into an apple slice.

"Bonjour," a voice called from outside the cabin, and Emilie felt a shiver run up her spine, thinking of its owner. Only minutes had passed since he left, and it had felt like years.

"It's Lorenz," Celestine announced, and the sound of his name made Emilie's heart skip.

Lorenz's tall form filled the threshold, and he greeted the women warmly. When he glanced Emilie's way, his eyes spoke volumes.

"We have bread and meats," Celestine announced proudly. "Breakfast for a king."

"Wonderful," Lorenz said, seating himself next to Emilie on the bed. "But I would hate to deny Emilie her breakfast." He was so close Emilie could easily bury her face in the midnight locks curling at his nape or taste the rough skin that needed a good shave. If she nibbled on his earlobe, she wondered if he would moan as he had the night before.

"Don't be ridiculous," Celestine said, breaking her

from her ardent thoughts. "Emilie couldn't eat all that food."

When Lorenz turned his black eyes on her, a sly smile gracing his lips, Emilie wanted nothing more at that moment than to have those exploring lips on hers. "Oh, I would suspect Emilie is quite hungry this morning."

Emilie wasted no time taking his bait. "And I suppose you aren't? After all that *dancing* you did last night."

Lorenz continued to grin while he reached across her and chose a crust of bread, purposely rubbing his arm against hers in the process. "Pardon," he whispered as he brushed past her, sending forth a round of goose bumps along her arms.

"By the way," he added, signaling to her vest with his eyes. "You missed a button."

Emilie blushed when she found a button out of place, then steeled her eyes when she realized Lorenz was laughing at her expense. But he didn't have the last word yet. "Where's your hat, Lorenz?"

The slice of bread froze on the way to his lips, and Emilie could have sworn his face colored. When he turned toward her, his eyes sparkling with merriment, she knew he loved the game as much as she. "Must have lost it in the passion of the dance," he said so softly, she felt her heart pounding in her chest.

"Why didn't you dance last night?" Celestine asked Emilie. The question caused the temperature in the cabin to drop significantly, for which Emilie was grateful. Their little game was going to get them in trouble.

"I wasn't in the mood for dancing," Emilie answered, picking up the slice of cake before Lorenz could grab it.

"I was trying to get information about my father and find someone with a boat to get us across the Mississippi."

"I already did find someone," Lorenz said between bites of bread. "Phillip knows a man a few leagues upriver who could sail us over to St. Gabriel."

"Blanchard," Victorine said. "Eraste Blanchard. Crusty old 'Cadien, but a nice man. He'll be glad to get you across the river as long as the weather holds."

Simultaneously, Lorenz and Emilie leaned toward the open window and examined the sky. Round puffs of clouds floated across their view, but the wind howled around the corner of the cabin, sending a slight chill from the north.

"Not a good sign," Lorenz said softly, confirming Emilie's fears that the pleasant spring weather they were experiencing would be short-lived. "It feels like inclement weather might be coming."

"If you don't sail over today, then you will soon enough," Celestine said with a hopeful smile. "I'm sure we'll be able to entertain you while you wait."

Emilie knew the young girl wanted Lorenz around as long as possible. She hoped the girl wasn't falling in love. They had to leave as soon as possible, for everyone's sake.

"They need to move on and find Emilie's father," Victorine said, patting her daughter lightly on the knee. To Emilie and Lorenz, she added, "She doesn't remember the exile. She doesn't know what it's like to be separated from family."

"I remember," Celestine argued, glancing at Lorenz

as if the knowledge would reveal she was shy of fourteen. "I don't want you to leave so soon."

"I have to get to St. Gabriel," Emilie said firmly. "I'll row the boat myself if I have to."

Victorine placed a hand on her arm and squeezed at the same time Lorenz picked up her free hand. Emilie wondered if her voice had betrayed her emotion. To her surprise, tears welled in her eyes.

"As I said before," Lorenz murmured softly in her ear, "I will find him if it takes the last breath in . . ." He paused, still rubbing his thumb across her knuckles. "Let me rephrase that. I will find him. And I will do it unimpetuously."

Emilie laughed while a tear stole its way down her cheek. "There's no such word."

"You're right," Lorenz said gently, wiping the tear away and taking the opportunity to caress the rest of her cheek. "No such word in our vocabulary."

"Well, it's getting late," Victorine said. "Come now, Celestine. We have chores to do, especially if the weather turns bad."

Celestine frowned, clearly unhappy to be leaving the man of her dreams and probably the most unusual woman she had ever met; but her mother pulled on her sleeve, and they made their farewells and exited the house. Lorenz saw them to the door, then turned and gave Emilie a questioning look.

"Do you think she suspects?" he asked.

"I don't know," Emilie said. "It is odd that she would leave us alone, unchaperoned. Maybe she's afraid her daughter might be falling for you and she'd hate to have such a louse in the family. But a cussing woman like me would deserve such a horrid man.''

Lorenz bounded across the floor, grabbed several apple slices, stretched himself across the bed and placed his head in her lap. ''Your mother and sisters have not complained about me,'' he mumbled between bites.

''My mother and sisters have not complained to your face,'' Emilie said, finishing off the cake and placing the empty plate on the tray. ''They're just used to you, that's all.''

They were so comfortable lying on the bed together, playfully fighting and enjoying breakfast after an endless night of passion. It would be so easy being married to Lorenz, no pretenses, no awkwardness between them. Gabrielle and Rose adored him, and Marianne considered him to be the son she never had. It was the natural course of action.

Still, doubts festered inside her, ones born of fear that her father would not be waiting for her in St. Gabriel. She kept seeing Joseph at the bow of a ship, moving farther and farther away as the pain of abandonment ripped at her heart. Was she becoming like her mother, experiencing visions of the future, or was her anxiety casting a permanent shadow over her soul, interfering with her ability to be happy?

''I miss my mother,'' Emilie said, trying to dismiss the aching in her heart, an anguish that only her family would fully understand. ''I wish my sisters were here.''

Lorenz captured her hand and kissed the inside of her palm. ''It won't be long, *chère*. Besides, your sisters are probably thankful to be rid of their overbearing head of the family."

Emilie withdrew her hand from his grasp and slapped him playfully. "I am not overbearing."

Straightening, Lorenz laughed. "You have never forgotten that your father left you in charge."

"And what if he did? I have to take care of my family; my mother cannot do it alone. And I have to look after my sisters; they are younger than I."

Twisting a lock of her hair in his fingers, Lorenz kissed her, melting her defiance. "Your mother is stronger than you think. And as for your sisters, they are of marrying age themselves, Em. Maybe now, without you around, a man might have a chance."

If he wasn't being so ridiculous, she would have punched him. "That's absurd," Emilie said. "Who would be courting my baby sisters on the frontier of Louisiana?"

"Emilie is going to kill us," Gabrielle said, staring at the roll of blue and white linen. "We can't keep this."

Rose fingered the store-bought fabric, a luxury they had never enjoyed. "It was a gift," she offered. "Could there really be harm in us accepting it?"

Gabrielle's instincts thought not, but her mind had more rational ideas. Besides, it wasn't proper for two young ladies to allow unchaperoned men to shower them with such niceties, especially since one was a pirate and the other an Englishman.

"I don't understand it," Gabrielle said, shaking her head at the sight of the beautiful fabric of white periwinkles on a pale blue background. "I would have expected this from Monsieur Thorpe, but the captain? Why would he wish to be so generous?"

Rose placed her hands on her hips and sent Gabrielle a scrutinizing look.

"What?" Gabrielle insisted.

"You know well what. That man couldn't keep his eyes off of you. Not to mention other things."

The thought of Captain Jean Bouclaire's lips on her hand, his thick mustache brushing against her knuckles, sent a shiver of pleasure through Gabrielle. She tried not to let Rose see her reaction, but the slight sigh that emerged gave her away.

"You have a lot of nerve," Gabrielle shot back, her face burning with embarrassment. "You have an Englishman professing love to you in front of Maman and the entire world."

Rose's smile disappeared, and she stared down at the miniature designs woven into the magnificent fabric. "I didn't encourage him," Rose said softly. "I had no idea he had such strong feelings for me."

Gabrielle stood and hugged her petite sister tightly. "Of course you didn't, my dear. Even the captain was shocked at his actions."

"You did promise not to tell Mother," Rose reminded her.

Gabrielle laughed, thinking back to the reaction on their mother's face that afternoon when Coleman Thorpe had released a long string of compliments. "I suspect she knows. But she hasn't said a word, and neither have I."

"What do you think will happen?" Rose asked softly,

and for a moment Gabrielle wondered if she had feelings
for Coleman as well. She surmised that Rose liked the
Englishman; Rose enjoyed just about everyone's company, holding no prejudices and seeing the good in even
the most abominable people.

But this wasn't a friendship between similar people.
This was a heartsick Englishman pining for an Acadian
girl. Rose wouldn't dream of pushing away the attentions
of a kind man simply because of his nationality, and that
scared Gabrielle the most. Without a man present, or
Emilie in her usual paternal role as family caretaker and
Lorenz as a protective big brother, Coleman could easily
sway Rose's emotions. Or at least he could convince her
to allow him to continue the courtship.

"You must not allow Monsieur Thorpe back," Gabrielle said, watching Rose carefully. As she suspected,
Rose's countenance revealed disappointment and hurt.
"If you see him at the fortress, you must not speak to
him. If he wishes to have his shirts mended, let Mother
deal with him."

"She doesn't understand English," Rose inserted.

"Neither do you."

Rose lifted her chin and met Gabrielle's eyes. The
confidence sparkling in her perfectly round bronze eyes
astonished Gabrielle, and she noticed for the first time
that baby Rose had matured into a woman. Her fears
intensified.

"Coleman," Rose began, then paused. "Monsieur
Thorpe and I know enough of each other's language to
communicate. It would be silly to have a man who is
offering us work struggle needlessly through conversation

just because you think I don't have sense enough to deal with a man who finds me attractive.''

"That's not it, Rose,'' Gabrielle insisted.

Rose tilted her head defiantly, but as usual there was no malice in her sweet face. "Of course it is, Gabrielle. You think he will become a pest. Or worse, carry me off willingly in the night with him.''

Gabrielle sighed. "Granted, I am a bit worried about the second scenario.''

Despite her height, Rose managed an arm about Gabrielle's shoulders. "He's a nice man.''

"You say that about everyone.''

Rose tightened her grip as if to shake sense into her sister. "No, Gabrielle. Coleman Thorpe is a nice man. I am sure of it. You have nothing to fear.''

"Except the fact that he is an Englishman,'' Gabrielle said, placing a hand on her sister's face. "A son of the Crown that caused us to lose our home, to be separated from our father.''

"He's not the reason we were separated from Papa.''

Gabrielle placed her own hands on her sister's shoulders. "What will Emilie and Mother say? Lorenz? What will Father think of this?''

Rose grimaced at the last thought, but Gabrielle was thankful she was finally seeing logic. "I speak a bit of English,'' Gabrielle offered. "Let me deal with him, then.''

Watching her sister's face contort with distress as she nodded tore at Gabrielle's heart, but she knew she was doing the right thing. Even if the man wasn't English, he was Protestant, which meant there would never be a future between them. Better to end the brief romance before it blossomed and caused larger problems.

Then, why did she feel as if she had crushed her best friend?

"Bon," Gabrielle whispered, pulling Rose into her arms. "He will meet an Englishwoman and fall in love again. And you will meet a handsome, rich Frenchman who will treat us like royalty."

What was she saying? Gabrielle thought with horror. Rose didn't care about material things. Neither did she. She stared down at the fabric, a testament to the lure of what money could buy. She had to return the material, make it known to Captain Bouclaire and Coleman Thorpe that their affections could not be bought.

Plus, it would give her a chance to see him again.

Gabrielle closed her eyes, trying to ward off the image of Bouclaire in his knee-high leather boots, his loose cotton shirt failing to hide a thick muscled chest. The brash man leaning forward ever so seductively to savor the taste of her fingertips. And she had the nerve to be worried about Rose.

"I'm sorry," Gabrielle whispered. "Perhaps I am wrong about this."

As Rose pulled away from her embrace to discuss the point further, both women were startled by a familiar, yet almost forgotten sound. They moved toward the window to listen more closely and recognized the source immediately as it made its way up the path from the river. At the same time, Gabrielle noticed Marianne pause at the well and Pélagie Leblanc gasp, her hand covering her mouth in surprise.

Walking toward the makeshift village of Acadian houses strode Coleman, a confident smile upon his lips and a violin upon his left shoulder.

Chapter Eleven

The tune was not familiar to Rose, a rollicking melody that reminded her of the music she heard in town at Port Tobacco. Something English to be sure, yet one could dance a jig to it, turn their favorite girl around the floor. Were their nationalities so very different after all?

Coleman's blond hair tousled about his face as he pulled the bow across the strings, but he didn't seem to notice. His concentration bent on the instrument in his hands, he continued confidently up the path as if walking into an Acadian village playing a fiddle was something he did every afternoon.

Rose couldn't help but smile, even though she knew Gabrielle was watching her carefully. Her sister feared she was losing her heart to the blue-eyed man, which, if she dared admit her feelings to herself, was probably the case. Rose wasn't going to think about it, however. He was a kind man offering work to her family and music to her village. Why shouldn't she be nice to him? She would treat him like any other good-hearted man. Besides, Gabrielle was missing a vital point: Coleman Thorpe dressed as a gentleman and lived as a Protestant. Why would he risk scandal marrying a poor Acadian Catholic girl?

None of this mattered at that moment. There was music emanating from outside, and she had to be part of it. Before Gabrielle could protest, Rose bolted out the door, joining the others gathering about the Englishman.

Coleman finished his tune with an exaggerated pull of the bow, then peered cautiously at the group, wondering, Rose supposed, if they would reject him for his audacity. Rose almost laughed at the sight of Coleman surrounded by foreigners, more than likely feeling as if he had stumbled into a nest of vipers and couldn't decide whether to run or stand still. But if there was one thing Acadians valued as much as family, it was music. She doubted any Acadian standing there would dismiss the chance to dance simply because the fiddler was not one of their own.

Suddenly, Coleman's eyes found hers, and his countenance shifted into a broad smile. The sensation of his eyes, the color of a summer sky, greeting her with affection caused her heart to skip. Before she dismissed the idea as absurd and reminded herself he was an Englishman, Rose remembered her dream and wondered briefly if Coleman Thorpe was the man she would marry.

Mathurin Leblanc urged him to perform another tune, and several of the group seconded the motion. Coleman beamed that he was finally accepted and lifted his bow in song. He started a slow jig, pleased to be of service. A buzz of excitement reverberated through the crowd.

The song featured several stanzas, but required constant jerking motions of the bow due to the elaborate melody. Rose watched in amazement as Coleman effortlessly met the task, his smile never faltering. He played as if the violin were an extension of his shoulder and the bow another limb. And the pleasure his talent allowed him was evident.

Just when Rose and the others felt comfortable with the melody and considered a dance, the tune shifted. The song remained the same, but the tempo increased a step. Rose began to alternate between watching Coleman's bow ride a wild wave across the violin and his foot stomping out the beat, because before she knew it, the tempo increased even more.

Mathurin let out a yell and grabbed his wife for a dance. Then Athanase Babin took his wife for a spin. Within seconds the group was alive in dance, mothers in circles of dance with their children, husbands turning their wives and laughing in the process. Even Gabrielle was whisked away by Joseph Blanchard, leaving Rose alone to watch the blue-eyed man with the strange accent making magic with a violin.

Coleman spied her and sent her a wink before launching into an even faster tempo. How on earth did he perform such a feat? she wondered, watching the bow fly across the strings. Perspiration flew from his forehead as his head vibrated from the music, but Coleman appeared as calm and surreal as if seated in church.

Father had said everyone had a special gift—Emilie

insisted Rose's particular talent was compassion—and watching Coleman delight in an aptitude that took no effort made her realize her father was right.

It wasn't possible he could play faster, but Coleman finished the slower set and began again at a higher pace. The men yelled their approval, but had a difficult time keeping up. Coleman's foot was now beating the ground at an alarming rate, the dirt packed tight beneath his foot.

When he took the tempo even higher, everyone stopped dancing to watch the bow fly at a dizzying rate. Coleman stopped smiling at this point and concentrated on the complicated turns of the bow. Perspiration flew about his head, and his blond hair was soaked from the powerful motions. Still, he appeared as if the performance had caused little effort.

When the song reached a wild conclusion and Coleman ran the bow across the strings in a grand finale, he finally appeared out of breath. Everyone cheered at the end of his performance, which pleased him as much as the playing. Rose's heart constricted, watching the usually solemn man's face radiate with delight.

The men began to make requests, others offering thanks. Coleman searched through the crowd until he found Rose, then gave her a smile and a shrug as if to ask, "What are they saying?" Rose couldn't help but laugh. She wanted to go to him, but the crowd was thick around him.

Pélagie handed Coleman a jug of water, and Coleman returned the favor by handing the violin to Mathurin, who promptly blew on the instrument as if it were on fire. The crowd laughed at the gesture, but Mathurin gazed at the instrument lovingly, gently stroking the smooth polished wood.

"Play," Coleman told him in English. When the older man looked up confused, Coleman motioned for him to perform. "Ah, *joue la musique.*"

Rose nearly laughed at the horrendous way Coleman spoke French, but at least the man was trying. And Mathurin understood every word. He placed the violin upon his shoulder and began "En Buvant," a song Rose had heard played as a child. The Acadians wasted no time resuming the dance, a smile on every face.

Coleman watched the process, clearly pleased to be of service, but distinctly apart from the revelry. Piernas had mentioned the Englishman suffered from family problems, something in his past that had caused a rift between him and his father. Piernas hadn't offered more, and it would have been poor manners on Rose's part to inquire further. Still, she couldn't help wonder why a man dressed as finely as Coleman, who more than likely enjoyed a prosperous living, would take comfort in pleasing a group of Acadian exiles, people thrown from their homes by his own government.

Rose might have assumed Coleman shared his riches to ease his guilt if Coleman had been in part responsible for the massive exile. But the man couldn't be more than twenty-five, she thought, gazing at high cheekbones kissed by the sun and accented by a proud, regal nose. He didn't stand very tall, which made him appear all the younger; Lorenz and Emilie would certainly tower above his thick locks of blond hair that repeatedly fell about his face. At the most he was Lorenz's age and had been too young to understand when residents of New France were being evicted from their homes thousands of miles away.

He needed a haircut, which confirmed that Coleman Thorpe lived in a household without women. The shape of his tattered clothes he brought to them to mend on a weekly basis was also evidence of that fact. Fine tailored clothes, imported fabrics. Tending to his rich attire was as enjoyable to Rose as his routine visits where they mostly smiled at one another, picking up small pieces of information in their respective languages. When Coleman would retreat back to the waterfront and Gabrielle and Marianne returned to their chores, Rose would lift the fine garments to her face, enjoying the smell of tobacco, manly perspiration and the smoke of well-chosen chimney wood.

What life did the mysterious Englishman live? she wondered. And was it childish fancy, or poor judgment on her part, to want to experience more of it?

Rose turned toward the dancing couples, watching with pleasure as Gabrielle turned her mother around and around the grassy area in front of their home. For the first time in weeks her mother was laughing. Dear God, Maman was actually laughing!

Looking back to Coleman, who stood awkwardly at the periphery of the action, she waited until their eyes met and sent him a grateful smile. The color of his aquamarine eyes intensified—if that was possible—and he bowed. It would have been so natural at this point for him to ask her to dance, but a chasm stretched between them. Instead, they stood apart, gazing at each other in mutual admiration.

"Rose," Mathurin announced when he finished the song, jolting her from her thoughts. "You must do us the honor."

A hot blush permeated her cheeks. It was one thing to sing before members of her community and family, but quite another before a foreign man who had taken a liking to her.

When others seconded his request, Rose hesitantly stepped forward near Mathurin, waiting for him to resume playing. Coleman stood at her side, so close she could smell the sweet tonic about him. Heavens, if only he wasn't watching her so intently.

Mathurin performed a soft ballad about lost love, and Rose closed her eyes and began to sing. The song referred to a lover lamenting a decision not to marry. When she opened her eyes and stared into eyes resembling a blue heaven, Rose wondered if she would someday regret the decisions she was destined to make.

The Mississippi glistened brilliantly despite the sliver of a moon rising on the horizon. Perhaps it was the torches burning at the fortress that reflected such a glow, but the muddy brown water appeared almost golden in the light.

The beauty of the massive river and the pleasant breeze caressing her cheek failed to lighten Gabrielle's mood. The familiar music, so long absent from their lives, infused her with a melancholy she couldn't shake. She thought of her father waiting at St. Gabriel for their arrival, of her mother's disturbing visions and the possibility that Emilie and Lorenz might have met with trouble on their journey upriver. It had been so long since the family parted ways in New Orleans, and the two-month deadline was approaching.

The weight growing heavy about her slender shoulders, Gabrielle had retreated to the only place that brought her comfort.

"It's not much of a boat."

Gabrielle pulled her shawl about her and turned toward the voice, straining in the darkness to make out its owner.

"Have no fear, mademoiselle," the voice continued. "You are in the company of a friend."

Gabrielle realized it was the captain who approached even before his long legs strode into the light and his tanned face underneath a wide felt hat came into view. He gazed at her intently, as if studying every feature of her face.

"You startled me," she said, trying to interrupt his staring.

The captain bowed gallantly, removing his hat in the process. "My apologies, mademoiselle. But you are standing on my threshold, no?"

Gabrielle blushed at the thought that Captain Bouclaire would assume she was waiting on the bank near his boat simply for the chance of meeting him. Even if it was true.

"This is the best spot on the bank for walking," she hastily told him.

He responded with a wry smile. "As I said, it's not much of a boat. In fact, it's a pitiful excuse for one."

Gabrielle turned toward his *radeau,* a wide, flat-bottomed boat whose sole purpose was to haul products up a fast-moving river. There was a makeshift sail, topped by a bottle of rum hanging from its mast, its presence indicating to all that Jean Bouclaire wished to conduct business. In the boat's center, amidst the endless crates, hides and lumber, was a raised deck where Gabrielle assumed the captain sought refuge during storms and to sleep. Its interior was lighted softly by a kerosene lamp.

"Would you like a tour of my magnificent vessel?" the captain asked, offering an elbow. "It requires getting your feet wet, but I do have something to offer you once aboard."

Gabrielle knew she must refuse; it was unthinkable to agree. And the sly twinkle in his eyes should have made her all the more wary. But she placed a hand on his arm and allowed him to lead her through several feet of water before embarking his rugged boat. His strong arms lifted her into the boat, and he combined two empty packing crates to allow her a seat. While she made herself comfortable, pulling her shawl about her in an effort at modesty, Jean disappeared into the cabin.

"I have some wine," he called out to her. "Some cheese and bread."

What was she doing here? she thought madly. Alone on a boat at night with a man professed to be a pirate? Gabrielle glanced toward shore and wondered how fast she could reach it if the captain attempted to compromise her. But when Jean emerged back on deck, a bottle of wine under an arm, two glasses in one hand and a plate of food in the other, her fears disappeared. Although she knew no earthly reason why, she trusted the man.

"You mustn't go to any trouble on my account," she said.

The captain spread the food on a neighboring crate, then uncorked the bottle and filled a glass. He sat opposite her on a barrel once used for gun powder.

"No trouble at all," he said, handing her the glass. "In fact, it is quite a pleasure. But I am surprised a lovely woman such as yourself is not enjoying the crazy Englishman's music. And I would suspect there are several young men wondering where their dance partner has gone."

If Gabrielle hadn't known better, she would have blushed at the comment. But she was too logical for such flirtations. "I am neither lovely nor missed," she said.

Jean regarded her above the rim of his wineglass, then stretched his legs before him and leaned back against the side of the boat. He ran a lazy finger across his mustache, studying her. His attentiveness was disconcerting.

"Why, monsieur, must you stare at me so?" Gabrielle insisted.

Jean straightened and rested his elbows on his knees. They were so close that she could make out the golden specks flitting inside his deep brown eyes. He was such an enormous, virile man. Gabrielle nearly dropped the plate of cheese in her lap.

"I am baffled, mademoiselle," he finally said. "Amazed that a woman as remarkable as you would not realize her beauty. I am equally astonished that a search party hasn't been ordered."

Gabrielle laughed at the thought, and the merriment broke the tension between them. Jean smiled broadly before refilling their glasses. "What is wrong with these men of yours?'' he asked. ''Is blindness a trait of the Acadians?''

Gabrielle placed a hand over her glass to keep him from filling it to the brim. She trusted him, but only to a point. ''Is charm a trait of French pirates operating on the Mississippi?'' she countered.

Jean mockingly placed a hand over his heart. ''Pirate?'' he asked. ''I am wounded to the core.''

Perhaps Rose was wrong, Gabrielle thought with horror. Piernas might have been joking about Bouclaire being a pirate, and Rose believed it as fact. Before she could retort, Jean leaned forward again. ''I prefer to call myself a maritime businessman,'' he said with a grin. ''Whether or not my business practices agree with the colonial powers I happen upon is another story.''

''Then, you are a pirate.'' Gabrielle couldn't stop the thrill that ran up her spine. She hoped it hadn't emerged in her voice, but feared it did.

Jean watched as the lantern's light reflected off Gabrielle's eyes, now widened as large as Spanish medallions. He didn't know why he didn't discredit the label. After all, he was at best a smuggler, and a good one at that. But a pirate? Hardly. He expected a gasp of surprise, an outburst of some sort, maybe a demand to be taken back to shore, safe from his pirating ways. Instead, the woman's eyes sparkled with rapture.

''Have you sailed to the Caribbean?'' she asked excitedly. ''South America? Have you robbed other ships, taken the jewels of monarchs and buried them on some remote island?''

Jean couldn't help but smile at her romantic notions,

no doubt gathered from the imaginations of bored ship-
mates on her sail from Maryland. His crew was quite
talented at weaving tall tales while at sea, outdoing one
another as the days turned into weeks without sight of
land. But pirates were a smelly, murdering lot. Jean only
wanted to haul cargo to places in need of such niceties
with men willing to pay top money for the luxury. Most
of it was illegal, but he considered himself too educated
and well-groomed to be labeled an ordinary pirate.

"Let me rephrase this," he said, hoping to set the
record straight without losing her esteem. "I have sailed
throughout the West Indies and South America. I have
had jewels and other riches aboard my ship. But I have
robbed no one. At least not at gunpoint. And I would
never dream of burying anything anywhere. There is a
great chance of never finding such a stash again."

Gabrielle peered down into her glass. "You must think
me very silly, indeed."

"Indeed not. I think you're charming. If being a pirate
raises me in your eyes, then I shall happily call myself
a pirate."

Gabrielle looked up then, and the smile she conveyed
struck him to the core. What was it about this dark beauty
that caused his blood to stir? "Why are you here?" he
asked.

Her smile disappeared, and she took a long sip from
her glass. "The music makes me sad, reminds me of
home," she said softly. "The water soothes me."

Jean wished there was something he could offer her

family besides a useless roll of fabric. Then a thought emerged. "I am leaving tomorrow for New Orleans," he said. "Shall I stop in St. Gabriel and inquire as to your father, your sister and the fellow she was with?"

Gabrielle instantly brightened. "I would like that," she said quickly, then frowned as if regretting her outburst. "That is, if it's not too much trouble."

"Don't be ridiculous," Jean answered. "It's on my way downriver. I'd be happy to."

"But you have done so much for us already," she insisted.

"I have only given you a gift of fabric."

"One we cannot possibly accept." She met his eyes, and for an instant Jean wanted nothing more than to meet those luscious lips with his own. Instead, he focused on the conversation.

"Mademoiselle, I found no buyer here for that fabric. I will lose money if I return it to New Orleans for market, and if I have to bring it with me, it will be one less space on this miserable craft. You would honor me if you accepted that gift."

Gabrielle bit her lip and stared off downriver. Her profile, Jean realized, was just as exquisite. Round, full cheeks, a petite nose rising ever so slightly on the end, deep-set, haunting brown eyes that threatened to engulf him every time they looked his way, and the fullest lips he had ever witnessed on a woman. Her silky black hair was gathered in a round braid at her nape and offered a startling contrast to the ivory color of her long, elegant neck.

But it wasn't one particular aspect of Gabrielle's beauty that caught his attention; more like a myriad of attributes. Her long, graceful fingers kept turning the wineglass round and round, making him wish they would navigate a course along his body. Her simple dress filled out in all the right places, causing him to imagine *his* fingers exploring her uncharted waters. The cross hanging from her neck descended into a steep valley beneath her breast bone, a spot now rising and falling dramatically with every breath.

Did he make her nervous? he wondered. Did she wish to be rid of him, to escape back to her solitude along the shore? As much as Jean swore off women, cursing their lot to be an endless stream of plagues and misfortunes, he longed for Gabrielle's company. He hoped she wished for his.

"Do you have family in New Orleans?" she asked softly.

Was she asking if he was married? His hopes soared. Then he remembered what family he did have in New Orleans. Perhaps Gabrielle would retreat back to shore sooner than he imagined.

"I have a daughter," he said, watching her for a reaction. "But I'm not married to her mother."

Gabrielle turned toward him and exhibited neither surprise nor condemnation. Jean never spoke much of Delphine, never wanted shame or scandal to figure into his daughter's life. But he felt the need to discuss her now, to share his life with this dark beauty, to share his pain.

"It wasn't for lack of trying," he continued. "But her mother set her sights on someone more important than a second son smuggling goods into the wilds of Louisiana. She married a count, a rich man with social ranking on both sides of the Atlantic.''

Gabrielle sipped her wine, her eyes soft from the lantern's light. They lacked the typical censure exhibited by most of New Orleans society, so he continued. ''I wasn't opposed to the marriage; there was nothing I could offer the child. I only asked to be a visiting uncle of sorts. But when Delphine was born, she was my mirror image. Only a fool would have missed the resemblance. The count gathered every coin of Delphine's mother's inheritance and left for France. Delphine's mother has the social standing she had always hoped for, but is now impoverished and without a husband. I support them both.''

Gabrielle reached out and lightly touched his hand. ''I'm sorry.''

If it hadn't been such a loving gesture, Jean would have laughed. ''Don't be,'' he said. ''Only Delphine's birth has kept me from cursing the day I ever laid eyes on Louise Delaronde.''

Gabrielle moved closer and refilled her glass. Clearly piqued with interest, she gulped down the wine and asked, ''Why?''

Jean refrained from cupping her adorable face with his hands and letting his thumb dance across those cheeks flushed from the wine. ''She is bitter because I have ruined her life.''

Gabrielle frowned. ''I hardly see how. It was her mistake marrying for a title and not for love.''

This time Jean did laugh. ''There was no love between us.''

"But how?"

"Too much wine one night at a garden party," he answered and instantly wished he could retract the words. Gabrielle cleared her throat, then placed the wineglass at her feet.

With lightning speed, Jean retrieved the glass and handed it back to her. "No, *chérie*. It isn't the same."

He expected a sigh of relief, but instead Gabrielle appeared disappointed. Or perhaps he was imagining things. "We are friends, no?" he asked her.

Now it was her turn to stare, gazing into his eyes with abandonment. "We are friends, yes," she answered softly.

Trying to ignore the pressure building inside him, reminding himself that it had been too long between females, Jean threw back his wine. "It's late," he said. "I should take you home."

Gabrielle nodded, then finished her own glass of wine. When she stood, she lost her balance and fell against his chest. He grabbed her by her arms, relishing in the softness of her body next to his. She smelled of cinnamon, of soap, of freshly laundered clothes, and her hair felt like silk against his lips.

She hesitated, then pushed away. "Pardon me," she said. "I haven't gotten my sea legs yet."

Jean laughed and noticed a twinkle in her eye. "Someday, mademoiselle, I shall show you my ship. She is a beauty, a feather on the waves of the ocean."

"Gabrielle."

"I beg your pardon?"

"My name is Gabrielle," she said. "Friends don't need to be formal, *n'est-ce pas?*"

Jean bowed before her. "At your service, Gabrielle. My name is Jean."

A smile erupted from her voluptuous lips, and it was everything Jean could do to keep his hands off her. Instead, an ingenious idea came to him. He jumped overboard, then leaned into the boat and pulled her into his arms.

"What are you doing?" she asked as he carried her toward shore.

"I'm carrying you off to my remote island, me lady, where I shall drape you in stolen jewels from my wild escapades at sea."

Gabrielle giggled, tightening her hold at his neck. "Louise Delaronde was a fool," she whispered into his ear.

Jean deposited her on shore, but her last remark tore at his heart. "Gabrielle," he said, still holding a hand at her waist.

They were closer than society allowed, but neither made a move to push away. "Yes, Jean."

"May I kiss you?"

Jean felt the waves lapping against the shore at their feet, saw the hawks chasing mosquitoes above their heads, but the only sounds he heard were Gabrielle's next words. "Yes, Jean, you may."

He leaned in ever so slightly and brushed his lips against hers, then slowly, gently, he deepened the kiss. With a chaste hand at her waist, he savored the taste of her ample lips against his, angling his head to gain better access, but not too evasive as to offend Gabrielle.

She evoked images of sweet wines, a warm hearth, fresh-baked bread. Everything Jean missed in his life. And as he refrained from delivering more powerful affections, she responded purposefully, her head tilted upward, her fingers grazing his neck. As their meeting several days before, their kiss seemed natural, as if destined to be.

Time seemed to stand still, yet he left the comfort of their embrace in what was surely only seconds. "Your family will be worried," he whispered, breathing in her delicious scent one last time.

When she opened her eyes, there were no regrets. Nodding, Gabrielle pulled the shawl about her, but hesitated and removed the mahogany cross at her neck. Placing it over his head, their lips almost touched a second time.

"God speed on your journey," she said, then led the way up the path toward home.

Piernas watched the Acadians rebuild the fire so they could continue dancing. It was well past midnight, and no one wanted to sleep. Coleman finished another jig, his bow sailing across the fiddle as if possessed by a demon, then followed Rose's lead as she sang a sad ballad about a lover lingering in prison. Amazing how happy these depressing songs made the Acadians, Piernas thought. He had never witnessed them so joyous.

Piernas hated being the bearer of bad news. Especially when the young Englishman was enjoying himself and the Acadians were happy for the first time since they had arrived. Still, he had a job to do and a governor to answer.

"Madame Gallant," he said, approaching Marianne. "I'm afraid time is running out."

Marianne's face turned ashen, but she didn't appear surprised. "I know," she said softly.

"I must send a dispatch to New Orleans and report your daughter and Lorenz Landry missing."

Chapter Twelve

Coleman slammed the bottle of rum before Piernas, causing the papers on his desk to scatter about the floor.

"I beg your pardon, sir," Piernas said, clearly displeased with Coleman's impertinence.

"How can you do that to Rose?" Coleman shouted. "How can you call the dogs on her sister and her friend?"

Piernas stood and gravely looked Coleman in the eye. "I gave them two months to return," he said. "Which is more compassion than they deserved considering their defiance. Any commandant would have reported them missing immediately, especially since I have distinct orders not to allow an Acadian to go to any settlement but the one to which he has been assigned."

Coleman began pacing the small office, his temple burning from the news, from the ridiculous rationale. "This isn't a game of chess between colonial powers, damn it," he said, turning back toward Piernas. "These are people. You are continuing to keep a family separated. A family that has not seen their father in thirteen years."

Piernas glared back at him, his dark eyes afire. Coleman knew the commandant called him a friend, a tentative one considering his nationality, but Piernas wasn't going to allow an upstart Englishman to address him in such a fashion, especially since his men were within earshot.

"I know the situation of every man, woman and child here," Piernas said sternly. "And they have all been treated with respect and provided shelter, food and materials to start a new life in a fertile land. I have not been unfair to these Acadians. God knows, they have made my life miserable."

Coleman erased the distance between them. "You can't do this to Rose," he said softly, hoping the Spaniard's feelings for the woman might sway him. "You're the one who introduced us, the one who begged me to help them."

"I'm going to the Illinois Territory to take command of a fort there," Piernas said. "I have to settle all business before then." Placing a hand on Coleman's shoulder, he added, "I know how much you love her, but I have done all that I can. It's out of my control now."

Coleman pushed his hand aside and strolled toward the open window. A cold, biting wind rattled the shutters, and he thought of Rose and her sister and mother shivering inside the cabin with a thousand holes in the walls. Without the father around, who would look after them, see to their needs? Who would plant and tend their crops, repair their roof when the violent rains of spring arrived?

"I am heading west," he told Piernas. "Today is my twenty-first birthday, and I come into my mother's inheritance. I have a land grant in the Opelousas District, and I plan to start a farm out there."

"I think that's wise considering everything," Piernas said. When Coleman turned, the Spaniard handed him a drink. "Come now, friend. One last drink among comrades?"

Coleman hesitated, then accepted the glass from Piernas.

"To your health and prosperity," Piernas said. "And may you find happiness wherever life takes you."

Coleman raised his glass and drank his fill, but he doubted he would be happy anywhere without Rose. Still, he couldn't stay and watch another man marry the woman of his heart, watch her be courted by men who understood her language, practiced her faith and shared her culture. Men who could stand in the shoes that he wished for himself.

But he had to relieve her troubles before he left her memory behind. "Is there nothing I can do?" Coleman pleaded.

Piernas poured them both another glass of rum. "Not unless you have five able bodies to take their place."

The rum burned Coleman's throat and seared his empty stomach, but his head remained perfectly clear. "I do have five able bodies," he said, his hopes rising, thinking of the slaves he had inherited that morning. His mother's slaves, who had been as miserable as he since her death three years before and who, like himself, despised the conditions they worked under due to his father's tyrannical hand. Slaves he planned to set free before he sought his own freedom out west.

"If I give you five able bodies and money for transportation, will you let Rose and her family go to St. Gabriel?"

Piernas leaned his head back and drained his glass. He didn't answer, but his eyes brightened as if he understood. The two men, miles apart in nationalities, extended their hands and shook.

"What do you mean another few days?" Lorenz took a deep breath to keep his anger in check. "The weather has cleared. We've been waiting several days already."

The elderly Acadian refused to budge either his assessment of the weather or his boat. "And you may have to wait several months if the river keeps rising," he added with a snarl.

"You don't understand," Emilie piped in. "We have to get to St. Gabriel as soon as possible. My father, whom I haven't seen in thirteen years, is waiting for us there."

Lorenz pulled Emilie aside when the man continued shaking his head. "He knows our situation. We've told him. He won't be moved as long as the wind continues."

Since their arrival in Cabannocé, the weather had deteriorated, a wet, cold wind blowing hard from the north. It wasn't a brutal blast, like the ones in Canada where spring buds were swallowed by several feet of April snow. Instead, the dampness penetrated their bones, giving them both an unabating case of the shivers.

"You're shaking again, *mon amour*," Lorenz said,

grabbing ahold of her sagging shawl and wrapping it tightly about her. "Let's go back to the cabin."

She obeyed, but reluctantly, casting a glance to the Mississippi, where whitecaps formed on its surface as it rounded a giant bend. "The rain has stopped," she offered. "Does the wind pose that much of a problem?"

"I don't know," Lorenz said with a sigh. "The man knows more about the river's currents than we do, Em. It doesn't look as strong from the bank, but the current could be deadly in the middle."

Emilie frowned as her eyes followed a log quickly drifting downstream. "He also said in another week the spring waters would make it impossible to cross. What do we do then, wait until August?"

Lorenz peered into her brown eyes and ran his hand up the length of her spine, then pulled Emilie tight into his chest. "We find someone else to take us across. We swim if we have to."

Gazing out over the top of Emilie's head, Lorenz couldn't help but be awed by the beauty of the great river. Its dark waters stretched out in a dramatic bend as it rounded the Acadian settlement, the surface glistening as if tiny nymphs danced upon it, dropping beams of light with their feet.

"It's called Brilliant Point," Emilie said. "Madame Blanchard told me."

Lorenz should have been surprised that she knew what he was thinking, but Emilie always seemed to be one step ahead of him. "How could you have possibly thought we weren't meant to be together?" he said softly.

Emilie placed a hand on his face. "I always thought

we would be together," she answered. "I was just hoping under better conditions."

"Better conditions?" Lorenz asked with a laugh. "Our circumstances haven't improved in years. If we wait for more prosperous times, we might be as old as that old curmudgeon who won't get us across the river."

She didn't answer, just quietly walked back toward the settlement. There was something else Emilie wasn't telling him, something else holding her back from wanting to marry him. "I don't like it here," she finally said, the emotions emerging in her voice.

"You didn't like it in Maryland," Lorenz said.

"Who would like it in Maryland? We were treated like dirt and practically begged to stay alive."

Lorenz took her hand as they walked down the path. "I can't say Louisiana has been ideal, especially having our freedoms taken away from us as soon as we arrived, but it has been an improvement. When we find your father, we'll be able to have our own land." He slid an arm around her waist. "You and I can build a house like the one you're staying in, only bigger, in case the Landry family increases by one."

"I don't want one," Emilie muttered.

Lorenz pulled her shoulders around so they faced each other. "You don't want children?"

"Of course I want children. I don't want a house like the one we're staying in." Emilie tightened her shawl about her shoulders. "The walls, for instance, have mud inside them. Mud, Lorenz. Widow Melancon says flax won't grow here so we won't be able to make our linens. And have you noticed, there are no rocks in this place.

Plenty of water, mind you, half stagnating on the ground and the other half continually falling from the sky. But no rocks.''

Lorenz watched her carefully, wondering where the conversation was leading. ''Since when are you so fond of rocks, Emilie?''

Emilie folded her arms across her chest. ''I don't want a life here. I want to go home.''

Lorenz didn't blame her for wanting to return to Canada, but the idea was ludicrous, especially since they were so close to recreating their beloved Acadie in Louisiana, their old friends and neighbors only leagues up and down the river from each other.

''We can make this work,'' he assured her. ''Somehow we can make this work.''

''How? With mud walls? And what shall we build a chimney with without any rocks about?''

''Those walls are ingenious,'' Lorenz explained. ''They mix the mud with that Spanish moss for extra insulation. You can hardly feel the wind blowing where the wall has been finished.'' Lorenz leaned in closely as he added, ''We used mud back home, too.''

The red flecks of Emilie's eyes lit up. ''We did not.''

Lorenz couldn't help but laugh at her indignation. He felt as though he were standing in the grassy marshlands of Grand Pré, staring at the skinny girl who followed him endlessly and always, always offered an argument. He couldn't help himself. ''Girls didn't build houses back home, remember? So how would you know?''

Emilie tilted her chin up defiantly, just the right angle for Lorenz to meet those saucy lips with a kiss.

"I'll build you anything you want," he said when he finally released her. "I'll build you a chimney of gold if that makes you happy."

They kissed again, this time Lorenz capturing her bottom lip in a playful bite. "I love you, Lorenz," Emilie said between kisses. "But I don't want a gold chimney."

Lorenz rubbed his lips against hers before exploring her mouth with his tongue. God, but she tasted delicious. He couldn't wait for nightfall. "Then, I'll build you a silver one," he muttered as his kisses drifted down to her neck.

Emilie pushed him away. "I don't want a silver chimney," she practically shouted. "I want to go home."

She stood before him defiantly, hands propped on her waist, as if nothing romantic had transpired between them. For the life of him, Lorenz would never understand women. He decided to meet fire with fire. "You're not going back to Canada," he retorted, placing his hands on his hips. "Get used to the idea and stop being so unhappy."

Emilie crossed her arms over her chest and looked away, and Lorenz immediately felt guilty. They were so close to finding Joseph, just a short boat ride away. He didn't blame her for being testy. He knew she missed her family; the past two months had been the first time Emilie had been separated from her mother and sisters. Then, to top it all off, they had made love. She could be with child, for all they knew.

The thought of being a father sent a surge of pride through Lorenz. Suddenly, nothing else mattered but keeping Emilie safe, making her happy. He wrapped an arm about her waist and let his free hand stray over her belly. Could it be possible? he thought. He almost felt drunk with giddiness.

"Emilie, you have to marry me," Lorenz stated firmly.

She gazed up to him with an annoyed look. "You promised, Lorenz, you wouldn't speak of it until after we arrived in St. Gabriel."

"A lot of things have changed since I made that promise."

"Not entirely," Emilie said. "You haven't proved you can spend a week without getting into trouble."

Lorenz gritted his teeth. She really was the most exasperating female. If he didn't love her as much as he did, he would get as far away from Emilie Marie Gallant as possible. "Forget all that for a moment. Think about what's important here."

Emilie shoved her arms against his chest to be relieved of his embrace. "What's important? Obviously you don't think making me a widow is important."

"Of course I do." Lorenz pulled his fingers through his hair, which desperately needed a haircut. "But we have to think of more significant matters here."

"Like what?" Emilie demanded. "Being able to sleep with me without leaving at daybreak?"

Lorenz grabbed her arms and pulled her close to him. He wanted to shake some sense into her, to make her realize the ramifications of what they had done. "You could be with child. Have you not thought of that fact?"

Again, Emilie released his hands and moved away. "Of course I have. But a week isn't going to make a difference there. Besides, if we are to marry, I want my family around.''

The last phrase gave him hope. ''Fine. We'll marry in St. Gabriel. We'll marry in Natchez. We'll marry in Canada if that's what it takes. Just tell me you'll marry me.''

The passion burned in Lorenz's eyes, and it took all of Emilie's might not to rush into his arms, to say yes, she would marry him and share her life gladly; but fear held her tongue. Fear and another emotion she had trouble naming. Weariness perhaps?

She was so tired of being denied passage across the river, having to wait yet another torturous day. It seemed as though all the Gallant women did was wait. Wait to hear word. Wait for the weather to clear. Wait until the boat arrived to take them somewhere else where they could wait in new surroundings.

If she must be forced to wait, why couldn't Lorenz?

But it was more than that. The familiar foreboding, the dark cloud of uncertainty, loomed over her heart. She could easily send it away at night when they lay in each other's arms, but the morning's light, coupled with a harsh north wind, blew a melancholy over Emilie's soul. Despite her love for Lorenz, despite his repeated devotion, her anxiety over her future held her back. Her heart shouted, ''Yes, oh yes,'' but her mind won over in the end.

''Please, Lorenz,'' she began softly.

Lorenz stepped back as if hit by a blow. Clearly wounded by her words, he could only stare at her, shocked that she had rejected him yet again. She had pierced him to the core, but all Emilie could feel was anger. If only he would let her be for a few more days, just until they found her father, until they were reunited with Marianne and her sisters. Why couldn't he give her that much?

"My father may be on the other side of that massive river, and I can't get there; so can we please talk about something else?" she shouted at him.

Lorenz leaned in close, his black eyes intense. "I would put up with your crazy moods, give you all the time in the world to decide, but we have crossed a line here that needs addressing." Crossing her arms about her chest, Emilie turned to avoid his gaze, but Lorenz took her chin and forced her to face him. "What we did is not something I take lightly, nor is it something we can dismiss. You can't possibly think to refuse me now."

Maybe it was Lorenz's authoritative tone or the pain ripping through her abdomen that made her doubt she was with child, but Emilie didn't want to discuss marriage one more moment. Her skin felt like the Spanish moss after it had been dried for mattress stuffing, and her head pounded from a headache. She couldn't decide if she wanted to cry hysterically or scream. "I can't possibly think of anything but my father right now," she yelled at him. "Please, can we talk about something else?"

Lorenz's eyes narrowed. He loved her, of that she would never doubt. But if they had crossed a line the night they made love, they were definitely crossing another one now.

"I'm tired of these games," he finally said. "I'm tired of waiting for you to make up your mind."

The anger returned, sending a flush through her head that made her almost dizzy. Before she had time to think, she blurted out, "And I'm tired of you asking."

This time, Lorenz didn't appear hurt. His eyes turned

bitter, and he sent her a scathing look. "Then, I'll ask
you no longer," he stated firmly and marched away.

Watching his retreating form, Emilie wondered what
had come over her. She was so irritable. Why did Lorenz
have to push the issue this particular morning?

She sat down on the cold ground and buried her head
in her hands. The pain in her womb increased, so she
pulled her legs into her chest and hugged them. The
tenderness in her breasts confirmed that she wasn't with
child; every ache and emotion was as familiar as the
phases of the moon.

She was such a stupid girl. When would she realize
that Lorenz's love was like a comforting blanket on a
frigid night and not a threat? He could be holding her
now, planting kisses on her head, telling her stories from
their childhood to make her feel at home in this dreadful
place. Instead, she wounded him and sent him away,
hurting the one person who owned her heart.

Emilie began to cry. If Lorenz were here, he would
help ease the emptiness the imaginary child left behind.
For those brief seconds when they had spoken of children,
Emilie's hope for the future had soared. She had actually
thought a happy life together was possible. But like the
promise of finding her father in a new territory and starting
anew, the hope was extinguished as quickly as it began.

"Another drink, Lorenz?" Simon Mire said, passing
the pitcher his way. Since early afternoon Lorenz had
sought refuge with the town's men, enjoying wine they
had purchased from traveling merchants with the meager

profits earned from winter crops. It was also a chance to be among the logical gender, men who spoke their minds and made sense.

Lorenz poured himself another, enjoying the warm path the wine led down his throat, along with the numb sensation it provided his mind. He didn't want to think of Emilie, of her stubborn refusals, of their endless frustrations to get to St. Gabriel and reunite the family. Of the family he had lost and the family he might never have. He wanted something to make the pain go away.

"So you don't remember a Joseph Gallant?" he asked Dominique Doucet, a resident of St. Gabriel who was visiting sick in-laws in Cabannocé.

"I remember a man of your description," Dominique said. "But it's difficult to say he was the same man. We were all sick with the fever, and he wasn't a member of our group. I believe this man came into Louisiana on an earlier voyage."

Lorenz straightened and attempted to clear his mind. "We got word in Maryland that a man of Joseph's description was at St. Gabriel looking for his wife and three daughters. There are people here who said a similar man came through saying the same thing, only that he was headed for New Orleans. We were hoping he had returned to St. Gabriel."

"Well, that's certainly possible," Dominique said. "As soon as we arrived in the territory and realized there was land to be had and freedom to practice our religion, we wrote back to Maryland encouraging others to come. But I personally cannot confirm that the man I saw was Joseph

Gallant. And I don't recall a Gallant living among us presently."

"It's possible he was there or that he settled nearby in a remote area," said Jacques Doucet, Dominique's brother. "Again, we were all very sick in the beginning. It was a harrowing journey from Maryland; then we arrived in deadly heat and were expected to clear land and build houses with few tools and hardly any provisions. It was merely a matter of time before we all became ill. Even the English near us were down with the fever. They claimed to have few supplies as well, and wouldn't offer us any."

Phillip snorted. "So they said, anyway."

"The Spanish did little to help either," Jacques continued. "We asked for more supplies, extra tools to help with our homes, but they maintained that the provisions were low and were forthcoming from New Orleans and the tools were only to be used on the construction of the fort. They called us lazy. We were starving, separated from each other and living in horrid conditions, and they had the nerve to consider us impertinent."

"Damn Spanish," Lorenz said to the inside of his cup before draining the liquid.

"I understand they forced you to settle in Natchez," Dominique asked.

Lorenz nodded. "They want to use us as a buffer to the English. Develop their frontier to hold back English encroachment in the Louisiana Territory."

"Same reason they gave us," Dominique said. "The English have a fort on the other side of St. Gabriel. We demanded the Spanish let us settle here at Cabannocé with the other Acadians, but Ulloa refused.''

"This Spanish governor is no better than Charles Lawrence,'' Lorenz said.

The sound of the Nova Scotia governor's name, the man responsible for the massive expulsion of the Acadians from their homes, brought up a round of grumbles. The deceased man's name was a cursed one, a name few repeated as if the words might burn their tongues upon being spoken. Lorenz almost regretted speaking it aloud for fear the curse would descend upon them. But he wasn't a superstitious man; he would rather say the name and wish Charles Lawrence to rot in hell, which was more than likely where he was.

"To our health and our prosperity,'' Lorenz said as he lifted his mug in a toast. "And to hell with Charles Lawrence.''

The other men, equally saturated with wine, saluted with their mugs and drank their fill.

"And to the memories of those absent,'' Phillip added, and the men lifted their wine once again. This time, a sadness descended upon the group as they all remembered the loved ones lost in *le grand dérangement*. The group of men continued to drink in silence, Phillip's eyes glistening with tears.

"You can sit here, drink until you're bleary-eyed and talk all you want, but your talking will get you nowhere.''

Lorenz looked up to find a Frenchman dressed in upper-class garments approaching the foursome on horseback. ''Jean Baptiste de Noyan,'' the man introduced himself as he dismounted. "Lieutenant to Attorney General Nicolas Chauvin de Lafrénière."

The Acadians stared at the finely dressed man, but were unimpressed with his long title. Living in the New World had taught them one important lesson, that every man was equal when fighting the elements for existence. Wealthy aristocrats failed to ignite their respect, but an Indian or clever farmer who could produce enough food to last a winter in the worst of conditions became a hero.

"Phillip Bellefontaine and Simon Mire of Pisiquid," Phillip announced. "Dominique and Jacques Doucet and Lorenz Landry of the town of Grand Pré."

The man bowed again, and Phillip motioned for him to join them. The Frenchman produced a dark bottle from his saddlebags and held it up as if to silently ask them if they would care to share his rum. The Acadians smiled at the invitation; rum was not an easy drink to find in primitive Louisiana. Phillip rose and gave the man a friendly slap on the back and handed him a mug.

"Now," the Frenchman announced, "I will tell you all the secret to getting our way in this Spanish-run territory."

Curious, Lorenz leaned in close to hear more of the man's secrets.

"The answer," the man continued, "is to revolt and take the colony for ourselves."

Chapter Thirteen

Darkness descended upon Cabannocé, but there was no sign of Lorenz. Emilie left her cabin for the third time since sundown in the hopes of catching him on his way to the barn.

"Have you seen Simon?" Marguerite Mire asked, rounding the side of the cabin.

"No," Emilie replied. "Have you seen Lorenz?"

Marguerite shook her head, and both women scanned the horizon for the men. The distant trees were hard to discern in the growing darkness; it was too late for the men to be away from the village. Emilie knew Lorenz would avoid her after their damaging conversation earlier, but it wasn't like him to remain gone for such a long period of time. She thought of the stories she had heard of cannibal Indians, and alligators, and other strange animals that roamed the swamps.

"Do you think they're safe?" she asked Marguerite.

"More than likely they're sampling Phillip's recently acquired bottle of wine," Marguerite said. "Still . . ."

There it was again, that unexplained emotion. A gloom fell upon Emilie's heart like a warning. She remembered that fateful afternoon in Grand Pré when her mother had experienced the same foreshadowing, the day her father had walked out the door of their home and into the trap of the English. Suddenly, nothing else mattered. She had to find Lorenz.

"I'm going to search for them," she said as she wrapped her shawl about her shoulders.

"Wait," Marguerite said, and ran toward her house. "I'll get you a lantern."

As Emilie waited for the woman to return, something caught her attention. The night was too quiet. The trees were silent, and a dog barked in the distance. The wind had finally died down.

Marguerite emerged and handed Emilie the lighted lantern. "Do be careful," she said.

"Those cannibals . . . ?" Emilie began.

"Lived in Louisiana before us in an area far from here. Believe me, we have other things to worry about."

"Such as?"

Marguerite leaned in close, allowing Emilie to make out her face in the dim light. "The Creoles who live nearby have a bone to pick with the Spanish. Poor trade, heightened regulations, lack of currency."

"What's this have to do with our men?" Emilie asked.

"They keep agitating our residents to revolt with them against the Spanish," Marguerite explained. "They want us to help fight their battle, and Simon is all too willing. Members of his family live in St. Gabriel. He was furious they weren't allowed to settle here with us.''

Emilie thought of Lorenz and his hotheaded reaction to the soldiers on the German Coast. ''What makes you think this is the case tonight?''

''Widow Melancon saw one of Lafrénière's men come through on horseback,'' Marguerite said. ''The man's notorious for inciting tempers around here.''

Emilie pulled her shawl tighter across her chest. She had to find Lorenz. Immediately. ''Where should I look?''

''Go to Phillip's house.''

Nodding, Emilie hurried away, her heart beating furiously. *Dear God*, she thought, *don't let Lorenz fall into their trap.*

The moon finally emerged as a sliver in the sky, and Emilie's passage down the winding road to Phillip's house was a slow one. As she held the lantern in front of her, watching its light cast ominous shadows among the bushes and trees that hugged the path, Emilie felt the familiar tightness in her chest return. This couldn't be happening, she thought. Lorenz had promised.

Finally, Phillip's house came into view, but Emilie's breathing failed to return to normal. The night was so still, the darkness so acute. She had to find Lorenz, know that he was safe. But something told her her travels had just begun.

Emilie knocked on the door and was greeted by Phillip, who appeared as worried as she when he caught sight of her at the door. ''He's not with you?'' Phillip asked.

Emilie shook her head and swallowed hard to keep the

fear from choking her. Phillip disappeared briefly inside, then emerged into the night, pulling on a jacket. "I can't leave my family," he said. "My youngest son is sick with the fever."

The last thing Emilie wanted to do was tear Phillip away from his family; but Lorenz had gone somewhere with this defiant Creole, and only Phillip knew of his whereabouts. "You have to help me," she pleaded. "Do you know where he is?"

Phillip rubbed her arms in a reassuring manner, but his frown convinced Emilie she had a lot to be concerned about. "The last I saw of him he was speaking with Noyen," Phillip explained. "They had plenty in common when it came to the Spanish."

"Who's Noyen?" Emilie asked.

"One of the Creoles who travels through here on occasion."

"Marguerite Mire said there was a Creole who tries to convince Acadians to help fight the Spanish with him." Emilie swallowed again to force down the panic rising in her chest. "Tell me you didn't let Lorenz leave with this horrid man."

Phillip stared down at his feet, deep in thought. "They had a few drinks with me, that was all, Emilie. I have no idea what they did when they left here."

Emilie grabbed the lantern and surveyed her surroundings. She had to find Lorenz. If Phillip couldn't help, then she would set out in all directions until she found him. "Which way should I go?" she asked Phillip.

She felt a jerking of the lantern as Phillip pulled the light from her hands. "You're not going anywhere but inside," he said. "Lorenz is a big boy, Emilie. He's old enough to make his own choices."

Imagining Lorenz being killed or exiled because he was too hotheaded to think things through brought forth a burst of tears, but Emilie fought them back, wiping her eyes to rid her face of the telltale moisture. "He can't make his own choices," she said, trying to hide the emotion in her voice. "He's young and he's angry. You would be too if you lived the life he's lived."

Suddenly, all her trepidation for her future, all the reservations she harbored about marrying Lorenz and his impulsive nature, disappeared. He was her soul mate, and she understood him clearly. Of course she did. She had been with him every step of the way.

The tears flowed down her cheeks, and this time she made no attempt to stop them. Standing there in the darkness of the mysterious Louisiana night, a place that felt as strange to her as a nightmare, Emilie wanted nothing else than to hold Lorenz in her arms, to have her best friend and lover safe within her grasp.

"I am such a fool," she said softly.

Phillip placed an arm about her shoulders and offered a sympathetic hug. "I will go see if my neighbor can help. Perhaps he knows where the men have gone."

Emilie wiped the tears from her face and straightened. "Where does this Noyen live?"

"You can't go there, Emilie," Phillip said sternly.

"Where does he live?" she repeated. She would crawl to the Creole's house if necessary.

"There is no way I will let you go after him," Phillip continued. "You are not leaving this village or my sight."

Emilie was about to launch into a serious argument, when a deep male voice sounded from behind. "I know where to find this Creole, mademoiselle, but your friend is right; you are to remain in the village. It's not safe."

It was difficult to make out the man in the darkness, but Emilie discerned a large, muscular shape approaching the lantern's light. When the man became visible, she was amazed at the broadness of his shoulders and the powerful forearms carrying a fat satchel and rifle. His eyes were invisible beneath his broad-rimmed hat, but she detected a mustache and a slight dimple. Then something else caught her eye. She knew she was imagining things, but for a moment Emilie thought she saw her sister's handmade cross lying against the man's shirt.

"Bouclaire," Phillip announced, extending his hand. The two men shook hands while the large man deposited his belongings on the ground at her feet. "This young lady is looking for her companion who has—"

"Run off with that insurgent Noyen, yes, I heard. I met with Marguerite Mire in the village."

"Then, you know where he is?" Emilie couldn't wait to be introduced. Time was of the essence.

The large man tilted his hat back, and two enormous brown eyes stared back at her. "You're different," the man said, examining her closely.

"Emilie," Phillip said, "this is Captain Jean Bouclaire. Jean, this is Emilie—"

"Gallant," the man answered, and Emilie felt a shiver run up the length of her spine. Oh, God, he knew who she was. The Spanish had finally caught up with them.

Then the man inched closer, and Emilie got a better

EMILIE   239

look at the pendant. It *was* Gabrielle's cross. The one she had carved from mahogany and religiously wore at her neck. The one she was waiting to give to Papa when they reunited. When she turned her eyes to his, to investigate the man wearing her sister's most prized possession, she found him examining her.

"No, you don't look at all like your sisters," he said as he took in her figure.

"How do you know all this?" Emilie asked. "What do you know of my sisters?"

As if the question reminded him of his manners, the captain bowed politely. "I am at your service, mademoiselle, at the request of Gabrielle Gallant. I am here to see you and Lorenz Landry safely to St. Gabriel. That is, if I can find the young man."

Emilie stared at him dumbfounded. They had spent two months alone in the wilds of Louisiana, accepting favors from the people they met along the way, favors that had kept them fed and healthy. But the last thing Emilie expected was a giant of a man popping out of the woods and offering them safe passage to St. Gabriel. At least, she imagined it would be safe. If Gabrielle, indeed, had something to do with this man, he was to be trusted. Still . . .

"There is so much to explain," Bouclaire said, as if reading her mind. "But there is no time. I will tell you the entire story after I go after Lorenz."

His last comment broke her from her thoughts and brought her to attention. "I'm going with you," she insisted.

The captain moved closer and sent her a stern look

with his bronze eyes, paternal eyes that wouldn't stand for defiance but offered a twinkle of comfort. "No, you're not," he said firmly, as a father would.

Despite the tone of his voice and his unwavering look, Emilie wasn't one to be left behind. "Yes, I am," she countered.

The twinkle disappeared. "No, you're not," he repeated, and Emilie stepped back at the power of that statement. "You're going to head straight to the river where my boat is docked and wait for me there. There's food and water and plenty of blankets. Here," he added as he thrust the lantern into her hands, "take the lantern."

Before she could retort, the robust man replaced the rifle on his shoulder and strode out of sight. She turned toward Phillip for support, but her friend was smiling.

"Well said," Phillip replied, then turned Emilie toward the river and pushed her forward. "Stay put," she heard him instruct her from behind. "Lorenz is in good hands."

The distance to the river was short, and a flat-bottomed boat was docked at the end of the path, just as the captain had said. Emilie waded through the water and climbed aboard, sitting cautiously on a crate so as not to cause movement on the small craft. She never understood what Gabrielle loved about sailing. Give her the solid earth— Louisiana mud if need be.

Afraid to move, Emilie sat stiffly on her wooden crate, staring out at the magnificent body of water silently passing. A slight breeze began from the south, warmer this time as if sending a slice of the tropics north.

"Strange weather," Emilie said to no one. "First winter, now summer."

She had to admit, the warm breeze felt nice against her neck and was complemented by the soothing sound of the river lapping against its bank. Bullfrogs offered a chorus among the rushes, and the slight moon sent down rivulets of golden light.

It wasn't so bad, Emilie thought, this swampland Lorenz called paradise. In its own way, it possessed certain beauties. But in the grand scheme of things, did any of it matter?

She was such a fool. What was she afraid of anyway, that she would be left behind, wondering of her man's fate, like her mother? Here she was on a boat on the Mississippi River, wondering where Lorenz was, worried about his safety. Should he meet with harm, her life would be devastated. What difference did it make if they were married or not? She loved him, he was a part of her soul and whether or not they traded marriage vows would never change that.

Anna was right. Love made a person whole. She had learned that the past few nights when he had come to her cabin and they had shared in each other's pleasures, becoming one in love. But it had been that way before their lovemaking. They were destined for one another. They were bound regardless of whether a priest made it so.

Emilie vowed that if she ever saw Lorenz again, she would make matters right. She would live in a house made of mud and sleep on mattresses made of Spanish beards if that was what it took. As the tears flowed in torrents down her face, Emilie prayed that she wasn't too late.

* * *

"I say we march on New Orleans and give Governor Ulloa his walking papers back to Spain," one of the Creoles announced, sending up a chorus of agreement among the drunk crowd.

"It's a difficult walk to Spain," Lorenz said, but no one paid attention. The group, consisting mostly of Louisiana-born residents of French parentage, was more interested in the next round of rum than in the common sense being spoken. Now that Lorenz thought of it, common sense had not reared its head once that evening.

"My brother has gone to Pensacola," Noyen said. "He is going to convince the English to fight with us to take over the colony. When the English get here, we'll show these Spaniards a thing or two."

Simon gazed over to Lorenz, and they exchanged a questioning look. It was one thing to admonish the Spanish, quite another to enlist the aid of the English. Lorenz had a serious quarrel with the Spanish and their determination to populate the frontier at the Acadians' expense. But the Spanish had welcomed them into a friendly environment and given them land, tools and provisions. Enough to barely survive, but what could one expect from a colony on the verge of bankruptcy? It was more than France had done for the scattered exiles. And certainly a better government than the damned English.

Simon placed his drink on the table and made his way to Lorenz's side. "I don't like this," he said.

Lorenz looked around the room at the wealthy Creoles and their problems of exports and outdated currency. This wasn't his fight. After listening to Noyen launch a tirade against the Spanish that afternoon, Lorenz had been more than happy to lend a hand, but he was a simple man who wished only to obtain a land grant, start a farm and raise a family. He didn't care about the problems of the transfer from one colonial power to another, of one crown's neglect to meet the financial needs of its colonists or the politics and ramifications of a years-old war. Like his father, he wanted to remain neutral in all the conflicts. Just give him a piece of land and . . .

"Simon," Lorenz asked, feeling as if a bolt of lightning had struck him. "What was it the English called us in Nova Scotia?"

"French neutrals," the man answered.

Lorenz thought of Joseph Gallant, who had stood proudly at the church that day when the edict was read, his head never bowing, even though the words were crushing. He thought of his father and the day he had swum leagues into Minas Basin to save a child caught by the incoming tide. The village men, so many now dead, who had worked twice as hard to bring in a good harvest to feed themselves and the English soldiers in an effort to keep peace. The men of Grand Pré were the bravest men he knew.

"We weren't cowards because we didn't fight the English, were we?" Lorenz asked Simon.

The Acadian sent him a powerful stare, but when Simon realized Lorenz was too young to recall the events leading up to the exile, his features softened. "No, *mon ami,* we were not cowards. We made an agreement with the English, and they failed to live up to the bargain."

Lorenz placed his drink on the table and retrieved his hat. "And killing a dozen Spaniards won't bring my parents back."

Simon placed a friendly hand on his shoulder. "No, it won't." Picking up his own hat, Simon added, "Let's go home."

The duo made their way to the door, making excuses to the drunk Creoles before emerging into the night air. The fresh breeze blowing up from the river was a welcome relief from the stuffiness of the Creole's study. Lorenz breathed in the humid air gladly, but nearly fell over from a wave of dizziness.

A pair of strong arms saved him from falling face first into the dirt, but they weren't Simon's. Although the older Acadian had not kept pace with Lorenz's drinking, Simon Mire was in no shape to catch a man of Lorenz's size.

"You made the right choice, Lorenz," he heard a booming male voice say behind him as his rescuer straightened and released him. "No sense losing your life over a rich man's problems."

Lorenz turned to find a man of his height but twice his girth staring back, a man whose stiff French accent was pronounced. *Now what,* Lorenz thought, *another Frenchman wanting help in a fight?* "Who are you?" he asked the stocky man.

Before the man could answer, Lorenz noticed the familiar pendant at his neck. "You're wearing Gabrielle's cross," Lorenz announced, shocked to see such an accustomed sight on a stranger.

The man clutched the pendant between his fingers, and his dimple deepened. "Your sister gave it to me for luck," he said. "After a long talk by the river, where she told me all about you."

Something in his smile touched a nerve; this man was too familiar with Gabrielle, speaking too intimately about a woman Lorenz cherished as a sister. Fear and anger surged through his rum-clouded mind, fury he had been saving up for the Spaniards. He grabbed the Frenchman by the shirt and threw him back against the trunk of a tree. "If you have harmed one hair of Gabrielle's head, I'll kill you," Lorenz shouted. "I swear I will."

The man didn't retaliate angrily, which infuriated Lorenz all the more. Instead, he grabbed Lorenz's wrists and forced them off the front of his shirt. "I appreciate the concern, Lorenz," the man replied gravely, raising the hairs on the back of Lorenz's neck. "But don't ever insult me like that again."

Lorenz examined the impressive man, wondering how much Gabrielle had told him. For an instant, even though the thought was absurd, he imagined the Frenchman in love with her. If only he hadn't drunk so much rum, he could make sense of this meeting. "Who are you?" he asked again as a wave of dizziness returned.

The Frenchman grabbed Lorenz's shirt this time, holding him upright as Lorenz felt the earth coming nearer once again. "Steady," the man said. "You have a long walk ahead of you. Perhaps dunking your head in the river might help."

Lorenz knew exactly what would help, and he was powerless to stop it. Before he could think to move his head aside, he heaved on the man's fine leather boots.

* * *

Emilie heard the sound of two men approaching, one she was sure was Lorenz, his voice booming over the other. She gingerly moved to the side of the boat, then jumped overboard and waded to shore. By the time she reached the bank, she recognized Bouclaire's large form hobbling up the path with his arm about Lorenz's waist. Lorenz was walking, but barely. Emilie's heart dropped.

"What has happened to him?" she asked, running up to the two men. "Is he hurt?"

Upon sight of her, Lorenz pushed Bouclaire away. "I'm fine," he said brusquely. But that didn't stop her from grabbing his shoulders and hugging him close. As she pressed her head against his cheek, so glad to see him alive and well, her arms roamed his back and arms, searching for injuries. All she could detect was a strong smell of rum. After several seconds, Emilie realized Lorenz wasn't hugging her back. He stood motionless and unemotional.

Emilie pulled away and stared into cold, dark eyes. She swallowed, wondering where to start in begging his forgiveness. "Are you hurt?" she said softly.

"Just his stomach and his pride," Bouclaire announced from the river's edge, where the man was cleaning his boots. Emilie's mind whirled from the thoughts. First, Lorenz left with a Creole threatening to revolt against the government, then returned drunk with a Frenchman wearing Gabrielle's necklace who was suddenly concerned with cleanliness in the middle of the night.

"Who are you?" she asked him.

Bouclaire frowned at his failure to rectify his boots, but he glanced her way and offered a smile. "All in good time, *mon amie*. Right now, we have to get you to St. Gabriel. Time is of the essence."

"But it's close to midnight," Emilie said.

"It can wait until morning," Lorenz added. "How are we going to find our way in this pitiful moonlight?"

Bouclaire laughed heartily, untying the bowline. "I know every league of this river," he said. "Every bend. Every current. I could find St. Gabriel with my eyes closed."

"But tonight?" Emilie asked. "Clearly Lorenz is in no shape to travel."

"I'm fine," Lorenz countered and headed toward the river's edge. "If we're going, let's go."

Bouclaire looked at Lorenz, surprised at his curtness, then up at Emilie. Apparently during their walk from the Creole's house to the boat, Lorenz had failed to inform the man that she had refused his hand four times. Well, that was a first. He usually told everyone. She caught up with him at the river's edge and grabbed his arm.

"Tu est tignon," Emilie said to Lorenz. "But that doesn't mean you have the right to be rude. The man is bringing us to Papa."

"Yes, I am drunk," Lorenz replied to her, then glanced over to Bouclaire. "And if I'm being rude, forgive me. I've had a trying day."

Before Emilie could react, Lorenz gathered her up in his arms and carried her toward the boat. "What are you doing?" she asked, before he gently deposited her into the boat.

"Being careful," he answered solemnly. "You may be with child."

Lorenz climbed into the boat and caught the bow rope Bouclaire sent his way. When Bouclaire moved several feet away to work at unfastening the stern rope, Emilie leaned toward Lorenz and whispered, "I'm not with child. I'm certain of it."

He appeared as disappointed as she, and knowing he cared enough about the prospect of a child warmed her. But as quick as that emotion crossed his features, another one replaced it. It wasn't possible for those intense black eyes to become colder, Emilie reasoned, but she was certain they did. A shiver ran up her neck, and she hugged her shawl tighter.

"Well, that's convenient," he said with a smirk. "That should solve all your problems."

The shiver multiplied, and Emilie worked her jaw to keep her teeth from chattering. How could he possibly think such a thing? She wanted children as much as he did. The tears welled in her eyes, and she stared at the distant shore to keep from crying.

"Let's be honest, Emilie," Lorenz said quietly. "We want different things. Let's be sensible and move on."

Emilie knew Bouclaire had joined them when the boat tipped in his direction. Lorenz stood and offered his services, and the two headed toward the bow of the boat. She heard them talking about sails and paddles and wind directions, but she comprehended nothing but Lorenz's final words.

He couldn't be dismissing her, not after all that they had shared, all the love they had expressed to one another. She had made a mistake, but she could reason with him. Couldn't she?

Suddenly, the boat drifted toward the center of the river, and the thought of heading to St. Gabriel gave her hope. She would reunite with Papa and head north to Natchez. There was a light to this nightmarish evening.

"About my family, monsieur," Emilie said eagerly to Bouclaire when he joined her at the stern to take command of the rudder.

"Your family is well," Bouclaire said. "They have constructed a house, received a land grant and supplies and been well taken care of at Natchez."

"And Gabrielle," she insisted, aching for news of her sisters and mother. "My mother, my baby sister Rose?"

Bouclaire stared in the distance, his countenance becoming grave. "All in due time, mademoiselle," he said. "What is most important now is getting you to St. Gabriel."

Emilie swore her heart ceased beating. Something was not right. Lorenz stopped his duties and turned to listen.

"Your sister sent me after you because the commandant at Natchez only allowed you two months to make your way upriver," Bouclaire began. "Those two months have come and gone."

Lorenz sent her a worried gaze. "We've been detained because of bad weather," he said.

"I understand," Bouclaire answered. "But Piernas has

already sent the dispatch. If the Spanish find you between here and Natchez, you will be arrested.''

"We've been fortunate so far," Emilie said.

Bouclaire turned to her. "I'm afraid, mademoiselle, your luck has run out. The Spanish soldiers were at Cabannocé this evening, asking for you both.''

Chapter Fourteen

The night dragged on forever. Lorenz's body ached from the rowing, the endless battle against the river's mighty currents. His head pounded from the lingering effects of the rum. His only respite was the gentle breeze to his rear that helped push the boat forward and the exhilarating feeling of standing in the midst of such an impressive body of water.

"She's an amazing river, isn't she?" Bouclaire asked him.

"It's an awe-inspiring territory," Lorenz answered, thankful that the man didn't hold grudges against drunkards who expelled their guts on expensive, store-bought boots. He glanced down to see if Bouclaire's boots had survived the ordeal.

"My boots are fine," the man said with a friendly

smile. "That's why I wear leather, because it's durable. They've seen worse, I assure you."

Lorenz shook his head, trying to make sense of the evening. "I swear I usually don't drink that much."

"Women will do that to you."

Who was this man who had appeared out of the darkness, who wore Gabrielle's beloved cross? Who knew of their secrets? Lorenz was thankful Emilie had finally gone to sleep. He was tired of remaining silent, tired of pretending to ignore her. He needed to confide in someone, and he wanted more information.

"It isn't hard to see that you two have had a lovers' quarrel," Bouclaire said. "When I first met Emilie, her heart was about to break at the thought of losing you. Don't be too hard on her. She loves you, that's obvious."

"She doesn't want to marry me," Lorenz said as he sat down at the stern, watching the steady breeze fill the boat's sail.

"Why?"

Lorenz sighed and rubbed his hands at his temples. How many hours before the pounding stopped? he wondered. How long before the searing pain in his heart ended?

"So many reasons," he answered. "Anxiety over her father, over starting a new life in this land." Lorenz laughed grimly, thinking of the promise he had made the night they first made love. "Then there's the problem of me being impetuous. She's afraid I might do something rash like revolt against authority and get exiled from Louisiana."

He expected a lecture of concurrence over the last

remark, but Bouclaire said nothing. The silence gave
Lorenz pause to think. Was he being unreasonable? Was
he crazy to ask this woman—who had traveled thousands
of miles to find her father, who was an outlaw traveling
through a land of swamps and marshes, who lived in fear
of her best friend and now lover acting impulsively and
getting himself killed—to marry him? Perhaps he had
misjudged Emilie. Always the pillar of strength, the leader
of her family. Could it be possible that deep down Emilie
Gallant was terrified?

Lorenz stared at her sleeping face that was anything
but peaceful. What demons raged inside? he wondered.
First her father disappearing. Now she worried whether
Lorenz might disappear from his constant lack of forethought. She had valid reasons to refuse him.

No. They loved each other. It was as simple as that.
Wasn't it?

"There's something I have to tell you," Bouclaire said.
"I was waiting for Emilie to fall asleep."

Lorenz rubbed his forehead harder. The horrid day
refused to end.

"Gabrielle asked me to check on you on my way downriver, so I stopped first in St. Gabriel." Bouclaire studied
him to gauge his reaction. Lorenz cringed, waiting for
the next shoe to fall. "Joseph Gallant's not at St. Gabriel,
Lorenz. In fact, he's not in Louisiana."

Lorenz shut his eyes as the pain ripped through him.
It was everything they had feared. "Are you sure?"

"When he received word his family was in Maryland,
Joseph traveled to New Orleans and took the next ship
to that colony." Bouclaire placed a hand on Lorenz's

shoulder to soften the blow. "As far as I could discern, he's on his way to Maryland or is there now."

Lorenz's stomach winced in pain, and his head's pounding doubled. They had been so hopeful coming to Louisiana. How would he break the news to Emilie? How would he tell Marianne? It wasn't possible. After all their traveling, Joseph couldn't be heading to Maryland. What God would be so cruel? For a moment, Lorenz understood Emilie's trepidations over marrying. Who could believe in happiness when life offered such trials?

"I thought it best for you to tell her," Bouclaire said.

Lorenz nodded. It was best that way. A weight as heavy as all the world's problems descended upon his shoulders, and he shut his eyes to brace himself.

"Get some sleep," he heard Bouclaire say.

Lorenz wanted to object, to offer his help in getting the boat upriver; but an acute tiredness overtook him, and he was powerless to confront it. He felt his head falling forward. Within seconds he slept.

The sun warmed Emilie's cheeks as she and Lorenz gathered apples from her orchards. From the tree's branches she could see the calm waters of Minas Basin and Gabrielle dancing on the shore. Marianne paced at the tree's base, singing to Rose in her arms.

All was perfect in the world.

Papa appeared from working in the fields and waved. Emilie waved back, reveling in his warm smile and blanketed by her father's love. Then Joseph turned and began to walk away.

An intense fear enveloped Emilie, and she looked to Lorenz for support. Lorenz sat in the branches of the neighboring tree, but all he could do was shake his head.

"No," Emilie shouted. But it was too late. When she looked back toward the fields, her father was gone.

Emilie bolted upright, the vision of the dream still fresh in her mind, the horror still vivid, the pain still choking her heart. When Lorenz appeared at her side, she grabbed him and held him tight.

Thankfully this time he returned the embrace.

"What's the matter, Em?" he asked softly, stroking her hair. "Another bad dream?"

"Oh, Lorenz, when is this going to end?"

Lorenz said nothing, just continued holding her close. When he finally pulled back, still lovingly stroking her hair, he appeared as if his night had been as disturbing as hers. "We have to talk," he finally said.

He was relenting, Emilie thought with joy. She smiled and captured his solemn face in her hands. "Yes, my love, we do."

Lorenz took one of her hands and buried his face into the palm, but his countenance never changed. Emilie felt the strings of her heart stretch. She had hurt him, pained him deeply. But she was going to change all that. It was a new morning, and they were on their way to St. Gabriel.

"Where are we?" Emilie searched the horizon. To the north, only a few leagues away, a village appeared around the bend in the river.

"We're approaching St. Gabriel," Lorenz said softly.

Emilie's heart leaped. Hope filled her being. She stood up, waiting to adjust to the movement of the boat—getting her sea legs, Gabrielle would have said—then moved as quickly as she could to the bow of the boat.

"Emilie." Lorenz had reached for her arm as he called her name, but she didn't have time to talk. They would discuss things later. They were approaching St. Gabriel!

She felt Lorenz's hands on her arms as she stared at the collection of houses so close she could make out the faces of the people on the shore. A young girl waved, and Emilie enthusiastically waved back. "We're here," she said to Lorenz, afraid that this, too, might be a dream.

"Emilie," Lorenz repeated, "we must talk."

Emilie turned and met his serious gaze. "We will. I am so sorry for everything I said yesterday." When she looked back toward shore, the little girl was following them upriver, waving as she ran. Others had gathered, too, waiting for the boat to make landing. "I'll make amends, I promise, as soon as we get ashore."

Lorenz placed his fingers on her chin and forced her gaze away from the village. "Emilie," he stated so gravely she shivered. "We need to talk now."

Then a wicked thought came to her.

"You're worried about what happened between us," she whispered with a grin. "I won't tell Papa about it."

When Lorenz didn't react, a fear ran through her. He looked at her as he had in the dream, as if he knew something horrible was about to happen and was powerless to stop it.

"Emilie!"

A familiar voice shouted from shore, and Emilie's fears lifted. When she turned and gazed at the riverbank, she realized she wasn't imagining the sound. Gabrielle stood ahead of the others, waving and jumping up and down.

"It's Gabrielle," Lorenz said. "How on earth?"

"Well, I'll be damned," Emilie heard Bouclaire say. When she turned toward the captain, she watched in amazement as his face erupted in delight. Dear God, Emilie thought, the man was in love with her sister! What on earth had happened during those two brief months in Natchez?

"It can't be," she said to Lorenz. "Am I dreaming?"

When Rose appeared next to Gabrielle, Emilie started crying from happiness. Lorenz pulled her close and kissed the top of her head, but he appeared as grim as before. She wanted to reassure him, tell him that things were finally falling into place and her anxiety over their future had been unfounded. She would marry him now. They would have a ceremony at the church in St. Gabriel—if they had a church—and Papa would give her away. For the first time in years, Emilie felt hopeful.

The boat quietly moved toward shore, but Emilie couldn't wait. She jumped into the muddy waters, feeling her moccasins sink in the river's bottom, then pushed herself through the waters toward the bank. Gabrielle met her halfway, and the sisters hugged knee-deep in the river. Rose joined them, throwing her petite arms about Emilie, but Gabrielle and Emilie had to grab her sleeves to keep her from succumbing to the river's currents, which ran fast despite their proximity to shore.

The three laughed at the sight they made. Their arms wound about each other, tears streaming down their faces. Their skirts were soaking wet, and Rose held on to their arms in a desperate attempt to remain standing. Emilie couldn't stop hugging them. Two months had been a lifetime.

A voice shouted from the bank, and Emilie looked up to see the group of spectators parting. She knew it was Maman, so she let go of her sisters and moved toward shore. Just as her feet met solid ground, Marianne appeared, her hand over her mouth to hold back a sob.

"Maman," Emilie said, the tears pouring forth, and they rushed into each other's arms.

It didn't matter that Emilie was now twenty-four and old enough to marry and begin a family of her own. She would never outgrow the comfort that only a mother could give. She buried her face into her mother's shoulder and sobbed while Marianne placed a hand at her cheek and swayed in an effort to soothe her. "Don't cry, my darling," Marianne said. "We're together now."

Something in her mother's tone wasn't right, Emilie thought. There was a trace of sadness perhaps, a catch to her voice. Instinct told her a piece of the puzzle was still missing.

Emilie pulled back and hastily wiped her eyes. "Father?" she asked, dreading the answer.

Marianne said nothing, simply placed a hand at Emilie's cheek and stared back sympathetically. The despair that had lingered in her mother's eyes for thirteen long years had not been relinquished despite the fact that they now stood at the spot where Papa was reported to be.

"He left for Maryland when he heard we were there." Lorenz's arms circled her shoulders and held her tight. "That's what I was trying to tell you."

Emilie's eyes shot up to her mother's for confirmation, and Marianne nodded gravely. Emilie felt Rose's hand on her forearm and heard Gabrielle whispering comfort while the tears poured down her sister's face.

This couldn't be happening. Not after they had traveled so far.

Just then Emilie remembered her dream, remembered her father walking away from them in the fields. Her vision where he stood at the bow of a ship, moving farther and farther away.

Her knees went weak beneath her, and Emilie felt Lorenz's arms catch her before she sank to the ground. The pain was too much; she couldn't weather the impact. The last thing Emilie witnessed before the darkness thankfully took her away was Lorenz's dear face, streaked with tears.

"It will be all right," she heard him say. Were those the same words she had offered him on the beach that horrid afternoon? She had meant it, too. She had believed they would find a better life, that they would escape the horrors inflicted on them by a greedy governor. But now all seemed lost.

As Lorenz's face slowly faded away, Emilie doubted they would ever have a happy future.

Days had passed since their arrival, but still Emilie refused to see Lorenz. She never rose from her bed and ate very little. Only Marianne could manage a word with her. Every day Gabrielle and Rose tried to be cheery, but by the fourth day they had given up the pretense.

"Why won't she let me come in?" Lorenz asked Rose. "It's not like her."

"No," Rose answered. "It's odd that she isn't following you everywhere."

The last thought brought forth an emotion Lorenz would rather not set free, but it lodged itself in his throat. He rose and moved to the table to pour himself a mug of water. Gazing out the small window of the meager cabin, Lorenz watched Gabrielle and Bouclaire deep in conversation outside.

The captain insisted on leaving every morning, but always found reasons to stall his departure. Lorenz was thankful for his presence. He liked the man, enjoyed his company. And helping him with his boat took his mind off Emilie and their troubles. Briefly.

"How did they meet?" Lorenz asked.

A sadness filled Rose's sweet miniature face, and she bit her lower lip to fight off her own unwelcome emotions. Lorenz slipped a lock of her hair behind an ear. "Rose, what is it?"

Rose inhaled and looked out the window. "It's nothing," she said, and Lorenz almost laughed at the lie. Dear Rose, so optimistic. And so transparent.

"It's not like you to be sad," Lorenz said. "Since it's so rare, it's also so obvious." Rose braved a smile, and Lorenz felt his chest constrict. "It isn't Emilie?" he asked, fearing the worst. "Tell me it's not—"

"No, it's not Emilie." Rose poured herself a mugful of water and took a long drink. "Emilie has received quite a shock, but I think she'll be fine in time. She has a backbone of iron, you know."

Lorenz winced. "She's not as strong as you think."

Rose pondered his words, then nodded. "I suppose you're right. I suppose we have tried to be strong, but we're all confused and frightened inside."

This wasn't the Rose he knew, not the child who had a smile for every occasion. "What has happened to you?" Lorenz answered. "Something has happened."

Rose placed a hand over her mouth, but the gesture failed to keep the tears away. "I have met a man," she whispered.

Lorenz placed an arm about her tiny shoulders. She was so small he often forgot she had grown to be a woman. But a man? He wasn't ready to let men near his sisters. Especially when he knew what fires raged inside them. "Who?" Lorenz insisted. "I'll kill him."

His words brought forth a laugh. "No, you will not," she said sternly but with a grin.

"Can I meet him at least?"

The sadness returned, and Rose shook her head. "He's gone west. He left Natchez without saying goodbye."

Good riddance, Lorenz thought. That solved that problem. "Then, perhaps it's for the best."

Rose stamped her foot and looked upon him angrily. "Why does everyone say that? How do you know what's best for me?"

He had never seen her this way, never heard her raise her voice before. This man had influenced her greatly, and he didn't like it. "Who was this man?"

"Lorenz," Bouclaire shouted. "I'm leaving. Walk me to my boat."

Lorenz grabbed his coat. "We'll talk later," he said to Rose, but she stubbornly shook her head.

"No, we won't," she said.

What was it with the Gallant women, he thought, that made it so easy for them to cut his heart in two? "Since when can't you tell me everything?" he asked her.

Whoever this man was, for some reason Rose guarded his identity. "Someday I'll tell you, Lorenz," she said softly. "When I'm older and he's only a memory. But for now, it's best we not talk about it."

Lorenz passed a hand across her delicate cheek. He adored his adopted sisters; he couldn't bear to see them troubled. "You can tell me anything," he said. But her gaze told him she would not say more that day. "If you need me, I'm here. Anytime. Anywhere."

Rose nodded and offered a faint smile. "Thank you, Lorenz," she said. "I love you."

He hugged her and kissed the top of her head. "I love you, too, pumpkin."

"Lorenz!" Bouclaire shouted again. "The wind won't last forever."

"What's the hurry?" he shouted back. "Little the wind does when you're traveling downstream." He gave Rose a squeeze, then passed Gabrielle at the threshold. "Please tell Emilie I was here," he said. "Again."

Gabrielle took his hand. "Time," she told him grimly. "Give her some time."

"It's what we're good at, eh, Gabrielle? Waiting is our middle name." Lorenz hadn't meant to be sarcastic, but he was tired of waiting, tired of the endless frustrations.

Lorenz didn't know why he grabbed his coat, for the

weather was as warm as a Canadian summer. Another
habit time would solve, he thought. A few years from
now he would be as used to the crazy weather as the
natives.

"What's that for?" Bouclaire asked, sporting a wide
smile. "Expecting snow to fall?"

Lorenz threw the coat onto the house's steps, another
thing he would have to get used to. All of the houses
were raised above ground in case of flooding, some so
high chickens and hogs passed underneath. "Where I
come from snow falls in April."

Funny, he was beginning to sound like Emilie. If truth
be told, he wished to be back in Grand Pré as well. They
could catch a ship for Maryland, meet with Joseph and
head north. It could be done.

"What are you thinking?" Bouclaire asked.

Lorenz shook his head, too weary to make sense of
what he was thinking. "I don't know anymore," he said.
"Nothing seems real to me."

"You've both had a shock. Emilie will pull through,
you'll see. You'll marry and move on to your father-in-
law's land grant and wait for him there."

That was Marianne's plan. Find Joseph's land grant
given to him by the Spanish and wait until he returned.

If he returned.

"Opelousas or the Attakapas District." Lorenz halted
when they reached the water's edge. "Somewhere else
to travel, somewhere else to wait."

Bouclaire roughly placed a hand on his shoulder, half
to wake him from his misery and half to offer support.
"Cheer up. It's not bad out west. There's a great swamp

between here and there, but beyond that it's prairie. Probably a lot like your home back in Canada. I've heard the Acadians there have made cattle raising a profitable business. Something to consider.''

''I don't know anything about cattle,'' Lorenz answered.

Bouclaire laughed. ''And I knew nothing about sailing until I joined the navy.'' He leaned in close and slapped Lorenz on the cheek. ''You'll learn.''

The sun had become so warm Bouclaire removed his shirt. It didn't surprise Lorenz that the captain was tanned all the way to his waist. ''I don't recommend it unless your constitution allows it,'' Bouclaire said when he noticed Lorenz staring. ''You can get quite a sunburn in this weather.''

''What's it like in the summer?''

This time, Bouclaire tilted his head back and let go a raucous laugh. ''Now, that's something you Canadians will never get used to.''

Lorenz untied the bowline while Bouclaire worked at the stern. Holding on to the ropes, he waded into the water and boarded his small craft. Turning back toward Lorenz, he threw him a bottle wrapped in calico.

''For your wedding,'' Bouclaire said.

Lorenz studied the bottle, appreciating the gesture. ''I doubt there will be a wedding.''

''Nonsense,'' Bouclaire answered. ''I know for a fact that woman loves you.''

''I know that, too,'' Lorenz said, ''but that doesn't mean she will say yes.''

Lorenz waded into the water to push the boat farther

out into the open waters and the currents that would quickly propel it downstream.

"You spent a lot of time alone with her these past two months, did you not?" Bouclaire asked him seriously.

Lorenz glanced up at the captain, wondering how much to divulge. "Yes," he said.

"It's hard to remain in control of your senses with a beautiful woman like Emilie," Bouclaire said with a wink. "Especially when the two of you are in love and have been since childhood."

Lorenz grabbed ahold of the boat, ready to push it away from the bank, but he was too curious where Bouclaire's line of questioning was heading to set it free. "And?"

Bouclaire sat at the stern and took control of the rudder. "And sometimes things happen."

When Lorenz failed to move or acknowledge his point, Bouclaire sighed and leaned a lazy elbow on the side of the boat so they were eye to eye. "When these things happen between lovers, it's best to confess them to a priest."

Now Lorenz was thoroughly confused. "A priest?" The last thing he needed was a priest interfering in their lives, forcing him and Emilie into a marriage. . . .

Lorenz grinned broadly. Bouclaire was a smart man. "Yes," Lorenz agreed. "A priest is exactly what I need."

Father Broussard was one of the few men lucky enough to have room to breathe in his small house, one of those constructed for the Acadians at St. Gabriel. Having no wife and no children allowed him the luxury of living a normal life underneath a roof. But when Lorenz stretched his long legs after the priest offered him a seat, the house became as confining as Marianne's.

"What can I do for you, son?" Father Broussard asked.

Now that he sat before the man, Lorenz questioned his motives. Never a religious man, Lorenz felt at once uncomfortable.

"You seem hesitant," the priest said. "Is there something on your mind that I can put at ease?"

Lorenz loosened the collar at his neck that suddenly seemed suffocating. "I'm not a church-going man," he said.

To his surprise, Father Broussard laughed. "Can I get you some coffee?" he asked, standing and moving into the kitchen. "I just made some."

"Yes, thank you." If sitting before a priest wasn't nerve-racking enough, having the holy man serve him coffee was. "May I help?" Lorenz offered.

"Yes, you can," Father Broussard answered, arriving back in the living area with two steaming coffee cups. "You can start by telling me why you have come."

Lorenz sat up straight and accepted his cup. He tried to avoid the eyes of the priest, but the man studied him intently. "I have been with a woman," he began.

"I see," Father Broussard answered without emotion.

"I don't consider it a sin," Lorenz added defensively. "We love each other very much, and I take complete responsibility for my actions."

The priest took a sip from his coffee, then placed it on the table beside them. "All right."

Lorenz waited for the man to continue, but he stared

at him silently. For reasons only God could understand, Lorenz began to rattle on incessantly, just as he had to Phillip, Mathias and Bouclaire. "She loves me, I know she does. Emilie's been crazy about me since we were children. But she's worried about our future together. Worried I might not make the most ideal husband."

"Will you?"

A passion lit up Lorenz's face, and his skin felt like fire. Even though his hasty trip to the Creole's house still lingered in his mind, he firmly stated, "Yes!"

"Then, what is the problem?"

Lorenz sighed and placed his coffee cup on the table and leaned toward the priest. "I've asked her several times and she keeps turning me down."

The priest rubbed the back of his neck. "I can talk to her mother if you like. Drop a hint that young lovers alone in the wilderness might be vulnerable to temptation, that it's a good reason to insist you two get married."

That would do it, Lorenz thought. Marianne would insist they get married if she suspected what had happened. "Fine. Tell her I confessed if you like."

The priest stared at him sternly. "That's privileged information, my boy. I would never speak of a person's confession." He folded his arms across his chest as he studied Lorenz further. "How long has it been since you've been in church?"

Lorenz leaned back in his chair and pulled his fingers through his hair, the fire returning to his brow. "I don't believe in praying to a God that has forsaken us."

Father Broussard uncrossed his arms and leaned forward, placing a hand on Lorenz's knee. "It isn't easy to comprehend God's plan when bad things happen, Lorenz. But if you can't believe in a future that includes love and peace, how can you expect Emilie to?''

He hadn't thought of it that way. Yet how could a benevolent God allow thousands of innocent people to die?

''You know, you look a lot like your mother.''

Lorenz's eyes shot up. ''You knew my mother?''

''Of course I did,'' the priest said. ''She had the loveliest voice in the choir.''

Lorenz felt ashamed he hadn't remembered Father Broussard. He had been young and impetuous even then, avoiding church to play among the fields and apple orchards, much to his mother's displeasure. What would Lisette Landry think of him now? he wondered.

''She would be proud of you,'' Father Broussard answered his unspoken question. ''She would have loved to sing at your wedding.''

Emotions rose inside him, and Lorenz could only nod his head. Father Broussard squeezed his shoulder. ''Things have not been easy for any of us,'' he said softly. ''But forsaking God is not the answer. Live in peace, Lorenz. Marry Emilie and live in peace.''

Again, Lorenz could only nod in agreement, wondering when priests had become so wise and thankful for the paternal guidance.

Chapter Fifteen

Emilie heard voices outside the bedroom and peered through the door to find Father Broussard speaking in hushed tones to Marianne. *What now?* she thought. First a doctor from the Spanish fort wanted to bleed her and administer leeches; now the priest would probably want to say prayers over her bed. What she needed was peace. And nobody had the power to give her that.

She hated herself for wallowing in self-pity, for never leaving her bed. But her body had refused to cooperate. She literally could not rise in the morning, her mind numb from the trauma and her body exhausted from her travels.

Poor Lorenz. Always visiting, always waiting. What would she say to him now? What possible life could they make together?

She missed him. Missed him terribly. Missed his warm body sleeping next to hers, his large, eager hands exploring every inch of her body, making her tingle at their touch. Missed his kisses. Missed his comforting hugs.

But he was one more problem to solve, and her mind couldn't cope with the load.

Emilie sat on the edge of her bed, waiting for Father Broussard to leave. She was ready to rise and face the world, but she dreaded seeing Lorenz again. What would she say to him?

The door opened, and Marianne appeared with a tray of food. "You're up," she said. "And dressed."

Emilie rose from the bed and took the tray from her mother's arms. "I'll eat this in the kitchen now, Maman."

The house they had been given belonged to the Doucets, who were visiting sick relatives in Cabannocé. It featured two small rooms surrounding a center fireplace, one of which housed a kitchen. Only when Emilie emerged into the opposite living area did she realize the rest of her family, excluding her mother who kept vigil in a chair by her bed, had been sleeping on the floor of the kitchen and sitting area. Emilie's heart dropped.

"I'm sorry," she whispered, thinking of her dear sisters sleeping on the hard wooden floors with holes big enough to spot the chickens scurrying underneath the house. "I have caused you all to be inconvenienced."

Marianne took the tray from her hands and placed it on the table. "You have done nothing of the sort," she said gently, then pushed Emilie into a chair. "But I would like a word with you."

Something in her voice sounded an alarm in Emilie's head. It reminded her of the time her mother caught her slicing the apple pie in the middle of the afternoon. Perhaps she was imagining things. Her mother had to be distraught over Papa. What quarrel would she have with Emilie? Then again, Emilie had disappeared from New Orleans, following Lorenz into the wilderness without so much as a goodbye. Her mother must be furious. And she had every right to be.

"I'm sorry, Maman," Emilie began. "I wasn't thinking."

"No, you weren't." Her mother picked up a napkin and placed in her lap. "Perhaps you want to tell me about it."

What was there to tell? Emilie wondered. She hated being left behind, as always, and followed Lorenz on his travels north to find Papa. "You know all the details," Emilie said, fidgeting with the napkin. "I wanted to be with Lorenz so I followed his lead."

Marianne crossed her arms and frowned. "So it was Lorenz's fault?"

"No." Her mother knew better than that. She was always following Lorenz like a shadow. Surely she didn't think Lorenz had talked her into such a dangerous mission. "No," Emilie repeated. "Lorenz would never allow such a thing."

Marianne planted her hands on her thighs and stared hard at her daughter. "But he did."

"No, it wasn't like that. I forced myself on him. He had no choice."

The staring continued, giving Emilie the shivers. She had known her mother would be furious at her actions, but Marianne's gaze was unnerving. Her mother stared at her as if she had lost her mind.

"It won't happen again," Emilie assured her. "I promise."

Marianne stood, folded her arms stiffly and gazed out the window where Rose and Gabrielle hung laundry. "Of course it will," her mother answered. "You will marry immediately."

"Marry?" Now Emilie was completely confused.

Marianne turned, fury in her dark eyes. "Emilie Marie Gallant, this is not something to take lightly. I would think you of all people would be more responsible than this."

Emilie had a bad feeling about where the conversation was heading, but she had to ask. "Maman, what are you talking about?"

Her mother's features softened, perhaps because she realized her daughter might not be following her. "I'm talking about you and Lorenz and a night of unbridled passion."

The hairs on the back of Emilie's neck rose, and she swore she stopped breathing. "I was going to tell you, Maman, I swear."

"When?" Marianne asked, her temper returning. "I had to sit here and listen to Father Broussard hinting that children left alone in unchaperoned circumstances might get into trouble and that it would be prudent to have a word with you."

"Father Broussard?" The man lived in St. Gabriel, and no one in Cabannocé knew about their actions. "Why would Father Broussard know?"

Marianne finally sat down, which relieved Emilie. Star-

ing eye to eye with her mother was a little less disconcerting than her towering figure. A little.

"Perhaps a certain young man was feeling guilty for his
sins and confessed. That's how Father Broussard knew."

Emilie bit her lip to stifle a laugh. Lorenz? Confessing?
The last time Lorenz confronted a priest was when the
Jesuit caught him stealing from the church fund. "He
would sooner fight an alligator," she said aloud.

Marianne sighed. She probably wondered the same
thing. "Be that as it may, my dear, he more than likely
did." Her voice grew warmer, and she took Emilie's
hand, massaging it gently. "I don't blame either of you.
I knew this would happen sooner or later. You two have
been crazy for one another since Grand Pré."

Emilie had to say something on her behalf. Guilt raked
her being. "Yes, but . . ."

Marianne stilled her tongue with a look. "Your father
and I loved each other like you two do. We never could get
enough of each other's company. You may be surprised to
know that we jumped the gun as well. We were fortunate
you weren't an early baby."

Emilie squeezed her mother's hand. "I suspected."

"But we got married," Marianne said sternly. "And
I expect you two to do the same as soon as possible."

Now it was Emilie's turn to stand and stare at her sisters
through the window. Oh, to be like Gabrielle and Rose,
so far removed from the complications of love.

"He's asked me," Emilie said softly. "Several times."

"And?"

Emilie swallowed hard. "And I turned him down."

Suddenly, Marianne was at her side, turning her to face her. "Why?"

Why indeed? Emilie thought. She wished she could figure it out. She wanted to marry him. Desperately. But always, something held her back.

"Oh, my dear," Marianne said, pulling her into her arms. "I have failed you."

Emilie clung to her mother, glad to be surrounded by her comfort and the smell of herbs and lilac soap, but Marianne's words disturbed her. "You have never failed me, Maman."

Marianne pulled away and took her daughter's face in her hands. "I have reared a daughter who is afraid of love."

Was it true? Emilie wondered. Was she afraid of loving Lorenz? "It doesn't seem to matter much what two people want when the whole world doesn't make sense," Emilie said, amazed that she had put the feelings into words. "How can love exist in such a time?"

Marianne grasped her daughter's hands and held them against her chest. "Love is the only thing that does make sense, my dear. It's the only thing that keeps us going."

"But Papa . . ."

"Papa is with me here every day," Marianne said passionately, raising one of her hands to her heart. "I wouldn't exchange one day of my life with him. Not one day."

Emilie nodded. She understood. Leave it to her mother to make sense of her conflicted emotions. How did mothers do that? she wondered. And would she excel at motherhood, too? The thought of bringing her own children into the world with Lorenz at her side brought tears to her eyes. Yes, she loved Lorenz. And she would love him for the rest of her life. Standing in the kitchen, the sunlight warming their faces as they embraced one another, Emilie felt the strength that only love could give. She knew then that nothing could keep her and Lorenz apart.

Lorenz pulled the ax up and over his head, splitting the log easily as he threw himself into the swing. Again, as a single man, he had been relegated to the barn. But he didn't mind. He was happy to be of service, happy to be a working asset to the new community. He could sleep anywhere.

Leger and Narcisse Landry waved from their house on the next land grant, and Lorenz returned the salute. His uncle's family, relatives he thought were lost from Pisiquid, a town located just outside of Grand Pré, turned out to be his neighbors. How ironic life was. He wasn't alone, after all.

There were others, too. A great-aunt he didn't know he had. A distant cousin who resembled his uncle Francois. Perhaps life would get better in this swampland called Louisiana.

Lorenz heard a twig break, and he turned to find Emilie standing by the side of the barn, scissors in her hands. She appeared pale and quiet, not at all like herself, until her hands found her hips and her chin turned upward in a defiant gesture. The Emilie he knew and loved had bounced back just fine.

"Are those for me?" he asked, pointing toward the scissors.

"Maman wants me to cut your hair."

She didn't smile, just stared at him, probably wondering what to do next with a man who shunned church, then spilled his guts to a priest about their lovemaking. Marianne must be furious. Lorenz was surprised she wasn't brandishing a knife at his throat. And Emilie, well God only knew what thoughts were raging inside that beautiful head.

"Are you sure you don't want to cut my heart out with those instead?"

A semblance of a smile curled at her lips, but she looked away before speaking again. "You have to be presentable for your wedding tomorrow."

Lorenz listened for the malice in her tone, but there was none. She didn't appear angry, or resigned to her fate. Instead, Emilie hovered somewhere in between, and Lorenz ached to know her feelings.

For an instant, Lorenz regretted his confession. He could have waited for her to accept his proposals, but knowing Emilie it might have taken years. No, he had forced her hand, and he wasn't going to back down now. They were meant for each other, better off married than sneaking around in the dark with the possibility of a child coming. She had to see reason, and this was the only way he knew how.

"Should I wash my hair, too?"

Emilie turned and frowned. "Of course you must." She rolled her eyes, the way she used to do when they were kids. Lorenz's heart warmed. "Lorenz Landry, you are insufferable. Do you wish to be married looking like that?''

As Emilie picked up the bucket of water and began to fill it at the well, Lorenz knew he was forgiven. He knew she loved him; he had known that since Cabannocé, if not before. But Emilie had needed a push.

Lorenz stood behind her and gently slid his hands up and down her arms. ''Are you happy with this?'' he asked.

''What difference does it make now?'' she returned, although again there was no anger in her voice. When she turned to face him, he wanted to pull her into his arms and plant kisses on as much available skin as possible, but Emilie pushed him aside.

''Your hair, Lorenz. I am not marrying a grizzly bear.''

Lorenz couldn't help but smile, even though Emilie still wouldn't. He obediently sat on a tree stump by the barn's side and waited for instructions. Instead, he was greeted with a shower of cold spring water.

''What the . . . ?''

Dripping from head to toe, he turned to look at the tormentor at his back, but she pushed his face forward. ''Sit still,'' she commanded. ''Unless you want these scissors in your neck.''

Lorenz didn't need to be told twice. Drenched in water, he looked forward and sat unmoving while Emilie washed his hair and trimmed months of growth off the back of his neck.

''Joseph has a land grant west of here,'' Lorenz began, hoping to talk of anything but forced marriages and sharp objects. ''We're not sure where, but it's in one of two districts, the Opelousas or the Attakapas. Marianne thinks

we should head west in search of it, then wait there until
Joseph arrives. It would be a way of sustaining ourselves
until he makes it back to Louisiana.''

Lorenz felt a comb slide through his thick locks and
heard the click of the scissors. He prayed she wouldn't
take revenge with those scissors and render him bald.

''Do you think he'll make it back to the territory?''
she asked softly.

Lorenz ached to touch her, to pull her into his arms,
but he thought it best for Emilie to make the first move.
''Yes,'' he answered. ''I think Joseph will swim back to
Louisiana if he has to.''

A silence followed with the clicking of scissors the
only sound. ''I think it's a good idea going west,'' Emilie
finally said. ''I choose the one without the cannibal
Indians.''

''That would be the Opelousas District, then. Although
I'm told the cannibals are gone now.'' Lorenz thought
of the absurdity of that statement. Maybe Louisiana wasn't
such a paradise after all.

''Is this Opelousas land farmable?''

''Nothing we can't handle.''

Emilie continued cutting, and Lorenz thought back on
their years in Maryland, when he and Emilie had managed
the planting and cultivation of their family's meager crops.
For being practically children, they had done well, managed to keep the family alive. But then, they had had
good teachers.

''My cousin . . .'' Lorenz swallowed, amazed at the
emotions that surfaced with such a simple word. ''He

says the Acadians in Opelousas have done well with cattle. It's something to consider.''

"I don't know anything about raising cattle," Emilie answered.

Lorenz thought back on what Bouclaire had said at the river's edge. They had a lot to learn in this new territory, and cattle was only one lesson among many. "I'm sure we'll do fine."

Emilie moved to his front to cut the hair surrounding his face. He ached to touch her, to place his hands on those generous hips and draw her close. If only she would give him a sign.

She must have felt him staring, for a slight blush spread about her cheeks. When she cut a lock of hair at his forehead, her fingers trailed behind, caressing the skin at his temple.

"We should name our firstborn son and daughter after your parents," she said softly.

Lorenz wasted no time placing his hands about her waist and sliding his fingers underneath the hem of her vest. He pulled her forward between his legs, so close he made out her heavenly scent, and buried his face in the soft material at her breast.

"Oh, Em," Lorenz moaned. "I have missed you so much."

Emilie responded by drawing her fingers through his hair, a simple gesture he had grown accustomed to since their first lovemaking, and an affection he had physically ached for since their argument at the riverside. Lorenz sighed, then tilted his head back and gazed into her eyes.

"Are you angry with me?" he asked.

Emilie's hazel eyes glistened in the dusk light, but no anger lingered there. "I would have liked to have been asked," she answered, a smile lurking.

The earth stopped moving at that moment; the heavens opened up and rained stars among them. It was possible to be happy after all, Lorenz thought, doubly determined to make their life together work. He would build her a chimney of gold if that was what it took. He would take her back to Canada in a chariot. Lorenz vowed at that moment he would spend his life making sure Emilie was content.

Lorenz stood and grasped Emilie's hand, motioning for her to take his seat on the tree stump. When she sat down, a puzzled expression on her face, he knelt before her.

"Emilie Marie Gallant," he began, holding her hand tenderly in his, "will you share my home, wherever that may be, bear my children, help me run a farm, grow old with me? Will you allow me the infinitesimal joy of being my wife?"

Emilie pushed a stray lock of hair from his forehead, then cupped her palm against his cheek. "Lorenz Joseph Landry, I would be honored to be your wife."

For the first time since Emilie had known Lorenz, he was speechless. He sat on bended knee, staring at her at a loss for words. She would have laughed had not the scene touched her heart so.

She leaned forward and cupped his face in her hands, then softly brushed her lips against his. "I will always love you, Lorenz."

She wanted to add that he was still the most agonizing, stubborn man she had ever met, but the gravity of the moment held her tongue. It was time to put away childish actions, time to leave Grand Pré behind and start a new life with her husband.

Quietly, Lorenz stood and held out his hand. Emilie accepted and rose to meet him. He placed her hand in the crook of his elbow and led her inside the barn.

"I suppose I would be asking too much of your mother if I were to steal a few minutes alone with you," he finally said.

A delicious shiver ran through her, thinking of the possibilities. "Maman doesn't expect me back soon," she said with a coy smile. Her mother had pushed her out the door, scissors in hand, stating firmly not to return until after dark. She had told Emilie she was creating her wedding attire, but Emilie knew Maman wanted them to have time alone.

Lorenz glanced around the barn, then led Emilie into the corner where he had made his bed. "All the animals are taken care of," he said as he pulled her into his arms. "No one will be coming here again tonight."

His kisses were gentle and hesitant, and Emilie wondered if he doubted she had agreed to marry him. He kept pausing, gazing into her eyes with wonderment as if he suspected he was dreaming.

"My dear Lorenz," she said, nuzzling her head to his. "I have made you wait far too long."

He slid a hand up the length of her back, but she felt his face break into a smile.

"No, *mon amour,*" he said so seductively goose bumps rose on her arms. "I was just thinking that I should listen to my elders more often."

Now Emilie was thoroughly confused. She drew back far enough to examine his countenance. Lorenz responded by grinning broadly. First, he chose a hand and tasted its palm, sliding his tongue along the inside, turning Emilie's goose bumps into sensual shivers. "Jean Depuis said it would take five proposals before you agreed," Lorenz said, moving his lips to her neck. "He was right."

Emilie tilted her head back so he had ample room for kissing. "Has it been that many?"

Lorenz bit an earlobe. "Tease," he whispered into her ear.

Emilie smiled, knowing they would always be dear friends and that some things, like their sparring, would never change. But as she ran her hands up his back, reveling in the feel of his broad, strong body, she knew childhood was over. Oh, yes, she thought, as Lorenz led a trail of kisses to her breastbone, things were going to be deliciously different between them.

Her head giddy with anticipation, she pulled away from his embrace and sat down on the makeshift bed. While his eyes never left hers, she slowly unbuttoned her vest and tossed it aside, then untied her hair and set it free. With a coy smile, she lifted her blouse above her head and relegated it to the floor. Leaning back on her elbows, with only a camisole to cover her, she sent him an inviting look with a rise of her eyebrows.

Lorenz knelt in front of her, but took no time removing his clothes. He discarded his vest and shirt by flinging them over his shoulder, then grinned slyly and grabbed her into his arms. Falling down onto the bed, giggling as they fell, Lorenz slipped his knee between her legs and lowered his lips to hers.

His wild, searing kisses were as monumental as the first time, only now Emilie felt at peace. Free to give her heart and soul to the man she loved. Free to face the next day as the rest of their lives together.

Emilie ran her hand up the front of his chest, threading her fingers into the dark hair. She paused at a nipple, then massaged it with the tip of a finger. Lorenz sighed, and his breathing became labored. Emilie wondered if her actions caused the same reaction as his tongue on her breast. She wondered so many things about lovemaking. She couldn't wait to try it all.

"Two can play at that game," Lorenz said. Placing a hand in the small of her back, he pulled her hips forward, at the same time lowering his head. Through the material of her camisole, Lorenz found her nipple and returned the favor.

His tongue worked magic, circling, teasing, suckling. A fire began deep in Emilie's core, and she moved her hips forward, aching to fill her need. Lorenz grabbed her bottom and pressed it closer, and his arousal only intensified her desire.

For a moment that seemed an eternity, Lorenz lifted his head and moved his hand back to Emilie's camisole and unbuttoned the wispy undergarment. Sliding the wet material aside, his hand cupping her breast, his mouth descended to her nipple, sending another rush of desire through her. This time, she didn't need help. Arching her back, she pressed her hips against him.

Lorenz moaned, but his mouth never left her breasts.

Instead, he let his hand wander, first down her stomach to her navel, then along the soft curves of her side. Emilie thought she would die from wanting.

"Lorenz," she whispered heatedly in an attempt to urge him on.

"All in due time," he whispered back.

Lorenz sat up on an elbow and gazed down upon her. What a sight she must make, Emilie thought, half-naked and burning with desire. She doubted her eyes were more than half open, for the fire burning within her consumed every bodily function. She grabbed the *clapet* of his breeches and began to unbutton them.

"Not so fast," Lorenz said, stilling her hand.

"Why not?" she whined.

Lorenz raised her hand to his lips and inserted her fingers into his mouth one by one. "Because it's better that way."

Lorenz leaned forward to her lips and kissed her again, savoring the taste of her mouth, nipping playfully at her lower lip. "Tease," she admonished him.

The familiar twinkle shone in his eyes when he pulled back once more to gaze upon her. "You are so beautiful," he whispered.

Lorenz slowly moved his hand across her shoulders, around the plump mounds of her breasts, down to her stomach. It took everything in Emilie's power not to unravel on the spot, her skin tingling from the places he had touched her, caressed her, teased her with his tongue.

When he reached her waist, he undid the buttons of her skirt and pushed the material over her hips. Her under-garments soon followed until she was completely naked, her body aflame with desire. Lorenz slipped a finger inside her, caressing the opening to her womanhood, and his thumb found the point where lightning seem to originate.

Emilie felt the wild spasms overtake her. She arched her back and called out his name. While wave after wave washed over her, carrying her to a higher pinnacle, she felt Lorenz enter her.

He moved slowly at first, then thrust deeper and faster until something larger, more fulfilling, began to build inside her. Emilie couldn't help herself. When the tidal wave came crashing to shore, she leaned her head back and cried out in pleasure.

She wasn't alone.

Chapter Sixteen

Emilie woke to find two smiling faces gazing down at her.

"Wake up, sleepy head," Gabrielle said. "Time to get dressed and get married."

Emilie leaned up on an elbow, wiping the sleep from her eyes. Was it possible that in only a few hours she would be Mrs. Emilie Landry? And was it possible that she had traveled to heaven and back only a few hours before?

Emilie grinned, thinking back on their lovemaking in the barn, when they had scared the animals with their cries. The horse had kicked out the back end of its stall, and the cow had bellowed so loudly Lorenz had thrown on his clothes for fear of the neighbors visiting to find out the cause of the disturbance.

No one came looking, however, and Lorenz managed

to calm the animals. But they had laughed long into the night, talking of their future and what kind of crops they would plant.

"What are you grinning about?" Rose said, jabbing her in the ribs. "You're not married yet."

"Doesn't matter," Gabrielle whispered, leaning in close. "She's already sampled the goods."

"Gabrielle!" Emilie had planned on telling her sisters in time. She also knew her mother wouldn't have exposed her. Was it possible Lorenz had told them? That was doubtful.

"Don't look so surprised, Emilie," Rose said. "You and Lorenz were alone in the wilderness for two months. We assumed as much."

Pulling her tousled hair behind her ears, Emilie smiled, happy to be in her sisters' company once again. "Do you know that Lorenz confessed it to Father Broussard and that Father Broussard hinted to Maman that children left alone might get into trouble?" For a moment Emilie felt like they were back in Grand Pré, telling secrets to each other in the apple cellar. "Maman asked me and then insisted we get married. That's why the quick wedding."

Both sisters grinned mischievously. "Mother didn't need a hint, Emilie," Gabrielle said. "She needed an excuse to get you two married."

"But she didn't know . . . ," Emilie insisted.

"I told her Lorenz proposed on the ship from Maryland." Gabrielle twisted her apron strings while she smiled broadly. "She was almost glad you ran off with him."

"Almost," Rose corrected her. To Emilie, she added, "She wants us all to be married these days."

Emilie thought of how happy her mother had been during the early years of her marriage, before politics had cruelly interrupted her life. Emilie vowed that no matter what misfortunes befell her and Lorenz, she would strive to be happy. For her mother's sake, as well as her own.

"Go away now, you have work to do," a voice announced from the other room.

Emilie looked over her shoulder to find her mother dressed in a well-pressed woolen skirt and linen shirt, clothes that had seen the worst for wear but were impeccably neat and clean. Her chestnut hair braided atop her head complemented the bright red stripes of her skirt. Her eyes, so routinely haunted by sadness, now glistened with happiness. Despite their impoverished circumstances, Marianne looked beautiful.

"Don't sit there staring," she said to Emilie, her hands planted on her hips, "we need you for the fitting."

Rose giggled, and Gabrielle nudged her and sent her a cautionary look. Emilie rose and straightened her chemise, playing along with the game. She knew there wasn't a wedding gown, and it didn't matter. She would wed in her everyday clothes, proud to be alive and to be given a chance at bliss.

"I appreciate the thought," Emilie said, following the three of them into the other room of the house. "But I know there isn't a wedding gown and I don't mind. You don't have to pretend . . ."

When Emilie crossed the threshold, she had to question her eyesight. There on the bed lay a pale blue gown dotted with tiny white flowers, its bodice graced by pearl buttons and a lace collar.

"Captain Bouclaire gave us the material," Gabrielle said. "We didn't want to accept it, but he insisted. As it turned out, it came in quite handy."

"The buttons were your grandmother's," Marianne explained. "And the lace was something I managed to steal away with us when we were exiled. If things don't improve for us, I hope you will pass these on to Gabrielle and Rose when their day comes."

Emilie stepped forward and lovingly caressed the soft material. Her dear sisters and mother must have labored into the night to produce such an exquisite gown. The tears poured down her cheeks.

"Now, don't cry," Rose admonished her, taking one hand. "You'll get the gown wet."

Emilie smiled through the tears and wiped her nose with the sleeve of her chemise.

"Let her cry," she heard her mother say to her back. "Do it now so you don't ruin everything when you're dressed."

Emilie heard the emotion in her mother's voice and turned to find her cheeks equally streaked with tears. The two women embraced each other, Marianne patting her hair as she had as a child and swaying soothingly.

"Be happy," Marianne whispered to her.

"I will," Emilie whispered back. "I want to be just like you."

After several minutes had passed, the two women reached for their handkerchiefs, and Emilie looked back at Gabrielle and Rose, who were now crying as much as she and her mother were. "I love you all," Emilie said, and the four women locked their arms around each other and laughed through their tears.

Marianne fitted Emilie into the gown while Rose touched up the hem and Gabrielle braided Emilie's hair with flowers. Both sisters made sure to place the first pins into the gown, items that Emilie would return to them as charms for getting their own husbands.

When all was finished, Marianne, Gabrielle and Rose stood back to appreciate their handiwork.

"You all are amazing," Emilie said, turning around to get the full effect of the wide skirt. "I can't wait to dance in this."

Marianne placed a hand at her throat to hold back her emotions. "You are so beautiful. But then, I always knew you would be on your wedding day."

"Now, don't start us crying again," Gabrielle chided them, although tears formed in her own eyes. "Your wedding time is near."

Emilie took Gabrielle's hand and squeezed. "I wish Father was here," she whispered.

She hadn't meant to say it. She hadn't meant to cast a gloom over the day's joyous event, but Emilie ached for her father. She wanted Papa with her today, dressed in his finest as he escorted her to the church. She wanted to receive his blessing on the happiest day of her life.

Her mother's eyes dimmed briefly; then she straightened her shoulders and lifted her chin. Marianne opened the satchel that contained all their possessions, mostly sewing instruments and bits of materials, and retrieved a handkerchief, the only item they had of Joseph Gallant's.

She pinned it to Emilie's gown. "Your father is here," she stated. "He is always with us."

Emilie felt another round of tears emerging, but a knock on the door interrupted her thoughts. "Is there a woman of marrying age about this house?" she heard Lorenz ask from the porch. "I am in need of a wife."

"There are three, sir," Gabrielle shouted back.

"Then, I am in luck," he returned.

Marianne opened the door to find Lorenz dressed in his familiar clothes, only they, too, had been meticulously pressed and cleaned. His haircut suited him well, no longer wild and untamed about his face, but distinguished and groomed. When had they grown up? Emilie wondered.

When Lorenz's eyes caught sight of Emilie in her new gown, they widened in surprise. He took Emilie in from head to foot, appreciating every inch. "How did you manage?" he began.

"Doesn't matter," Marianne said. "Sometimes miracles do occur in the worst of circumstances."

"Like you two getting married," Rose interjected.

Lorenz sent her a playful nudge on her chin, and she returned the affection with a hug, wrapping her petite arms about his waist. Gabrielle threw her arms around her adopted brother and squeezed.

"I do believe he is intended for me," Emilie said with a laugh.

"You have to wait your turn," Marianne said, and tearfully hugged her future son-in-law. "I always wanted you as my son, Lorenz," she whispered.

Lorenz's eyes glistened with moisture, and Emilie feared they would all start another round of tears. "I think we should all make for Father Broussard's before we drown ourselves.''

Marianne released Lorenz and wiped her eyes. ''Not until I say what I have to say.'' She captured Lorenz's hand and then Emilie's and pulled them together. ''As you know it's a father's duty to speak to the couple before the wedding. Since your father cannot be present, I will speak in his absence.''

Emilie and Lorenz knelt before her and waited for Marianne's blessing. ''My children, I bless upon you the same happiness that was given to me with your father, and I charge you to love one another as your parents have loved you. If you fail along life's path, and you will, be kind to one another and forgive the other his faults. Above all, strive to be happy and make this world a better place because you have lived.''

Marianne paused to collect her thoughts, and Emilie saw tears well up again in her eyes. Collecting herself, Marianne concluded, ''And may you have children as insufferable as you two have been.''

Jean Depuis escorted Emilie into Father Broussard's house, which was now suffocating from the amount of people and the temperatures more natural to a summer's day. When Lorenz's cousins arrived, and the heat became unbearable, they all agreed to have the ceremony outside beneath a stand of cypress trees.

''We need a church,'' Father Broussard reiterated. ''The next thing we build in this wilderness should be a church.''

Gabrielle and Rose lined up next to Marianne while Leger and Narcisse Landry stood next to Lorenz in front of Father Broussard. Jean brought Emilie to the center, and Lorenz took her hand.

Father Broussard began the ceremony, speaking of the duties of married life and the responsibilities of raising a family. Emilie heard some of the words spoken, but mostly she comprehended the tall, handsome man at her side, the man whose life she would share. When Father Broussard finally called upon her to recite her vows, she almost didn't respond.

"Yes," she said, hoping no one noticed her preoccupation. "I do."

She expected a glance from Lorenz, a smile perhaps, now that she had announced before God that she would finally be his wife, but he stared unemotionally at the priest. When Father Broussard asked him to agree to his vows, Lorenz remained silent.

Emilie's eyes shot up, staring at the man who had relentlessly hounded her about marriage, but still he said nothing. Finally, after several moments of silence, he turned toward Emilie with a frown on his forehead. "Perhaps we should think about this," he said.

Emilie couldn't believe her ears. She was ready to shout "What!" when the edges of his lips turned up in a smile. "I do," he said, a sly grin emerging.

Emilie knew they were crossing a threshold that day, entering adulthood as man and wife. But she couldn't help herself. She threw Lorenz a solid punch in the arm. Lorenz laughed, then snaked an arm about her waist and pulled her into a kiss.

"I haven't finished," Emilie heard the priest say, but Lorenz refused to obey his orders. As Lorenz held her tightly and delivered a slow, seductive kiss, Emilie heard Father Broussard sigh. "I now pronounce you man and wife."

Lorenz released her, then let out a cry of happiness. Suddenly, everyone was at their sides, congratulating them, patting them on the back, offering hugs and kisses. When Emilie looked over at Lorenz, he was grinning broadly.

The entire town joined the festivities, and everyone brought forth food and drink. Emilie and Lorenz sat at a special table while those who knew them stood and told anecdotes or offered a toast. Then one of the townspeople brought out a fiddle, and they all began to dance. As was the custom, Emilie danced with every man present and made sure every maiden girl had a partner. They enjoyed jigs, reels and group dances, thankful to be together and rejoicing as free Acadians.

As evening descended on the small community of St. Gabriel, women of the town approached Emilie and presented her with gifts, items useful in beginning a household. Two of the bachelor men offered Lorenz use of their home, which Lorenz gratefully accepted. The thought of a real bed, as opposed to one made of hay, was the best gift anyone could give, Emilie thought with relief.

When the fires waned and the children grew sleepy, Marianne proposed one last toast. "To Emilie and Lorenz," she began. "And to those who love them who are absent today, may you look upon them and guide them on their journey."

Marianne then sang "A La Claire Fontaine," and Emilie and Lorenz danced one last dance. As they turned around the floor made of dirt and damp grasses, Emilie gazed up into the black eyes she had adored since she had first noticed them staring back at her across an apple tree. She wanted to tell him how much she loved him, how silly she had been to doubt of their marriage, how her whole life had led up to this moment, but words were not needed.

Lorenz gazed back lovingly, and his eyes spoke volumes.

Chapter Seventeen

The Reverend John Leggett stared at the destitute man before him, wondering if the papist French problem would ever be solved in Maryland. Acadian refugees still remained in the colony, but most had chartered ships for the Louisiana Territory, several at the expense of the Maryland government. Anything to rid their land of the unappreciative exiles thrown on their hands by the governor of Nova Scotia.

"They should be grateful for the colony's assistance," John told his wife on a weekly basis. "We give them food and shelter. But they refuse to work on farms throughout the countryside for fear of separation."

His portly wife, never looking up from kneading bread, always offered the same answer. "Imagine the prospect of losing your religion," she had told him. "Imagine losing your family."

John tried to remember her compassionate words as he watched the pale, thin man devour his offering of soup and bread. He didn't like the French, had never approved of them in North America. They incited the Indians to attack, hoping to secure the continent for their own greedy country. They were papists and not to be trusted.

Yet this poor man had traveled thousands of miles to be reunited with his family, arriving in Port Tobacco to find them gone to Louisiana, and John could feel only sympathy.

"*Merci,*" the Acadian said, trying to employ an ounce of dignity while wiping his face, heavy with weeks of beard growth.

"You can use my barn to rest," John said. "My wife will make us a proper supper when she returns."

The man's eyes met his, and John shivered at the pain reflected in them.

"Are you sure?" the man asked. "My wife is Marianne Gallant. I have three daughters."

John shook his head. "I'm sorry, sir. I know for a fact that the Gallant family traveled on the last Acadian ship headed for New Orleans. I took the roll myself. There were five of them, a mother and three daughters and a young man named Landry."

The pain in the man's eyes intensified, and John turned away to escape it.

"I do have something to offer," John said, rising from his chair. "My wife bought something from one of your daughters, the dark one who resembles you."

"Gabrielle," the man whispered as if the sound of her name would unravel him on the spot.

"Yes," John answered, watching him intently in case he might faint. The Acadian was much too thin. More than likely he had spent every dollar on the ship from Louisiana and had little left over for provisions. It was doubtful he would be able to pay for a return voyage. "She carved crosses and sold them to villagers to help support the family," John continued. "My wife bought this one."

John placed the small oak cross in front of him, and the man quietly slid his fingers across the elegantly carved wood, closing his eyes to mentally call Gabrielle to his side. When he finally opened his eyes, John saw the tears lingering there. Uncomfortable at the sight, John moved to his desk to retrieve what the man would need, anything to send the Acadian on his way.

"I have maps, and will give you some provisions to take with you," John said over his shoulder. "You must stay the night. Annie will never hear of anything else." Searching through his desk drawer, he finally spotted the crude map showing the neighboring town. "There is a farmer in the next village, Patrick McConnor. He has seven daughters and is always in need of help running his farm. You could stay with him until you earn enough to pay for a ship . . ."

"*Non, merci.*"

When John turned, the man stood before him, pulling on his coat.

"You can't leave without supper," John insisted. "And rest. You need rest. You won't find his place easily after nightfall."

The dark-haired man placed his hat on his head and

tilted the rim for a snug fit. "My name is Joseph Gallant," he said confidently in a thick French accent. "I have been without my family for thirteen years. I will not waste another moment of your time or mine."

"But it is hostile territory out there," John began. "You can't possibly think to walk to Louisiana."

Instead, the man tipped his hat politely and headed for the door. "Again, *merci,* monsieur."

He was crazy, this Acadian. John imagined himself party to a suicide. "You have no maps, no guide to help get you there," he pleaded. "You will never find it."

The Acadian paused at the threshold and smiled knowingly. "I will find Louisiana, monsieur. I will follow the sound of my wife's singing, and she will bring me home."

And with those final words, the Acadian walked out of the door, heading west toward the territory of Louisiana.

ABOUT THE AUTHOR

Cherie Claire has no problem dreaming up great characters for her Louisiana historical romances. A native of South Louisiana, she was raised saturated in the colorful culture and traditions of the Bayou State. A newspaper journalist, Cherie makes her home in Baton Rouge with her husband and her two sons.

Cherie loves to hear from readers. Visit her web site at: *www.geocities.com/BourbonStreet/Bayou/4745*

BOOK YOUR PLACE ON OUR WEBSITE
AND MAKE THE
READING CONNECTION!

We've created a customized website just for our very special readers, where you can get the inside scoop on everything that's going on with Zebra, Pinnacle and Kensington books.

When you come online, you'll have the exciting opportunity to:

- View covers of upcoming books
- Read sample chapters
- Learn about our future publishing schedule (listed by publication month *and author*)
- Find out when your favorite authors will be visiting a city near you
- Search for and order backlist books from our online catalog
- Check out author bios and background information
- Send e-mail to your favorite authors
- Meet the Kensington staff online
- Join us in weekly chats with authors, readers and other guests
- Get writing guidelines
- AND MUCH MORE!

Visit our website at
http://www.zebrabooks.com

Book Two
The Acadians: Rose

Englishman Coleman Thorpe threw off the shackles of an overbearing father, traveling to the Louisiana prairies to begin a new life, but the miles fail to extinguish the memory of the Acadian woman he left behind, a Catholic woman he could never hope to court.

Rose Gallant and her family continue their travels throughout Louisiana in an effort to reunite their Acadian family. The bountiful prairies of Opelousas offer them hope of establishing a new home, but when Rose realizes she is neighbor to Coleman Thorpe, the only man she has ever loved, hope of a new kind surfaces. If only they can bridge the chasm between their nationalities.

On sale November 2000

We're sure that you have enjoyed this BALLAD
romance novel and we hope that you are looking
forward to reading the other wonderful stories in this
series, as well as sampling many of the other exciting
BALLAD series.

As a matter of fact, we're so sure that you will love
BALLAD romances, that we are willing to guarantee
your reading pleasure. If you have not been satisfied,
we will refund the purchase price of this book to you.
Send in your proof-of-purchase (cash register receipt
with the item circled) along with the coupon below.
We will promptly send you a check.*

Offer valid only to residents of the U.S. and Canada. Offer expires on 9/30/00.
* Refund check will be for U.S. purchase price in U.S. dollars.
BALLAD Romances is an imprint of Kensington Publishing Corp.

www.kensingtonbooks.com

Mail coupon and receipt for **EMILIE (0-8217-6648-1)** to:

BALLAD Romances
Kensington Publishing Corp.
850 Third Ave.
New York, NY 10022-622

Name:_____

Address:_____

City:_____

State/Zip:_____

Offer expires 9/30/00